THE
EVIDENCE
ROOM

THE EVIDENCE ROOM

CAMERON HARVEY

MINOTAUR BOOKS
A THOMAS DUNNE BOOK
NEW YORK

A THOMAS DUNNE BOOK FOR MINOTAUR BOOKS.
An imprint of St. Martin's Publishing Group.

THE EVIDENCE ROOM. Copyright © 2015 by Cameron Harvey. All rights reserved. Printed in the United States of America. For information, address St. Martin's Press, 175 Fifth Avenue, New York, N.Y. 10010.

www.thomasdunnebooks.com
www.minotaurbooks.com

Designed by Omar Chapa

The Library of Congress Cataloging-in-Publication Data is available upon request.

ISBN 978-1-250-03115-0 (hardcover)
ISBN 978-1-250-03114-3 (e-book)

Minotaur books may be purchased for educational, business, or promotional use. For information on bulk purchases, please contact the Macmillan Corporate and Premium Sales Department at 1-800-221-7945, extension 5442, or write to specialmarkets@macmillan.com.

First Edition: June 2015

10 9 8 7 6 5 4 3 2 1

32005 4206

For Mom and Dad

ACKNOWLEDGMENTS

I am so grateful to everyone who was a part of this journey. Thank you especially to Kat Brzozowski, for believing in my story and making this book a reality with your generous spirit and insight. Thank you also to my incredible mentor and teacher, Louella Nelson, and the extraordinary members of her writing group, who taught me so much. Mom, Dad, and Alissa, whose boundless love and encouragement kept me afloat, and finally, to the memory of Jayne and Diana, among the stars.

THE
EVIDENCE
ROOM

CHAPTER ONE

July 17, 1989

Dr. James Mason was more comfortable with the dead than the living.

It was morbid, sure, but sitting alone in his office, James had to admit it was true. At no time had his distaste for the living been more palpable than this week. He was interviewing new techs, and the process was exhausting. The spelling errors on their applications were beyond atrocious—since when was "morgue" a difficult word? And the outfits that some of them wore to the interview? Well, they absolutely defied description. There was no question about it; the world was getting dumber, and he was getting older and less able to tolerate it.

He could have gone home. That was the reason he had the beeper that clung to the inside of his coat like a troublesome insect. James neither liked nor trusted the little machine, and so he preferred to stay in his office in the Cooper County morgue during peak hours—between two and six in the morning—and wait. A multicar accident on the causeway had consumed the bulk of the night. Now it was almost four-thirty, and he could catch up on some paperwork.

James caught a glance at his reflection in one of the stainless-steel refrigerators. Not bad for forty. His hair was now almost completely the color of burnished metal, except for his two short sideburns, which stubbornly retained the reddish auburn of his youth. His face was smooth, having not yet fallen victim to the relentless Florida sun. He still had a lot of good years left, James thought. It was a good thing too, because there was certainly nobody else in the office with half a brain, let alone the smarts and patience it took to do his job.

Buzz.

The sound of the intake door buzzer jolted James out of his chair to a standing position. He glanced at the police scanner, still humming and gurgling incoherently on his desk. Protocol mandated that the responding officers notify him in advance if he was needed so that he could prepare—call one of the techs for help or head for the crime scene himself in the beat-up blue van. He was always reminding the cops: the medical examiner had primary jurisdiction of the crime scene.

Buzz.

Showing up unannounced ranked high on James's somewhat lengthy list of pet peeves. Ringing the buzzer twice was just rude. James stalked towards the garage door, punching the button to lift it with an angry closed fist.

With a chorus of squeaky protests, the door began its slow ascent, revealing the feet, pants, untucked shirt, and finally the blotchy face of Detective Floyd Rossi, squinting in the rain. James hated Rossi. He was one of those irritating people who was perpetually in a good mood for absolutely no reason. You would think a cop, of all people, would know better. Even at this ungodly hour, Rossi wore a clownish lopsided grin.

Frowning, James looked past him for a van, for a body.

All he saw was a little girl.

"Oh, Doc. Thank God," Rossi began, ducking under the door before it was fully opened, accompanied by a cloud of bugs from the humid night. Without bothering to remove his shoes or even wipe his feet, he marched past James into the pristine autopsy suite, half leading and half dragging his small charge by one of the puffy sleeves of her bubble-gum-pink windbreaker.

"Detective—"

Rossi clamped his hands on James's shoulders, and for one awful moment, James was sure he was going to hug him. Instead, he looked straight into his eyes and spoke.

"Doc, I really need you to watch her for a little while. Just a little bit."

"Rossi, have you lost your mind? You want me to babysit? Here?"

"Listen, Doc. We found her about half an hour ago, outside Margie Belle's mini-mart. Social services won't be here until nine, and I would keep her with me, but I just got a call that there's a"—here he paused and lowered his voice, eyes flickering towards the little girl, who remained expressionless—"body out on the water. I can't take her with me."

"What about the hospital?" James swept his eyes over the autopsy suite behind them. In the half-light, his spotless examining table and the rubber biohazard bins took on an otherworldly sheen. "Or the station? This is no place for kids."

Rossi covered the little girl's ears, his meaty hands framing the oval of her upturned face. "We think she may be related to the vic we found on the bayou. She may have witnessed something, and the killer's in the wind. I can't risk him finding her at the hospital. We've got every cop in the department down at the scene. The night shift dispatcher's at the station by himself, but I'm afraid the perp might show up there too looking for her. I've got nowhere else to bring her. Please, Doc. She's just a kid."

For some inexplicable reason, James felt himself nodding.

"Thanks, Doc." Rossi released the little girl from his grip and ruffled her hair, as if he were greeting a beloved pet. "Bye for now, sweetie."

The girl shot Rossi a look of unbridled reproach, which James found immensely endearing.

Rossi frowned and rose to his full height. "She hasn't said a word since we picked her up."

"We'll be fine," James heard himself say, even returning Rossi's silly thumbs-up sign. He hit the button for the garage and watched Rossi jog back to his cruiser.

The little girl turned her face up to James. Someone had brushed her dark hair into pigtails, and the humidity had curled them into two damp spirals. Someone had buttoned her jacket that morning, tucked her feet into white Velcro-strap sneakers with rosebuds emblazoned on the sides, even dotted her tiny half-moon fingernails with glittery polish. Someone loved this child, so why had she been left alone?

"I don't know much about children," James admitted out loud. The girl regarded him blankly. "My sister has two kids," he continued. "They're younger than you, though." James thought about his twin toddler nephews, with their constant earsplitting screams and perpetually runny noses. "I don't know if you'd like them very much. I certainly don't."

He led the girl into the autopsy suite and gestured towards a stool, as though he were seating her in a fancy restaurant. She instantly turned to the glass jars of tools on the counter. He liked that she didn't seem afraid of the place; just curious. James wasn't sure what a kid this age knew about death. Nowadays, everyone believed in sugarcoating everything until kids reached a certain age, when they would be abruptly informed that there was no Santa Claus, bad things happened to good people, and everyone they knew, including themselves, was someday going to die. It was better—and surely less traumatic—to just be up-front from the get-go, James thought.

"Those are my tools," he began in what he hoped was not too academic a tone. "I use them on my patients. When they come here, it's my job to figure out why they died. Like a puzzle. Do you like puzzles?"

The girl nodded so vigorously that the pigtails bobbed up and down. She drew a breath, and James felt sure that she was going to speak, but she stayed silent.

"Well, then maybe you'd like to be a doctor someday." James was beginning to get the hang of this one-sided conversation thing. In fact, he rather liked it.

"How about something to drink?" James had no idea what kids her age drank. Undoubtedly some sugary concoction. The morgue refrigerator yielded a sorry selection—some diabetic-friendly shakes from one of the techs, and his secretary's six-pack of Tab. James tugged one of the sodas free of its plastic harness and opened the pull tab too quickly, sending a spray of soda across his eyeglasses. He turned to see the little girl staring at him with an amused expression, the corners of her mouth twisting into a tiny smile.

"Yeah, that's funny, huh?" he said, removing the glasses and wiping them with the cuff of his shirt. "Here you go." She took the can from him with both hands and returned to her perch.

The back closet was stacked high with unclaimed property from the deceased who had come through, ready to be boxed up for the evidence room. James wondered if there were some kids' toys or games back there.

"I'll be right back," he told her, but when he turned on the light in the closet, there she was right at his heels, a solemn little soldier, grasping the leg of his pants in her fist. It was a small gesture, the kind of thing that kids probably did all the time, but James felt an odd tightness in his throat, and an unfamiliar warmth bloomed in his cheeks. He looked down at her, and she yawned.

"Are you tired?"

She nodded. He was an idiot. Of course she was tired; it was almost five in the morning. James steered her towards his office and pointed to the couch.

She shrugged off her windbreaker, clambered up on the couch, and curled into a ball, hugging her knees to her chest. The first few fingers of sunlight were beginning to poke through the blinds in front of them. James pressed the blinds closed and folded the small jacket over his chair.

And then he noticed it.

Underneath the tag inside the little jacket, printed in runny blue Magic Marker letters.

Aurora Atchison. The name hit him like a fist, the shock of it traveling the length of his spine.

"Aurora."

He said it out loud without thinking. She bolted up and stared at him, her eyes somehow clearer now, as though she had finally been able to hoist herself out of a dream. She closed the distance between them quickly, scrambling into his lap, clutching the lapels of his lab coat, burrowing into the folds of his shirt. Soundlessly she clung to him, but the face she pressed against him was wet with tears.

"Aurora." He whispered it like a prayer, over and over, rocking her gently back and forth.

Outside, the sound of sirens split the dawn, and James covered Aurora's ears as Rossi had, protecting her against the terrifying crescendo, bearing the news closer and closer.

CHAPTER TWO

July 17, 2014

The police department's booth at the Cooper's Bayou Annual Founders' Day Fair was occupied by the oldest beauty queen Detective Josh Hudson had ever seen.

Josh had volunteered for set-up duty, and the booth was supposed to be empty; but somehow he wasn't surprised to see the elderly woman in a tiara, reclining barefoot in a plaid lawn chair in the center of the enclosed space. Coming across the unexpected just went with the territory around here.

He took a few steps closer to investigate. The woman's shiny chartreuse satin gown was hiked up around her knees. A German shepherd sprawled on the burned grass at her feet, its velvety tan-and-black head pressed against her alabaster shins.

Josh slid the backpack from his shoulder, and the folder filled with photographs of missing people shifted in its depths.

He had planned on getting here early enough to post the pictures, culled from a daylong dig through the county case files. It was a long shot, but these fairs brought all kinds of people out from different places; you never knew who might have a key to finding someone who was lost. He dug out the fair map, sure he'd written down the incorrect stall number.

Nope, he was in the right place.

"Excuse me, ma'am. I think you may be in the wrong—"

"Hush!" The woman brought an index finger to her lips. The motion woke the dog, who exhaled loudly and settled back down without glancing in Josh's direction. "Keep your voice down." She motioned Josh closer.

Josh slid his backpack from his shoulder and knelt at her feet. In a town like Cooper's Bayou, nestled in the swampland south of Tampa, Florida, a tiny enclave of only two hundred residents, everybody knew everybody else, but this woman was a stranger. She had the tiny, fine-featured face of an old-fashioned doll, her eyebrows carefully penciled on, her lips outlined in a crimson bow shape. Above her tiara, her silver hair rose in a gravity-defiant funnel, to which several glittering butterfly clips clung for dear life.

She was sizing him up too; he could see that. Her rheumy eyes traveled the length of his T-shirt and alit on the badge clipped to his waist.

"You're a policeman," she breathed. It wasn't relief in her voice, but something else, something halfway between surprise and mild amusement.

"Yes, ma'am. Here to set up our booth for the fair. I'm Detective Josh Hudson." Josh flinched inwardly at the sound of it. Two years on the force, and the title still fit him like a bad pair of pants, clinging in all the wrong places. Detectives solved mysteries; they found lost people. Josh had spent the last two years chasing possums out of locals' yards and letting people out of speeding tickets.

And he hadn't yet found the one person he'd returned to Cooper's Bayou to find.

The woman tipped back her head and laughed, a booming, unexpected guffaw that did not match her delicate frame. "Of all the hiding places—I chose the police fair booth. I wouldn't make much of a criminal, would I? Lord mercy." She adjusted the tiara. "And it seems I lost my manners along the way! I'm Iola."

Josh grinned. There was something of his Tennessee grandmother in Miss Iola; genteel and headstrong. "And what, may I ask, are you hiding from, Miss Iola?"

"Oh, please don't take me back there, Detective Hudson," Miss Iola stammered. "I can't go yet. I'm not ready yet." The stark longing in her voice compelled Josh to take her hand in his own. Her skin was almost transparent, the blue patchwork of veins so close it seemed as though they might break the surface.

"You don't have to go anywhere you don't want to."

She squeezed his hand. "You don't understand, Detective."

"Tell me."

"She's a witch," Miss Iola confided.

"Excuse me?"

"Trinity Patchett. She's a witch."

Josh suppressed a smile. Trinity Patchett was one of the fair's administrators. Josh had worked with her on a police fund-raiser. A mean-looking brunette with a too-high pony-tail, Trinity had a voice that could shatter glass and a leadership style that would make Stalin blush. He didn't blame Iola for running away; he admired her for managing to escape.

"And what business did you have with Miss Trinity?"

"She's in charge of the pageant this year. She's bringing us all back, all the past winners. I thought it would be fun, but once I saw that she was going to be parading us around like a sideshow—I took off running. You should see these women, Detective. It isn't right. And those unruly children in this year's pageant! They raise them like wild animals. You never heard such a racket in your life."

Josh fought to keep a straight face. "So you won the pageant when, last year? Year before?"

"Something like that," she said with a wry smile. "I was born and raised in Cooper's Bayou, but I haven't been back here since. And what about you? I seem to recall some Hudsons living over by Bayou Triste. Is that your kin?"

"Yes, ma'am. My father's family." It was an important distinction in Josh's mind. He searched Miss Iola's face for signs that she knew something of his father, but she was spellbound by some other memory. "He followed my mama to Tennessee, where I was raised."

"A man from Tennessee asked me to run away with him all those years ago." Her fingers ghosted across Josh's stubbled cheek. "He was a handsome fella, had those Windex-blue eyes like you."

"And he let you out of his sight?"

Miss Iola turned her attention to the dog, patting his belly in concentric circles. It was a moment before she spoke again. "Not while he was alive. He passed on a few years back."

"I'm sorry, Miss Iola."

"Don't be," she said. "Time's a funny thing. You think your world's going to end when you lose somebody, but life just goes on. It's cruel, in a way. I thought coming back here would be a way to move forward, but there's nothing here for me. Nothing but memories."

"I understand," Josh said. And he did, in a way that she didn't realize. He'd returned to Cooper's Bayou for the same reason; trying to find a past he couldn't fix.

"So, Detective Hudson, are you going to turn me in?"

There was no way he was going to, and she knew it. She was playing him like a fiddle.

"No, I'm not, Miss Iola. But if you're going to stay for a bit, you can't just sit there lounging in the sun with your dog. I'm going to have to put you to work."

Miss Iola made a humphing noise. "My daddy was a shrimper. I'm not afraid of a little hard work. And this lovely creature isn't my dog. He just took a liking to me, my little beau. Somebody's probably looking for him too."

Josh bent down and scratched the dog behind the ears. "Well, we'll handle one mystery at a time. First, I need some help hanging these up." He opened the manila folder and laid the photographs on the picnic table in front of them.

They were all shapes and sizes, the faces of the missing staring back at them from yellowed family snapshots, school photographs with blue-sky backgrounds, candid images of birthday parties and beaches. Some of them had been cut from group photos, so that an arm or shoulder reached out of frame. Some had been missing for longer than Josh had been alive.

"All these people are missing?" Miss Iola ran her fingers along the edges of the pictures, cloaked in plastic. "Lord Mercy. Veda Fontaine." She tapped a black-and-white portrait of a brunette, eyes wide and lips pursed, a cluster of pearls resting in the hollow of her throat. "That's Miss Veda. My mama knew her. She disappeared when I was just a kid."

Miss Iola nudged another photo aside, revealing the picture of Liana. Josh's sister. An ache split Josh's insides, an old stitch giving way to a wound underneath. Nobody would ever notice a family resemblance; Liana had their father's fair skin and hair, while Josh, like his brother, had the dark curls and olive skin that were their mother's. She shouldn't be in this array; Liana wasn't really missing. Not in any official police sense of the word, anyway. Josh felt Miss Iola's gaze and turned away from Liana's image.

"I don't know how we're going to hang these pictures, Miss Iola." Josh scanned the tent. Someone was supposed to drop off easels, but they hadn't. The tent walls weren't an option either. Around them, drops of moisture saturated the canvas enclosing the stall, the day's humidity clinging to every surface.

"I've got an idea," Miss Iola said, scooping a plastic bag out of the supply bin at the back of the enclosure. "Clothesline. We could hang the pictures that way." She held up the bag of clothespins for Josh to see. Together they stretched the cord the length of their stall and pinned up the pictures, one by one along the line. *Forgotten Faces*, Josh scrawled in marker on a piece of shiny poster board, and below that *Help Solve My Mystery*. The two of them stood back and admired the display.

"Nothing tastes better than a hog on a log," announced a voice behind them.

Josh turned to see Boone Lambert holding aloft a pork drumstick. Boone, Josh's partner on the force, was the redheaded reincarnation of Paul Bunyan, with a little more padding. A third-generation cop, Boone had treated Josh like a kid brother since his arrival in Cooper's Bayou. Josh was a regular at Boone's Sunday barbecues, along with whatever local single woman Boone's wife, Laura Jane, was hoping to set Josh up with.

"Have you seen some of the food they've got here, Josh?"

Josh chuckled and feigned surprise. "And here I was, thinking we were on the clock."

"I was working," Boone insisted. "The Good News Bible Camp people called in a complaint about the voodoo woman's booth." He tore a hunk of meat off the drumstick caveman-style and spoke as he chewed. "Also, we've got a missing person—a lady from the pageant."

"Yeah, I might have a lead on that."

Miss Iola, who had retreated to her lawn chair, appeared at Josh's side. "I guess it's time for me to turn myself in. I've taken enough of your time, Detective Hudson. You have been so gracious."

Boone raised an eyebrow at Josh. "Miss Iola Suggs?"

"Guilty," Miss Iola said.

Boone chuckled. "Well, ma'am, I can't say I blame you for hightailing it out of there. That Trinity Patchett and her pageant cronies sure are crazy. All the same, it's best to let them know you're safe." He glanced at the clothesline of missing faces. "Is this what y'all have been working on?"

"It's just marvelous, isn't it?" Miss Iola winked at Josh.

"You really think someone might give us a tip?"

"You never know," Josh said to Liana's picture. "Just takes one."

"That's what I like about you, Hudson," Boone grinned. "You're an optimist. Some might say a fool."

"One of those," Josh agreed.

On top of the folding table, Josh and Boone's scanners began to crackle in unison.

"Here we go," Boone said. "Ten bucks says we have to haul someone's drunk rear end out of the creek again. Excuse me, ma'am." He spoke into the receiver. "Go ahead for Boone and Hudson."

"Niney Crumpler went missing this morning." Captain Rush's voice, veiled in static, sizzled and popped through the speaker.

Boone gave Josh the thumbs-up. "Told you. Damn, I'm good."

"Lucky guess," Josh returned. "I'll go." Niney was probably passed out after raising hell somewhere, but even so, he needed to be brought home safe. Josh took a step towards Miss Iola to say good-bye and almost tripped over the German shepherd.

"Boone, do you know anything about this dog?"

"Oh, yeah, I forgot to tell you about him. He's from Hambone PD."

"Did they loan him to us or what?" The dog lifted his head and unfurled his enormous pink tongue in their direction, as though aware they were discussing him.

"They wanted to know if we had a use for him before they hauled him off to the pound. I guess he failed out of K-9 training." Boone laughed. "Pretty dumb, huh? I thought shepherds were supposed to be smart."

"Well, I don't know about that. You failed out of what, sixth grade? And you didn't turn out so bad."

Miss Iola chuckled.

"Is that what passes for humor up there in Tennessee?" Boone scoffed. "Let me know when Niney is home safe and sound. Come on, Miss Iola. Let's get you back to your kingdom."

Josh pecked Miss Iola on the cheek. "Take care, now, Miss Iola. That Trinity gets out of line, you give me a call."

Miss Iola pressed a kiss into Josh's cheek and whispered into his ear. "I hope you find who you're looking for," she said.

The words flooded Josh's insides, filling in the hollow places. He steadied himself, reaching down to pet the dog. Beneath his palm, he felt the animal's heartbeat, even and steady. "Well, Miss Iola's beau, I guess you're coming with me," he said. "C'mon, Beau. Let's find old Niney."

With the German shepherd matching his stride, he trotted in the direction of his car.

CHAPTER THREE

"We've got a list of cocktails that'll make you feel single and see double," Mama Brigitte boasted. "Or if you're on call, I could fix you a Shirley Temple."

Mama Brigitte, the bartender at Dalhart's, winked at Aurora Atchison over the shoulder of her unsuspecting date, a new MRI tech named Mike. Everyone who worked at St. Agnes Hospital knew Mama, who had that preternatural ability shared by the best bartenders of knowing exactly what you needed. Aurora had seen her serve coffee floats to exhausted interns and had also seen her boot one of the most respected surgeons in New York out on his ass for being rude. She could see Mama sizing Mike up and was sure she'd be getting a full report later.

"I'll just take a Blue Moon," Mike replied, glancing back at Aurora. "And of course, whatever the lady wants."

"Diet Coke, please, Mama," Aurora said.

Mama shook her head and slid their drinks across the bar. "Someday this girl's gonna let me fix her a real drink. Now, you let me know if you need anything else."

Mike led the way to a booth in the back. "So you're one of

Mama's favorites, huh? You must have done something special to earn a lifetime of free drinks!"

Aurora waved away the compliment. "I treated one of her relatives." Aurora had treated Mama's mother in the ER a month before. Pulmonary edema. She remembered putting a hand on the older woman's back, feeling the patchwork of bones under her fingers. When Mama Brigitte had arrived, she could feel the older woman breathe easier, felt her lungs open up. *Make sure you love somebody and somebody loves you*, the older woman had told her later. *Then you can do anything.*

Mike pointed to her Diet Coke. "Sure I can't tempt you? Those cocktails sounded pretty good."

"No thanks. I'm on call," Aurora said. "What time is it? I have to be at the softball field at eight-fifteen." Aurora smiled at his pouting expression. "Coach's orders."

Mike checked his watch. "Let me at least get you a refill."

"Sure."

Aurora tipped back in her chair and caught sight of her reflection in one of the cloudy mirrors that lined the bar. She'd tried to coax her curls into a twist, but they were escaping over her shoulder. *Mermaid hair*, Nana used to call it when Aurora was a kid and she'd fussed as Nana tamed it into braids before school. She'd teased her about it with a sad smile, and Aurora knew without asking that her hair, along with her lanky frame and her green eyes, were all reminders of her mother.

Mike was cute. She let this thought nudge all the other ones out of the way. They'd struck up a conversation in one of the break rooms last week, and there was something about him that had put her right at ease. He waited at the bar, Mama commanding his attention, probably interrogating him. It had been a while since Aurora had brought a date here. She had met Mike at work—where else? She spent most of her time there. A nice guy. Maybe there was a chance she could be his girlfriend. But she couldn't hide her past forever.

Mike returned with the drinks. "Is Mama always so—chatty?"

"She likes you," Aurora said with a laugh. "What did she say?"

"Oh, the usual twenty questions," he joked. "I thought I was getting to be a local, but the first thing she asked me which hick state I came from."

"And what hick state is that?" This was always the part of dates that made her nervous, the exchange of personal information that led to the inevitable family questions. Aurora took a swig of her soda.

"Indiana. Been here two months, and I'm never going back."

"So you like it out here."

"It's cool." His smile was like a little kid's, part smirk. "I've still got a bunch of family back there, though. I miss them." Aurora imagined a mom and dad, an SUV, a golden retriever. "What about you? Where are you from?"

"Connecticut." It was only partly true. She didn't have many memories of the bayou, but it would always be her birthplace, rooted deep in her bones in a way she couldn't explain.

"So you stayed close to home, then. Is your family still there?"

"I don't go back too often." She knew there was something awkward in her tone, some note of warning. She was willing to bet he could see it too. Danger—seriously fucked-up family shit ahead.

In her lap, Aurora's cell phone buzzed. *Play ball!* the text said. She would have to hustle to be there in time for the first pitch.

"I'm so sorry, Mike. I have to go."

"Hey, that's what I get for going out with the team's big slugger."

"And pitcher," Aurora added. "Double threat."

She stood and he reached for her hand. "I hope we can do this again," he said. What could she say to that? Maybe this was the beginning of something. Maybe Mike was the one who could handle the whole story, if she could summon the strength to tell it.

"Sure."

"And next time tell me to shut up so I can learn more about you. Aurora Atchison, international woman of mystery."

"Sounds good," she said, and in her mind she added, *You have no idea.*

Outside, darkness was beginning to fall, the lights of the Williamsburg Bridge reflected in the iridescent slice of the East River. Aurora loved that no matter when her shift in the ER ended, the city was always waiting for her outside the door, a living, breathing thing. Two blocks away, she could see the lights on the baseball diamond, casting an otherworldly glow on the trampled grass. Aurora broke into a jog.

Behind home plate, Dr. Tusharkanti, a pediatric doc and the self-appointed coach of the Public Enemas hospital softball team, gave instructions that were lost on an unexpected twist of breeze that wound through East River Park.

"Aurora! Hey! Over here!" Nicky, another ER nurse and Aurora's closest friend on staff, bellowed from behind home plate, where she was struggling with her spikes. Nicky had rolled the cuffs and twisted the sleeves of the softball uniform. It reminded Aurora of the way she'd tailored her scrubs at work; always a fashionista.

"Hey, Nic!"

Nicky gave Aurora the once-over. "You wore your softball uniform on the date? It's a good thing you're so cute. How'd it go?"

"I had fun."

"Really. Don't spare any details." Nicky rolled her eyes.

"I had fun," Aurora repeated. "But we'll see what happens." She fit her fingers inside the baseball glove.

"You know what I think?" Nicky planted a hand on her hip.

"Please tell me. I'm dying to know."

"He's just not your type. You have to find someone who is."

"I guess." Aurora wanted someone strong. Strong enough that she could lay down all her weapons for a change and stop fighting everything alone.

"So it isn't Matt. So what? On to the next."

"Mike."

"Whatever. All those blond techs look the same to me. Good genetic material for a baby, but about as interesting as unflavored oatmeal." She turned towards the dugout and cupped her hands around her mouth to yell at Dr. Tushy. "Where do you want us, Coach? Let's get this show on the road."

"Aurora, you take shortstop tonight," Dr. Tushy hollered from the bench. "Nicky, you're at third base." He slapped an unenthused-looking resident on the back. "Dr. K, let's see if you can pitch!"

"Shit," Nicky muttered. "I hope nobody hits it this way."

"I've got your back."

"So anyway," Nicky continued, "my friend's band is playing at this festival out on the Island on Friday. It's at the beach, so there's gonna be food, drinks, all kinds of summer fun. And I checked your schedule, and I know you're off, so no excuses. Are you in?"

"I'm supposed to see the lawyer on Friday about Papa." She had been putting off the appointment with Luna Riley for weeks.

"Oh, I'm sorry, hon. I forgot."

"I can probably reschedule." What was one more time?

Nicky linked her arm in Aurora's. She had been witness to Aurora's grandfather's slow decline from lung cancer. Papa had loved Nicky. She had shown him a thousand tiny kindnesses that Aurora would never forget—played cards with him, slipped him an extra pudding cup, got the maintenance guys to bring him one of the TVs with the good channels. She'd even helped Aurora compose his obituary for the funeral home. Loving husband of Laurel. Adoring father of Raylene. Beloved grandfather of Aurora. A life expressed in terms of connections to other people. What Nicky might not realize was that Aurora was the end of the line. *Make sure somebody loves you.* But what if nobody was left?

The first baseman caught a pop fly for the third out, and Nicky and Aurora jogged together to the dugout. "Did you scatter his ashes?"

"Not yet." Aurora ignored the tightness that gripped her throat. Papa's remains were still tucked under her bed. She knew he wanted to be on the bayou for all eternity, but she just couldn't take him there. Not yet. It was funny how Aurora could bear witness to other people's tragedies, could be the one to make the death notification, to rub the back of the crumbling family member while she delivered the news—but when it came to dealing with her own tragedies, she was useless.

"He's at peace," Nicky told her. It was the kind of thing they were supposed to say to patients' family members, a cliché that rang hollow to Aurora at work but, coming from Nicky at this moment, seemed oddly comforting. The idea that Papa now looked down upon her from paradise, all of his questions answered and his fears soothed, fortified her. Aurora gave Nicky's hand a squeeze.

"Aurora! You're up!" Dr. Tushy held out a batting helmet.

Aurora stood in the batter's box. Had her mother played sports? She herself had been a decent athlete in high school; Nana and Papa had attended all of her games, pushed her feverishly into any and all after-school activities in their campaign to give her a normal life.

"Come on, Aurora! You got this." Dr. Tushy was growing hoarse. "We want a pitcher, not a belly itcher!" His spirit, even in the face of the team's consistently terrible record, was what made Aurora keep signing up to play.

She settled into her stance, pictured her swing, fluid and easy. She connected on the first pitch, the ball carrying over the second baseman's head and into center field. Aurora sprinted to first base and smiled at her teammates' applause. Nothing to it . . .

Something buzzed in her pocket. Probably the hospital. Well, she'd had a good run of it so far this evening. Aurora made a time-out signal and took the call without checking the caller ID.

"Hello?"

"Aurora! I'm so glad I caught you. This is Luna Riley." A tiny surge of anxiety shot through Aurora. Papa's attorney.

"Hi."

"I just wanted to make sure that our appointment on Friday at eleven thirty still works for you." Luna's voice was friendly, but something in her voice told Aurora the lawyer was onto her, knew she was ducking the appointments.

"Sure, I'll be there."

"Great," Luna said brightly. "We can go over all the issues related to the estate, and I can answer any questions that you might have. We're working under a deadline here, so—"

"Issues?" Papa had held the same job at the bank for forty years, and his military upbringing had made him a meticulous man, tidy about everything from his sock drawer to his bank account. The luxuries in his life were in his relationships with other people, not in material possessions. *Live simply,* he'd always told her, *so that others may simply live.* What possible issues could there be?

"Oh, we'll discuss all of that in person on Friday," Luna replied. "I'll let you get back to your evening." In the background, Aurora could hear the hum of chatter amidst the thin strains of orchestra music. So Luna was calling after hours, from her cell phone, to confirm their appointment? What could be so urgent?

"Can you just give me an idea of—"Aurora began to formulate the question, but Luna had already ended the call. She slipped the phone back in her pocket and walked back onto the baseball diamond.

"Everything okay, hon?" Nicky said with a frown. "You didn't get called in, did you?"

"No, no, everything's fine." Aurora gave Dr. Tushy the thumbs-up, and the batter stepped back into the box. Luna's words burned a trail through her mind. Estate issues could mean anything, she told herself. Maybe a bank account that hadn't been closed, or a bill that hadn't been paid. But something told her it was more than that, something related to what had happened a thousand miles away from here, on the violet shores of a bayou, a tragedy she had survived but could never outrun.

And Friday morning, like it or not, she was going to have to find out.

CHAPTER FOUR

Josh stood in line for his coffee at the Java Jive Café and tried to shake the feeling that he was being watched.

He glanced around the café. A man in his forties sitting at the booth in the corner folded his newspaper, met Josh's eyes, and then returned to the sports section. Just a regular guy enjoying breakfast, Josh told himself. Not everyone was a suspect. Everything was fine. The day that he'd crossed paths with the Shadow Man was a lifetime ago; it had happened to a different person. He was a cop now. Not a victim.

Josh focused on the case at hand. Niney Crumpler was safe and sound, passed out in a beery slumber on his front porch after being hauled out from behind a Dumpster at the local watering hole. And now Josh was here to refuel. At his side, Beau was alert, his ears perked. Did he sense something too?

Josh's right hand closed around the printout in his pocket, the results of the previous night's search of the missing persons database. *She was eighteen the last time you saw her*, the first detective he'd ever visited back in Tennessee had told him. *She had the right to go missing.* As though Liana's disappearance from his life had been some kind of expression of civil disobedience. During downtime at work, he searched property records and DMV files, but only at night in front of his laptop did he log on to the national database of unidentified victims and allow himself to consider the darker possibilities. There were so many girls who were beyond saving in those nameless profiles. Josh tried to remember each one. Sometimes the details made it easy to tell the girl was not his sister; the dead girls were the wrong age, or height, or ethnicity. But then there were the other details: *Healed fracture of the left elbow. Tattoo of a sunburst, right ankle. Evidence of childbirth.* Each one was a reminder that so much time had passed, a reminder that there were things about Liana he could not know and might never know.

But he would never stop looking.

A little boy in a red-sleeved baseball jersey nudged past Josh, and the man in front of him in line scooped the boy up in an easy motion, so that Josh could see the kid's face, flushed with delight, against the man's shoulder. Something black flapped its wings in Josh's chest. He saw the Shadow Man, Jesse unconscious against his shoulder, carrying him away. Now, at thirty, the desire to be a father had begun to take root inside of Josh. But how could you bring children into this world when there were no guarantees that you could protect them?

Over beers last week at Crabby Jim's, he'd confided in Boone about the Shadow Man. Boone had asked about the Shadow Man's record, and Josh had rattled off the information. He had a name, of course, and an inmate number. But in

Josh's memory he would always be the shadow on the bath-room wall, a faceless shape that bloomed and shrank in the light. *Sometimes I think I see him now,* he'd said. *Even though it's impossible.* To Boone's credit, he hadn't blinked an eye, just drained his glass and leaned forward. *We all got some-thing that haunts us, Josh. Ain't nothing to be ashamed of.* Boone had leaned close to him, spoken with a fervor Josh had never heard in his voice before. *You can have that crazy voice in your head,* Boone had said. *You just can't let him drive.* He hoped that somewhere Liana was finding a way to heed that advice.

Josh reached the front of the line.

"Shit," the barista, a long-haired kid with sleepy green eyes, said, staring at the remains of a frozen cappuccino, upended on the counter, that had begun to rush in an icy waterfall over the edge towards Josh's feet. "I mean, welcome to Java Jive. Can I help you?"

Josh smiled and picked up the overturned cup. "I'll keep it simple. Cuban coffee to go." The brunette standing next in line smiled, and Josh smiled back. The feeling was already begin-ning to loosen its grip.

Outside, his cell phone began to chirp. Josh glanced at the caller ID. Boone.

He fished the phone out of his pocket. "Don't tell me Niney woke up and wandered off."

On the other end of the line, Boone let out a breath. "Not yet," he said. "But the guys from Hambone showed up a while ago looking for you. Said you're supposed to meet them over there—they need you."

The drug squad. What the hell time was it? He was late for the operation. He began to jog towards the car, the details of it clicking through his mind, the thought of the Shadow Man already retreating from his consciousness like an unpleasant dream.

"Tell them I'm on my way," he said.

CHAPTER FIVE

"It's Hudson. I'm at the—um, the beauty parlor."

On the other end of the phone, Officer Clifford Fizzard, Josh's partner on the tri-county narcotics interdiction force, clucked with laughter. Police chief of Hambone, five counties over to the east, Fizz also worked part-time as the owner of the Pig Squealer BBQ, but brought his best work to his full-time job as a Class-A ballbuster.

"You gonna ask her for a perm before you take her down, Princess?"

Josh suppressed a smile. "Now, that's just the jealousy talkin', Baldy," he said. "Tell you what, I'll see if I can grab ya some cans of spray-on hair on my way out."

Fizz snorted. "Laugh it up, young buck. It happens overnight. One day you're running around chasing ass, next day you're balder than a peeled egg and three days older than dirt." He cleared his throat, and his voice took on a grave tone. "You ready for this one?"

"Sure am."

"Atta boy. Just get her talkin' on that tape. Fix a time for the buy tomorrow, then we'll let the DEA know, and they can bring in the big dogs."

"Got it."

"And, Hudson?"

"Yep?"

"Be careful. None of this bravery garr-bage," Fizz said, his Cajun accent stretching the word out as far as it would go. "If shit gets bad, just get your ass out of there."

"I got it, Fizz. Call you later." Josh ended the call, the adrenaline molten in his veins. The tri-county narcotics force had only been in existence for six months, created at the feds' direction to help fight rural Florida's worsening drug problem, and already they'd taken down two prescription drug rings and were close on a third. They'd gather the evidence and then turn things over to the feds. The fact that ten cops from three hillbilly towns with a combined population under twenty thousand had made the busts was beginning to garner attention from larger cities and had even been profiled on a local news station.

Josh didn't give a shit about that. He liked the job because it was always different; every operation brought something you didn't expect, so you always had to be ready for anything. The youngest on the force, with a tall, lean frame, stubbled complexion, and no girlfriend to force a haircut on him, Josh was the natural choice to play the role of Matt Saunders, drug seeker. Josh glanced down at his battered jeans and work shirt with the sleeves cut out. The transformation was almost too easy.

Josh parked across the street from the Kut and Kurl, the salon they believed was a cover for a multicounty drug ring. In the backseat, Beau chewed a pulled pork sandwich, the remains of Josh's lunch.

This whole block on the outskirts of Hambone had once been the slave quarters for a Confederate general's plantation. Now it was a neglected row of failing businesses. That was how things were down here; they upgraded without getting better. Someone had made an effort with the Kut and Kurl, though; its exterior had been painted an aggressive shade of pink, and the cloudy front windows had been cleaned and fitted with cheap lace trim curtains.

Inside, Josh could see his target, Pernaria Vincent. She was seated at a desk, three chairs and mirrors behind her, il-luminated by a square of fluorescent light that made the out-side darkness seem threatening, as if at any moment, it might consume the tiny shop.

Josh exited the car and checked around the building. No other cars; was she really alone after hours? People were in-credibly stupid, Josh thought. Women disappeared every day, plucked from their lives by men who looked like the boy next door. Bad things happened in ordinary places.

Josh completed his perimeter sweep and peered in the win-dow. Pernaria was concentrating on something, her head bent over the desk like a schoolgirl taking an exam. Josh would chat her up a little bit, work his way up to asking about a buy. He pushed open the door.

"*Je ne vous dois pas un sou,*" the woman said in a me-chanical voice. She registered Josh's arrival with a tired nod, but her heavily-lashed green eyes swept over him from head to toe. Her hair was tucked into a twenties-style bob wig, and her eyeliner was drawn out beyond the curve of her eyes in a dra-matic sweep. The effect was a cross between something feline and a bad Cleopatra costume.

"I owe you nothing," the woman went on in a spiky tone, but winked at him. Josh realized that she was mimicking a voice on the digital recorder that sat in front of her, not unlike the recorder that nestled in his pocket.

"Well, now, that's not quite true, is it?" Josh said. "You do owe me something."

The woman giggled, the easy laugh of a woman used to male attention. She was lovely in an unexpected way, with pearl skin and soft features. "Sorry. I'm learning French. Planning on moving to Paris soon. And what is it that I owe you?"

"How about an explanation for why a beautiful woman like you is sitting here alone on Friday night?" Josh infused the cheesy line with Tennessee charm. Women had always loved Josh. Maybe they sensed how much he wanted to protect them.

"I guess I was just waiting for you," the woman said. "I'm Pernaria, but everyone calls me Pea." She stood up, revealing a pair of perfect legs set off by sky-high heels. Josh tried to gag the male part of his brain, which was now drowning out the cop part. What was this woman's role in the drug ring? Fuck your brains out and rob you blind?

Behind her, the woman on the tape prompted in a strident voice. *Pouvez-vous m'aider? Can you help me?*

"I'm Matt." Using the alias was getting easier every time, softening up like an old pair of jeans. Josh averted his eyes and looked at the yellow wall behind Pea, where faded beauty-queen photos, curling at the edges, were displayed in a crooked row. There was a dimpled toddler, then a little girl in a sailor dress, then a teenager in a gypsy costume holding a tambourine aloft, and then the pictures stopped.

"So you're a beauty queen, huh?" He saw right away that it was the wrong thing to say, that he had crossed some sort of invisible border. Her face darkened, and she crossed her arms.

Je me suis perdu, the woman on the tape said, this time speaking in a breathy tone. *I am lost.*

"That's my sister," Pea said. She frowned and perched on the edge of the desk. "I told her to take those down. Bunch of perverts running those pageants." And then Josh saw it, the damage just underneath the surface. She was like him; someone had stolen something from her, something that could never be replaced.

She had seen something in his expression also, because now she came closer and dug both her hands into his hair, drawing her nails across his scalp. Josh stood perfectly still, the digital recorder beating in his pocket like a second heart.

"You're not here for a haircut," she said.

"You're right."

"So why are you here, Matt?"

"Turner said you could help me out."

She nodded, pleased with this answer. "What do you need?"

"He said you could get me started. Just something to tide me over."

Pea tucked a stray synthetic hair behind her ear, a girlish gesture. *C'etait amusant*, the tape said. *That was fun.*

"Well, any friend of Turner's is a friend of mine," Pea purred, opening a drawer. "I'm sure he told you, we don't keep any product here at the salon, but we could get you a sample, just to get you started." She rummaged around and then pouted. "No more samples."

"That's all right. I can come back tomorrow."

"Guess you'll just have to see me again, Matt."

"Sounds good to me," Josh said. "Same time tomorrow?"

"I'll be here, all by my little old self." Pea returned to her seat behind the desk and crossed her legs. "*Je suis désolée*," she repeated with the woman on the tape in a singsong voice that was slightly unnerving. "I am sorry."

"Well, I'll leave you to your French lesson, then," Josh told her. "Good night, Pea."

"Good night, Josh."

The sound of his real name sent a sizzle of shock down Josh's spine. He slid his hand into his waistband and fitted it around the gun, his eyes darting to every corner of the room, sure that any second Pea's associates would be on him from all sides. How the hell had she made him?

Pea approached, a wry smile on her face. "I guess I ruined all the fun, didn't I?" She held up her hands in mock surrender and fluttered her fingers. "You could still arrest me, but I'm not the one you really want. And I think you'll be interested in what I have to say."

Josh considered this. Pea was a smart woman; she probably knew the bigwigs of the operation. Maybe he could turn her, get her working for the narcotics force. It might be worth a shot.

"I'm listening," he said.

"I know where Liana is."

The phrase hit him like a punch to the gut. Liana. He tried to keep the shock from rising to his face.

"Bullshit."

Pea shrugged. "Believe what you want. I heard you were looking for her, saw that picture you put up at the fair, the ones around town."

"How do you know her?"

"I met her when I used to live in Sarasota."

"And how do I know you're not full of shit?"

Pea rummaged in her bag and handed him a photograph. "She left town about two years ago, right when you came looking for her. I met her a little while after that. Here we are."

In the picture, Pea and his sister toasted the camera with

oversized neon mugs. All these years, and he would still have known his big sister anywhere. Liana had always made goofy faces at the camera, pulling a face in all their family pictures, making their mother crazy. She had a hyena laugh and loved orange Popsicles and Kurt Cobain. She had punched Butch Sheridan in the face at the bus stop in second grade when he'd told Josh and Jesse there was no Santa Claus. A terrible longing flooded Josh, all the memories hurtling to the surface. Where had she been these seventeen years? Why didn't she want to be found?

"You know where she is?"

Pea nodded. "I do," she said.

Josh felt the breath leaving his body.

She tugged Josh's phone free of his front pocket and began tapping the screen. "Take my number."

"What do you want from me?"

"I'll tell Turner to set up a buy for tomorrow, and your guys can bust him. That piece of shit broke my heart. I've got enough saved up. I can hop on the next flight to Charles de Gaulle."

"Pea. I can talk to the guys about cutting you a deal if you give us Turner. But I can't just let you slip through my fingers."

She waved the Post-it note in his direction. "Would you rather let Liana slip through your fingers?"

It was an impossible choice. You couldn't trust drug dealers. In his pocket, the recorder ticked the seconds away, preserving his hesitation on tape. Fizz would hear all of it; the mention of his sister and his father, Pea's offer. He trusted Josh, sure. But how much?

He plucked the Post-it from between her fingers, knowing he was crossing a line, breaking a code. It wasn't the first time he'd gone out on a limb for Liana, and it probably wouldn't be the last, either. He'd used the police database to try and find her, stuff that wasn't exactly legal but didn't keep you up at night, either. But this was worse. Making deals with bad people; that had his father written all over it. The decision should have been tough; he should have hesitated. But it was his sister. Blood was thicker than water. "We'll be here tomorrow, opening time. You make sure Turner gets here, and then get the hell out of the country and don't look back."

"Fair enough," Pea said. She reached up as though she was going to embrace him, and instead slid her hand between his top two shirt buttons, freeing the digital recorder from his inside pocket. He could feel her cold fingers through the fabric of the shirt. She pressed it into his hand.

"*Bonne chance,* Josh," she said. "Good luck."

CHAPTER SIX

"All that money, and she left it to the cat. Can you believe it? What's the goddamn cat going to do with two hundred thousand dollars?"

The disgruntled woman sitting next to Aurora in the waiting area of Benedict & Riley aimed this rant at the law office's receptionist. When no response was forthcoming, she made a huffing sound and returned to fussing with the diamond collar on the hostile-looking Himalayan perched on her lap. Aurora avoided eye contact and slid a Christmas issue of *Southern Living* free from the stack of magazines on the table and waited for her appointment with Luna Riley.

The entire office, the first floor of a Park Avenue brownstone, seemed to have frozen in time somewhere in the seventies. Mossy shag carpeting covered the walls, paisley curtains clung to the windows, and rusting ashtrays were carved into the faux-wood arms of every chair and couch. Shiny pamphlets with ominous titles like—*What a Will Won't Do* and *Living Trusts—Why You Need a Professional* were stacked in front of the reception area like travel brochures.

Aurora wondered how many people had sat on the stained

olive-green couch and contemplated life's eternal mysteries. In the emergency room, there was no time to think about these things. Death was part of the job; it had to be endured. You had to continue, because what choice did you have otherwise? It worked well until it happened to someone you cared about. Papa's death was different; it made her want to bury her face in the smoke-stained cushions and sob.

One foot in front of the other, she told herself.

"Aurora?"

Luna Riley appeared in the doorway and swept Aurora into a rosewater-scented embrace. Her silver hair was sprayed into stiff wings that framed her owlish face, and she wore a coral-colored suit adorned with gold buttons the size of quarters. Aurora had met Luna for the first time at Papa's funeral and been surprised to learn that they were old friends "from a hundred years ago." There was a warm competence about Luna that Aurora liked. Maybe this would be easier than she thought.

"Thanks for seeing me," Aurora said. Luna led them into her office and shut the door. The office furniture was sparse, but pictures crowded each other for space on every surface. In the largest photo, on the wall, a group of older women barefoot in bridal gowns, Luna among them, posed on a beach, held champagne flutes in the direction of the camera.

Luna followed Aurora's gaze. "Wedding dress party," she explained. "We get together every summer down South and wear 'em. Crazy old Southern belles." She touched the photo briefly. "Most of these gals are divorced now, but Grant and I are still going strong. Forty-three years and counting. Anyway"—she gestured for Aurora to sit on the yellow plaid couch—"you're not here to listen to an old lady's stories. Again, I was so very, very sorry to hear about your grandfather's passing. Hunter Broussard was one of the kindest, smartest men I've ever known."

"Thank you," Aurora said, a catch in her voice. "He was a wonderful man. More like a father to me." The only father she'd ever known. "You said you were longtime friends?"

"Oh, yes." Luna smiled. "You wouldn't know it now, but I'm a bayou girl, born and raised in Hambone, just north of where your folks are from. I used to wait tables at one of the fried fish joints on the causeway, and your granddaddy was a regular customer. Always respectful, always left a big tip. He teased me that I'd forget about all the bayou folks back home once I became a lawyer in the big city." She held up a charm that dangled at the end of a gold chain wrapped around her desk lamp, and in the light, Aurora saw an image of an out-stretched palm with stars protruding from the fingertips. "I never forgot where I came from. Still got my voodoo charms."

"So you knew my family, then?" Aurora searched Luna's face.

Luna nodded. "Oh, yes," she said.

Of course she did.

Luna leaned towards Aurora. "I've seen a lot, Aurora. I know that what your daddy did casts a long shadow."

"Yes."

Wade Atchison, her father, had murdered her mother in cold blood when Aurora was a toddler. When Aurora was growing up with her grandparents, she had looked for him in the dark corners of her room, under the bed, in the back of the closet. *Wade's dead in a ditch somewhere, by the grace of God*, she'd heard her grandmother say one morning when she was supposed to be out of earshot.

But there was always the possibility that he wasn't.

"Your grandfather, he loved you so much," Luna said.

"And he was so proud of you. 'My granddaughter,' he used to tell me, 'she saves lives every single day.'"

Aurora managed a smile, but the pinprick sensation was beginning behind her eyes, the swell of grief rising in her chest. Luna slid a velvet-covered tissue box in her direction, and Aurora plucked a tissue free.

"I understand he was ill for quite some time," Luna continued, hoisting an accordion file in front of her. "Had he spoken to you at all—about the estate?"

"The estate? You mean the house?" Estate seemed like a fancy word for the tiny two-bedroom in Connecticut where Aurora had grown up.

"No, the estate refers to all of his property—assets, real property, all of that." She began pulling papers from the file, her voice shifting into a businesslike tone. Luna dealt with death every day, just like her. It was in every file that cluttered her desk. Did she see it as a series of calculations, an ordered list of possessions?

"We really didn't talk about that."

"That's okay! That's fine." Luna beamed at her. "It's my job to deal with these things, and I can answer any questions you might have. But I have to let you know, there are some things here that I'm not licensed to handle, with regards to the real property, the house. I do have some great contacts down there, though, and—"

"Down where?"

"In Florida. Cooper's Bayou."

Aurora's breath caught in her throat. Papa had left Cooper's Bayou behind after her mother's death. It was another world, a place where terrible things had happened that were never discussed, all vestiges of that prior life scrubbed free from their lives in Connecticut. In her face, Aurora saw that

Luna Riley knew the whole sad story, and that there was much, much more than Aurora had imagined.

"There's a house in Cooper's Bayou?"

Luna swiveled a color printout to face her. The house was a plantation in miniature, blue with delicate white trim the color of birthday cake icing. Beveled glass doors opened onto a patio half obscured by the aging knee of an oak tree. The front yard glowed with clusters of flowers shaped like pink pinwheels.

Cajun hibiscus. Aurora almost said it out loud. It had been her mother's favorite flower, one of the few facts she knew about Raylene. She loved Cajun hibiscus, her favorite food was fried okra, and she was afraid of thunder and lightning. Each detail of her mother that Aurora had caught she had treasured like a jewel, repeated like a mantra. They breathed life into the photographic images she had; they were something to cling to after the sound of her mother's voice had faded from her memory.

Papa had known, too. He'd kept his daughter's favorite flower blooming in the front yard; had cared for this place for twenty years from thousands of miles away, without ever mentioning it to her once. Aurora's eyes flicked over the photographs on Luna Riley's desk, photographs of a real family, their arms entwined on beaches and in front of a Christmas tree and at an outdoor wedding. They were making memories for themselves, creating legacies, leaving something real behind, not just a file full of papers and a secret house on a bayou.

"When did he get this house?"

"Your mother grew up there," Luna said gently. "Your grandfather built it with his own hands. It's been in your family for quite some time."

Aurora stared without replying, hypnotized by the photograph. "Does anyone live there now?"

"No, but your grandfather hired a local gentleman to help with the day-to-day upkeep. He wired him money every month for maintenance, repairs, that kind of thing. His contact information is somewhere in here, along with the deed. Here we go." Luna held up a page. "Jefferson Gibbs. I have a phone number there in the file."

"I'm sorry, Ms. Riley, I just—I didn't know any of this. It's just a lot to take in." Aurora felt warmth rising to her face. She closed her eyes and took a deep breath.

"Well, of course it is." Luna reached across the desk and patted Aurora's hand. "I wish there was more I could do to help, but I'm not licensed in Florida. I've done some research to point you in the right direction."

"What do I need to do next?"

Luna indicated the pile on her desk. "Florida law requires that you file the will in local circuit court after learning of the death. Then they'll decide whether or not it has to go through probate."

"I have to go to court?"

"Maybe, maybe not. A good attorney should be able to figure out your options. Then if you want to sell the house, you'll need to get the title cleared, get the property inspected, that sort of thing. It may take some time." She handed Aurora a business card. "Royce Beaumont is a dear old friend of mine. He knew your family, and he handles these matters. You can trust him."

She was going to have to go back. Cooper's Bayou. Aurora wanted to slide time back a few weeks, before Papa's death had brought the past hurtling into the present. The thought of returning to the place of her birth—alone—brought a chill with it. She would have to ask for bereavement leave from work. How long would it take to sort through all of this?

"Did Papa know about all of this? That I would have to take care of it?"

Luna folded her arms. "I told him that you would have to go to Florida to handle the property. He was aware of it."

So he knew. "He never wanted me to go there when he was alive. Cooper's Bayou—he never talked about it." Papa had hidden the past for twenty years to protect her from the ghosts that waited there. There had to be a good reason.

Luna nodded. "Maybe," she said, "he was ready for you to find out why."

CHAPTER SEVEN

"I need to see you in my office first thing, Hudson. We need to talk. Now."

The voice mail Captain Rush had left on Josh's cell was not the harbinger of a good day. Josh took a long swallow of his coffee.

He walked the two blocks from Java Jive to the Cooper's Bayou Police Department headquarters, an unassuming gray building squashed between two halves of the Curtain Call Pawn Shop. A flag outside the shop proclaimed JESUS SAVES on one side and WE BUY GUNS! on the other. The police department consisted of five police officers—Rush, the chief; one sergeant, Donovan; Josh and Boone; and one part-timer named Bay who was also a third of the fire department.

Rush was waiting for Josh at the door, his pudgy arms crossed, already sweating profusely at this morning hour.

"Hudson. I need to see you in my office. Now." Captain Rush worried the edge of his mustache, a recent addition that gave him an unfortunate passing resemblance to a wayward pirate. During the course of his lengthy divorce, he had tried out several new looks, much to the delight of his coworkers.

"Can I finish my coffee first?" Josh raised the paper cup in a toast to Rush, who frowned.

Pea's face floated in his memory. *I know where Liana is.* Pea should be somewhere over the Atlantic Ocean by now. Would she have gone to the police, burned him before she left?

"Now, Josh." Rush opened the door to his office, revealing Sergeant Donovan in the middle of a swing at an imaginary baseball. Donovan was a local, the son of a shrimper. He was a Bible-thumper and a bit of a blowhard, but he knew it and took Josh's ribbing with a good sense of humor.

"Hey," Donovan said. He brandished the autographed baseball bat, one of his prized possessions. "Big game against Hambone's coming up. You're looking at the MVP." Both Donovan and Josh had captained their high school baseball teams, and the creation of a police department softball team had led to a friendly rivalry.

"I've seen better swings on a porch." Josh mirrored his smile and slid into a chair. Rush was a stickler for administrative details; Josh never turned in reports on time. There was still a possibility that this had nothing to do with Pernaria Vincent.

"Listen, Josh. I've got to talk to you about something."

"I don't know if I can fix your swing in two days, D. I need more time."

Donovan chuckled, but there was something shuttered in his expression. Rush nodded at him. "Leave us be a minute, Donovan. I need a word with Josh."

Donovan closed the door, and Rush removed a folder from the top of the file cabinet, extracting a large glossy booking shot. For a moment, Josh imagined that it was his sister, that she was being held somewhere, that this morning was the end of his search.

But when Rush slid the photo towards Josh, it was Pea who scowled at him from the photo, red-eyed and wild. Rush averted his eyes and spoke.

"Do you recognize this person?"

Josh exhaled.

"Well? Do you recognize her?"

Josh refused to meet Rush's gaze, hypnotized instead by Pea's booking photograph. Pea had been true to her word; she'd led Turner right into their hands. Josh had kept his end of the bargain—so how had Pea gotten herself caught?

"Where is she?" Josh forced his voice to sound casual. Pea should have been in Paris a week ago. A dozen times over the last couple of days, he'd pictured her at an outdoor café, those incredible legs crossed underneath a delicate wrought-iron table. What had happened to her?

"So you admit that you know Pernaria Vincent." There was a tremble in Rush's voice.

"Yeah. She helped us out on a drug case."

Rush averted his eyes and spoke in a voice Josh had never heard before, a voice tinged with disappointment. "Why don't you tell me about that, Josh."

"Sure," Josh said. "We're working two separate groups. The first one was part of the same group who sold to Haylee Graves." The Graves case was the one that had secured Josh an invite to the squad. Haylee was a local Hambone student, a golden girl who'd been found dead of a heroin overdose. Josh had been the one to collar the scumbag who'd sold to her. It had earned him some attention, a medal of recognition and other bullshit that didn't change the fact that Haylee was dead and there were a hundred lowlife dealers waiting to take her killer's place.

Rush nodded. "And the second one?" He shuffled some

papers. "According to Fizz, it's some Hambone ring, oxy and other pills, using Ms. Vincent's beauty parlor as a front?"

Josh swallowed. "Yes."

"Fizz told me that you went undercover to make a buy at this shop, right? And what happened?"

Josh forced himself to look Rush square in the face, to make the lie sound as earnest as possible. "When I went there, I spoke with Ms. Vincent. She gave me the information I needed. The next night, I came back, and we shut down the operation, made several arrests, including the head of the group, Turner Randall. My understanding at that time was that Ms. Vincent had already left the country."

Rush frowned. "Ms. Vincent told the investigators that she had a deal with you, but Fizz tells me he never authorized it. He says your orders were to take the pack of 'em into custody, including Ms. Vincent. Instead, it seems you warned her, because she was pulled over on the interstate with Turner's money, headed for the airport." Rush tilted back in his chair. "Ms. Vincent was speeding, and the officer who pulled her over had a bad feeling and decided to run her license. It was a lucky break, really. Or unlucky, I guess, for you."

A thin ribbon of dread began to unfurl itself in Josh's stomach.

"We pulled Ms. Vincent's file, Josh. It seems that she wasn't taking orders from Turner Randall. She was making weekly visits to an inmate at Craw Lake." Rush slid another booking photo over Pea's. Doyle Hudson leered at the camera. The face had aged, but the smirk was the same.

His father.

Josh brushed both pictures aside. "What the hell is this?"

"Tell us who's involved, Josh. We've got to get a handle on

this thing before it gets out of control. And you need to start by telling me the truth."

"It's not what you think, Cap," Josh began, realizing how lame it sounded.

To Josh's surprise, Rush slammed a closed fist down on the table. When he spoke, he spit the words out in short trumpet blasts.

"Fizz asked me about you, Hudson. Before they picked the narcotics team. And you know what I told him? I said, Josh Hudson is the best we got. Doesn't matter that your old man went sideways, I told him you do things the right way. We're lucky to have him in this department, I said. Donovan and I, we both vouched for you. So you fucking tell me, Josh—what am I supposed to do when this shit lands in my lap?" He gestured at the pictures. "So I'll give you one last chance here. To explain yourself. To tell me what's going on with you and your dad and this woman and this drug thing."

"Cap, I didn't do anything," Josh said, fearing it was far too late for the truth. "Pea—Ms. Vincent—I let her go. I did. Because she wasn't a major player in this thing—and because she told me she could help me find somebody."

"Who?"

"My sister. Liana." He was unprepared for the rush of emotion that the simple act of speaking her name evoked. "I don't know where she is, but I know she's in trouble. She's the one that put my dad behind bars. I need to find her. Cap, I swear to you. I'm not into drugs, I'm not part of some big conspiracy, and I had no idea Pea was involved with my father. I just want to find my sister."

A flicker of understanding crossed Rush's face, quickly replaced by the same disillusioned frown. "I don't have a choice here, Josh. You'll be placed on probation, on desk duty in the evidence room, until we can look into the matter further."

"But, Cap—"

"It's not permanent," Rush said. "You can use your time there to think."

Josh was going to be a powerless desk jockey. This was a nightmare.

"So that's it? I'm done?"

"I'm going to need your weapon. While we sort this out," Rush said quietly.

Josh unclipped the gun from his waistband and slammed it on the desk along with his badge. "Y'all have a great day now," he said.

Outside, Josh leaned against the building, the relentless Florida sun scorching his brain. In his pocket, his cell phone buzzed. Josh dug it out.

Pea.

Bonjour, the text read. *Just made bail.*

He hesitated. *I had no idea*, he typed. *Just found out. I didn't turn you in.*

I know, sugar plum. I'm sorry I had to tell them about our deal. But we all have to save ourselves in the end, don't we? You understand.

He did. Pea didn't have to know what he'd discovered about her and his father. How much could Doyle do from prison? And she was still a connection to Liana. He had to see it through. What did he have to lose?

Of course, he wrote. *All we can do is try to do right by each other.*

The words appeared before he'd finished typing.

Tell me what I can do.

Something inside Josh leapt at the words. There was still

a chance he could find his sister. Pea had her picture. She knew something.

I need a favor, Josh typed. He couldn't be too specific, not on this cell. He made a mental note to buy a throwaway.

The reply was almost instant.

Anything you need.

CHAPTER EIGHT

Aurora's return to the place of her birth had been strangely serene. Her nerves, usually strung as tight as guitar strings, had unwound on the plane ride, and driving the hour and a half to Cooper's Bayou, she had even rolled down the windows of the steaming rental car and hummed along to the morose strains of an unfamiliar country song on the radio. For once she was like all the people in the other cars on the road—just trying to get home.

Shiny strip malls and car lots gave way to swampland, the road ahead of her thinned to a one-lane strand winding through the bayou, brimming with earth-colored water. In the passenger seat, the keys to the house on the bayou anchored the fluttering road map from the rental car company, the location of her hometown outlined in a red circle.

It was only now, two miles from the turnoff for Cooper's Bayou, that the reality of where she was going began to settle around Aurora's shoulders. She'd been vague when requesting the time off from work, telling them she had to settle some affairs for her grandfather. Now she wished she'd confided in someone. She was the person people turned to at work to make death notifications, to handle the unbearable things that no-body else wanted to do, and now here she was, falling apart on a country road. She was stronger than this. She knew it, and Papa had known it too. He had entrusted her with this task. There had to be a reason.

Aurora searched her memory for the day she'd left here in Papa's peach-colored Buick. She remembered the stifling interior of the car, the bugs clinging to the window. Nana had stroked her hair and drawn hearts and smiley faces on her back with her index finger, one of Aurora's favorite games to play with her mother. She remembered the pink satin suitcase at her feet with the wheels covered in sparkling stars. She'd thought they were going on a vacation, that they'd be back and she would tell Mama and Daddy all about the adventures she'd had.

It was only later, when they had been in Connecticut a couple of months, that she realized that day in the car was the moment that everything had changed, and that everything in her old life was lost to her forever. Papa had sat on the edge of her bed in the guest room in the unfamiliar Connecticut house and told her that Mama was in heaven and that Daddy was a terrible man who had hurt Mama, and God had somehow delivered Aurora from that night. The same God who had spared her life had taken everything else away with no reason, no explanation. What kind of God could let that happen? She would never understand it.

The last turnoff, according to Luna's directions, was little more than a dirt road leading directly into the bayou. The rental GPS was useless in the tangle of roads. She was going to have to find her own way into town later. She pulled off on the shoulder and stared at the map. She had to be close.

Aurora threw the car into reverse, and with a turn of her

head, caught sight of the house. It was set off the road at an angle, as though turning a shoulder to her, its shuttered windows facing the bayou. Aurora pulled into the driveway and cut the engine, stepping outside into the slickness of the late afternoon humidity. The last of the sun's long fingers grazed the bayou's surface, the last slice of light hovering on the horizon, outlining the husks of half-sunken cypress trees. Aurora was a city girl and never had been much for nature, but there was something about this landscape that commanded her attention in a way that was more than a little unnerving.

Aurora turned back towards the house. Nobody had lived here for twenty years, and yet it glowed, emanating warmth. Four freshly painted white columns supported a delicate latticed porch like upturned palms. Papa had built this place with his own hands, for his wife, for his children. Wings beat in Aurora's chest, her spine hardening. This was where she was supposed to have grown up. This should have been her home.

She climbed the steps slowly, drawing her fingers across the polished wood railing. A kiddie pool was wedged in one corner of the porch, one of the cheap plastic ones, translucent with age. It seemed out of place on the otherwise pristine porch. From this vantage point, Aurora could see something rippling the surface of the water. She moved closer.

It took her a moment to identify what they were; four black shapes arrayed in a diamond at the pool's warped plastic bottom. Alligators. Baby ones, it appeared, each one no longer than her forearm. Aurora knelt by the pool's edge and dipped a hand in the water, running her index finger along the ridges of one of the tiny prehistoric bodies.

"Dadgummit, they sure are cute, ain't they?"

The voice behind her had the same sugared drawl as Papa. The man crouched next to her, his sun-battered face next to her own. He looked to be somewhere in his seventies with a thick beard and an Army-fatigue-colored fishing hat.

"They're so tiny—it's amazing."

"Jefferson Gibbs," he said, grasping her hand. "And you must be Aurora." He scooped up one of the baby gators and held it aloft, like an offering. "I've been looking after these little fellas since your family left. Didn't have the heart to just release the little fellas. You remember the gators? I remember when you were just a teeny little thing, your papa used to put you in here with the gators. Man, your mama didn't like that one little bit. But you was just as happy as a puppy with two tails." He grinned.

Papa had put her in a pool with alligators? It seemed so cavalier, so unlike him. "I never knew that," she said. "Wasn't he scared? Wasn't I scared?"

"Nah," Jefferson said. "Gators, they're easy to predict. It's people you got to watch out for." This statement hung in the air between them, and Aurora held out her palms so that Jefferson could place the baby gator across them. She marveled in the perfection of it, the scales etched in miniature on the curve of the animal's back.

"Your grandpappy," Jefferson said in a reverent tone, "he was the alligator nuisance man. Nobody in this county knew more about gators than him. He taught me everything I know about 'em."

"The alligator what?"

"He was the alligator nuisance man for Cooper County. Anybody had a problem with gators, they called your grandpappy, and he'd come out. Wouldn't shoot 'em, no, not unless they hurt somebody. He'd truss 'em up and relocate 'em."

Aurora searched her memory for any mention of alligators. Papa had always worn a suit and tie to his job at the bank, but insisted on pairing it with snakeskin boots. "Guess I'm still a country boy at heart," he used to tease when she asked him about it.

"I guess he never mentioned it when I was growing up." She lowered the gator down to the water's surface and watched it submerge in one smooth motion.

Jefferson shrugged. "Not much work for an alligator man up north, I guess." He laughed, but averted his gaze, as though afraid he had said too much. "Well, I'd better let you get settled. The house should be stocked with everything you need. I do hope you'll let me know if there's anything you need, Miss Aurora."

"Thank you so much. I guess I need to find my way to the courthouse to file some papers about the house."

Jefferson nodded. "I would start at the police station. They handle all manner of stuff down there, records and deeds and whatnot. It's right in the middle of town. You can't miss it."

"Great."

"I'll let you get settled, then." He gave her a salute and started down the steps.

"I'm sorry—Jefferson?"

He turned.

"Did you know my mother?"

"For true," he said softly. "Raylene was prettier than all the stars in the sky." The grief was written in bold strokes across his face. Her mother had meant something to Jefferson Gibbs. "For her to leave this earth that way—it wasn't right. And your grandpappy, he never gave up trying to find out what really happened to her."

Something fluttered in Aurora's chest. "What do you mean?" The story was simple. Aurora's father had strangled her mother on the shores of the bayou, then disappeared into the night, leaving Aurora on the steps of a local store. In her presence, they'd never mentioned her father. When she pressed Papa for details, he'd told her Wade was an evil man who'd killed her mother in a fit of rage. She'd never questioned the story, and to her knowledge, neither had he.

"Hunter came down here, every couple of months or so. Said it was to take care of the house, but I know different. He was working on something. He told me last time he was in town, he says, 'Jefferson, I'm getting close to finding out what happened that night on the bayou.'"

"I don't understand. The case is closed. We know what happened." Even while she spoke, the pieces were falling together in her mind. The fishing trips before he'd gotten sick. 'The fishing was good, just the catching was bad,' he'd joked when he'd returned to the house empty-handed. Papa had been here. All this time, she'd thought he'd put her mother out of his mind, but he'd been coming here, trying to figure out what had happened to his only daughter that night on the bayou. She should have been stunned, she should have felt betrayed somehow—but she felt none of those things. Papa had always been her hero, her defender, the person she turned to for help. Knowing that he'd been the same for her mother, even after her death, just made her feel that he was the man she had known all along.

"Do you know what he thought? What he was working on?" The questions tumbled in her brain.

Jefferson shook his head and gestured towards the set of keys in Aurora's right hand. "It's not for me to know," he said. "You take care, now, Miss Aurora. Call if you need anything at all." He plodded back down the steps and then paused, turning back once again. "I left everything the way it was," he said, "just like your granddaddy told me to."

"Thank you." She wasn't sure what he meant, but she nodded in gratitude. "Thank you for everything."

Aurora twisted the key and pushed the heavy door open. She flipped the light switch and then covered her mouth, grasping the elbow of a stately armoire to steady herself.

Crucifixes covered every available wall space. Silver and gold, plastic and wooden, large and small, they stretched in uneven rows around the length of the great room, floor to ceiling. Papa had been religious, but the sheer number of them suggested a fervor that Aurora had never experienced from him.

More unnerving were the objects that seemed significant but foreign to Aurora. The side tables, desk, and dining room table were littered with them; tiny jars and vases, some filled with liquid, others clear; bundles of sticks and rolled-up paper tied with string, and rows of bags, cinched at the top.

Aurora jumped at the sound of her cell phone, trilling somewhere in the depths of her bag. A familiar name flashed on the screen. Luna Riley. She picked it up.

"Hello?"

"Hi, Aurora. Just wanted to check in with you and see that you made it down there in one piece. Everything okay?"

Aurora turned away from the mantel, where a felt doll crowned in purple feathers leered at her. "It's not what I expected."

"Is everything all right?"

"There's just a lot of—well, I don't know how to describe it. He has these bags everywhere. They're kind of like sachets, tied with ribbon." She knew she sounded insane, but miraculously, Luna Riley hummed in agreement on the other end of the phone.

"Gris-gris," Luna said.

"What?"

"That's what the bags are called. They're for luck. Good fortune. It's nothing bad, Aurora. I promise. Your grandfather and people like him who grew up on the bayou, it's just a part of life for them to have those. Like a talisman."

"Do you know anything about why he'd have these jars? And pieces of paper with string?" Aurora perched on the edge of the satiny yellow sofa. Beside her, the waxy, bubbled remains of several violet candles dotted the windowsill.

"I'm not an expert in that stuff, so I'm not sure," Luna admitted. "There's somebody in town who is, though—you can be sure of that. I'll let you settle in. Mr. Beaumont, that attorney I mentioned, is expecting your call."

"Terrific, thanks." Aurora ended the call. Shadows had begun to creep across the ceiling. She walked from room to room, flipping every switch, drenching the house in light. What had Papa been doing with these religious objects? Aurora had assumed that Jefferson meant Papa was reviewing her mother's case, looking through old files, but the truth appeared to be something more supernatural.

She put the kettle on, the purr of the stove reassuring. Her grandfather grinned at her from a picture magnet on the refrigerator, one of those plastic ones you buy at a gift shop. *World's Sweetest Grandpa!* the frame in the shape of chocolate bars proclaimed. Tears of recognition sprang to Aurora's eyes. Papa must have brought it down here on one of his trips back to the bayou. She had bought this for him on their sixth-grade class trip to Hershey, Pennsylvania. The man in the photo was the grandpa she loved, stalwart and solid, a man who handled everything in his stride. It was hard to picture him lighting these candles, tying the bags of gris-gris, summoning the daughter that was never coming back.

Aurora leaned against the counter. For as long as she could remember, she had felt her own sense of responsibility. *Be a good girl, be kind, be the best you can be.* She'd had to do it because Raylene could not, because her mother's death had to mean something. She had to save people because if she didn't, what was left? The other part of herself. She was Wade Atchison's child too. He'd killed her mother and spared her. *What your daddy did casts a long shadow.*

Maybe Papa had stumbled across a dark truth that he could not handle. Maybe that was up to Aurora.

There was nobody else to do it. She was the only one left.

CHAPTER NINE

"They ain't critter bones. I told you, Doc. I knew it. I was right. Wasn't I, though?" Zeke Crumpler demanded.

Slowly, in a way that he hoped conveyed the annoyance he felt, James brought himself to a standing position and turned away from the duffel bag and its grim contents.

Zeke Crumpler hovered nearby. Everyone in town had hoped that age would settle the Crumplers, maybe smooth out some of the rough edges, but that had turned out to be overly optimistic. Zeke and the older generation, now no longer able to participate in the petty crimes of their youth, continued to cause trouble by poking into everyone else's business, running illegal poker games out of the Sunny Land Rest Home, and terrorizing anyone who dared to complain about the herd of barking dogs or incessant four-wheelers on their property outside town. Barred from his brother's autopsy, Zeke had once called James "a pansy-ass, real light in the loafers." It had been a long time ago, but then again, it wasn't the kind of thing you forgot.

"I'm going to need you to step back, Zeke," James said. He

drew his handkerchief across his forehead, an instant sheen of new sweat rising in its wake. Summer in Cooper's Bayou was getting more brutal with each passing year. Days like this, he wished for more help in the field, but explaining everything to the tech was more trouble than it was worth, so these things had to be borne alone.

James knelt back down. According to Zeke, the neon pink duffel bag had just shown up on the shore, and he'd opened it up to find the bones tucked inside. It was a dubious tale at best, but it was all they had to go on. James surveyed the shoreline. Someone could have tossed it from a boat, or the bayou itself could have deposited it on the beach. James's father had told him stories as a kid about the magical things hiding in the bayou; skeletons of pirate ships and sea creatures. *Bayou's dark and deep,* he'd tell James, *but even the bayou can't keep a secret forever.*

He would have to call the police department, maybe find the name of the forensic anthropologist that he'd spoken with at the medical conference last year. The list of procedures stretched ahead of him, but for now, one fact crowded out all the rest.

It was a child.

He was pretty sure, given the size of the remains. James imagined the forensic artist who would press clay around the skull to re-create the face. Bayou John Doe, or Bayou Jane Doe. It had to be done, but James hated that it would become a sensational news story instead of being treated with quiet reverence as the tragedy it was. Death investigation was the telling of a personal story, not for public consumption, in his view.

James surveyed the area around the body. Whoever had left the bag had done so on a small curve of beach outside Baboon Jack's, Cooper's Bayou's kiddie arcade. James had attended two of his nephews' birthdays here. WHERE KIDS RUN WILD! proclaimed the sign, and in James's experience, it was true. He recalled the cavernous interior, a maze of blinking video games, yellow plastic slides, and a noise level unmatched by anything he had ever experienced. He was grateful that none of the kids inside had witnessed the discovery.

"How long you think this will take, Doc?" The proprietor of Baboon Jack's, a humorless middle-aged man named Walter Coggins, hovered over him. "We've got a zombie dodgeball tournament in about half an hour."

"This is a possible crime scene, Walter," James told him. "I've got to call in the troops. Crime lab, police. You probably need to start shutting it down for the day."

"Aw, hell, Doc. You gotta be kidding me." Walter raked a hand through the greasy tendrils of his comb-over. "What am I gonna tell these parents? And I ain't gonna get my money back on these zombies."

"It's a potential crime scene," James repeated and extracted his cell phone from his pocket, turning away from Walter.

Mary Earl, the dispatcher, answered on the third ring.

"Hello there, darlin'." Her pleasantries always caught him off guard. He'd said to Rush that they needed to answer the phone in a more professional manner over there, but the truth was, he liked hearing the words, even though he never knew what to say back.

"Um, good afternoon, Mary Earl. We've got a body here, down by Baboon Jack's. They're skeletal remains. I'm going to need whoever Rush has available."

"Lord mercy," she breathed. "Rush and Boone went out on a call a while back. Gators in someone's yard up by Bayou Triste, and some hillbilly shooting at 'em and carrying on." Her voice faded and then returned. "Hello? Doc Mason?"

"Yes, yes. Sorry, Mary Earl. You know how the cell service is out here. Just please have them get here as soon as possible." He ended the call.

"You all right, Doc?" Zeke was staring at him.

"Hot day," James managed.

"Yep," Zeke continued. "And ain't none of us getting any goddamn younger, that's for sure. Well, I best get going, Doc."

"Zeke, you've got to stick around, tell the police what you told me about finding the body."

Zeke shook his head. "Ya'll know how to find me. I gotta go. I'm helping Jefferson Gibbs take care of the Broussard place, least until they sell it. I need that cash, you know?"

The Broussard house had stood empty for years, perched on the bayou's eastern shore, one of the town's historic landmarks. James drove past it every evening on the way to his own house.

"Hunter's selling the place?"

Zeke frowned. "Hunter went to be with the Lord, couple weeks ago. They said it was some cancer, but I said it's that Northern living that'll kill ya. You didn't hear about that?"

James hadn't heard. A memory kicked its way to the surface of his consciousness unbidden, and there she was in his mind's eye: Raylene Atchison, Hunter's daughter. The last time he'd ever seen her alive was in his autopsy suite, asking questions about being a nurse. She'd lingered in his doorway then, and even James, adrift in all his cluelessness about the opposite sex, had known she wanted to say more. He remembered the patient who'd been on his table that day, an escaped convict from Craw Lake who'd drowned hiding out in the bayou. *You treat 'em the same, no matter what they done?* she'd asked, pointing to the fragmented cuff that still hung around the patient's graying wrist. When James nodded, she'd smiled. *I could do that. Wade's always saying I see the good in people, sometimes when it ain't even there.* Even all these years later, the memory of that statement sent a ripple of sadness through him.

"So what's going to happen to the house?"

"Dunno," Zeke said. "She just got here, but Jefferson said didn't feel like it was right to ask her on her first day in town. Even though my daughter-in-law Renee, she won't shut up about it. She's a Realtor, you know. Got one of them glossy billboards on Route Seven and everything."

"Who just got here?"

"Hunter's granddaughter. Aurora. You remember, they took her away all those years ago? I met her yesterday. Good-looking girl, did well for herself up North, she's a nurse. I'm guessing she won't be hanging around here long."

Aurora. So many times James had thought about her since that night, wondered where she was, hoped that she had gone out into the world as fearless as her mother. He felt a little tick of pride at hearing that she was now a nurse.

"Well, keep your phone on you. I'm sure someone will be wanting to ask you some questions."

"Much obliged, Doc." Zeke gave him a salute and headed back in the direction of the parking lot.

James sat down by the edge of the bayou. He wanted to stop by the Broussard house, to pay his respects to Aurora, but what if she didn't want to see him? He was a part of the worst night of her life; he wouldn't blame her if she just wanted to forget.

James thought about his own father. After his death, James had sought out every one of his father's shrimping buddies, yearned for stories, anything to breathe life into that memory again. Grief was a funny thing, though; everyone walked along its path differently.

His cell phone buzzed and shifted in his pocket. All these years, and it still gave him peace, knowing that someone was looking for him. It was the being needed that counted, even if it was only dead people who needed him. He answered the call, just as the whine of a distant siren rose above the noise of the water. The police were on their way.

CHAPTER TEN

Josh's new place of work, a sprawling old wooden warehouse perched on the scorched riverbank, had all the traditional markings of a haunted house.

This far out of town, the bayou was no more than a thin chocolate strand that yawned into a swamp choked with black gum trees and buttonbush shrubs, and the vegetation seemed to be strangling the building itself. Surrounding trees covered the roof in long, gray plaits of Spanish moss, and woolgrass rose in thick clumps around the base of the splintering structure.

The only sign of life was an eggplant-colored Corvair parked at a dramatic angle in the weeds. This had to be his new boss's car.

Something shifted in the tall grass, and Josh reached for his gun without thinking. Of course, there was nothing in his waistband. He was a member of the Rubber Gun Squad now. Administrative leave in the evidence room. *It's not permanent,* Captain Rush had said, avoiding Josh's gaze, pretending this job wasn't the last stop on the loony-tune express to nowhere. *Use your time there to think.*

As if he didn't think too much already.

"Hello?" Josh shouted in the general direction of the front door and was answered only by the whine of a swarm of insects. The relentless Florida humidity smothered him from all sides. What were the chances this place had air-conditioning?

Josh edged his way around the back of the building to the crumbling remains of a porch, complete with an ancient double-paned white door. Next to the buzzer was a plaque that read EVIDENCE ROOM, COOPER COUNTY. PLEASE RING FOR ASSISTANCE.

Josh pressed the buzzer twice. Above him, the leaden sky growled and snapped, a finger of lightning reaching down to touch the bayou. Josh turned the knob and went inside.

"Hello?" Josh was beginning to feel like this whole exercise was a joke. Boone and Donovan were probably crouched in the bushes outside, howling at Josh as he circled the building and then let himself in the back door.

The walls of the massive indoor space were painted in bright pastels like a kindergarten classroom. Rows of metal shelves twenty feet high stretched across the massive warehouse interior, boxes bursting from every shelf. From deep inside the warehouse, Josh could hear the faint lilt of music.

He followed the sound down the first row of metal shelving, a creaky ceiling fan sending a plume of hot air down on him. Cardboard boxes, wrinkled with age, slouched on each of the shelves, marked with a case number and a curling piece of colored tape. The boxes gave way to rows of skateboards and then bicycles suspended upside down, their streamers brushing against Josh's shoulder. All of them evidence; all of them had once belonged to someone who had been the victim of a crime.

The music was louder now, and Josh stepped out of the row into a clearing where a pudgy man with salt-and-pepper curls swayed to the strains of a Dylan song that Josh half recognized.

"Christ on a bike!" the man shouted.

"Sorry," Josh said. "Didn't mean to interrupt."

The older man chuckled. "Not at all! You just gave me a scare. Thought it was those ghosts again." He extended a sweaty hand in Josh's direction. "Mike Sambarello. But everyone calls me Samba. And you must be Detective Hudson!"

"Josh. Pleased to meet you."

"So what do you think, Josh? Is this a cool place or what?"

There was something about this man, with his outward pointing feet, that reminded Josh of a clown, and he could not suppress a grin. "Sure. I like the music."

Samba grinned. "Hey, you gotta do something to lighten the mood around here, you know? Dealing with this stuff gets kinda . . . you know. Heavy." He clicked off the paint-splattered boom box. "So this is your first time here, huh?"

"Yep," Josh said. "I worked narcotics. Not a lot of cold cases." *Except my own*, he added to himself.

"Where you came in, that's where law enforcement comes if they want to request any evidence we might have. Then we have two days to find it. That's the fun part."

"Is there an automated system?" Josh hadn't passed anything resembling a computer.

"Sure is," Samba said, tapping his wrinkled forehead with his index finger. "It's all up here. We have almost two thousand pieces of evidence housed here, and I've organized it into categories."

"But what about the state? Don't they make you log everything in a database?"

Samba frowned. "I don't trust those state guys," he said. "I've been cataloguing evidence for thirty years. I know how to preserve things right and how to find them. I don't need a computer. They can send me all the nasty letters they want, I'm not changing." He lowered his voice, as though afraid someone might be listening. "Fuck the establishment."

Behind them, Josh heard the high-pitched bleat of a cell phone. Samba ignored it, leading Josh in the other direction.

"Is that your phone?"

Samba laughed. "No. That's from our electronic evidence aisle. There's always something chirping over there. You'd be surprised; sometimes these old machines still have a spark in 'em."

Samba led them down a row of enormous yellowing refrigerators, all buzzing at different frequencies. "This is all the biohazard stuff," Samba said. "But if you decide to bring lunch—and I know every man's got his own preference for barbecue, I myself am partial to Piggy Jim's on the corner—you can put it in the big silver one on the end." Josh stepped over a puddle of stagnant green liquid seeping from beneath one of the refrigerators. Samba had placed a plastic CAUTION sign next to the spill. Who was he warning, Josh wondered. Did anyone else even work here?

"So how often do you get a request for evidence?"

"Oh, you know, every so often," Samba said. "I think the last one was two months ago, May. You know, the newer evidence stays with the property clerk of the PD for about a year before they bring it to me here. There's less demand for older stuff, but I make sure everything is where someone can find it."

"How long do you keep the evidence here?"

"Eighty years is what the statute says," Samba confided.

"Plus they ask us to dump out anything that'll get you drunk or high. Those cops are no fun. But I've never thrown anything away, and I don't think the guy before me did either."

Samba reached the end of the row and plopped down on the arm of an overstuffed paisley sofa with its entire midsection cut out, right down to the foam. "Everything we have in here—every piece of evidence—well, to me it represents an injury to somebody. Just 'cause it's old, that doesn't mean you forget about it. It's never too late to get justice. Believe me, I should know."

Josh nodded. Here was a person who cared about his job, a custodian of tragedies, his own and others'—a guy who thought that maybe the system didn't have all the answers. A guy who worked in a warehouse full of unsolved crimes and somehow still believed in justice.

Josh's second cell phone, the throwaway, began to vibrate in a circle on his abandoned table.

"One of your girlfriends, I bet." Samba winked, and Josh reached for the phone.

"*Bonjour,* Josh." Pea.

Josh ducked behind one of the rows of boxes. "Hey. I'm at work. I can't really—"

"I have a lead on Liana." He heard her quick intake of breath, a split decision not to finish the sentence.

"What is it?" The desperation was naked in his voice. Pea was free; he had nothing left to barter with, and she knew it. Still, there was a goodness in her, he could see it. She wanted to help him.

"Pea, please. Whatever it is—I need to know. I need to find her."

"She's in trouble, Josh. She's involved with some bad people. You need to be careful."

When they were kids, Liana was the one who had first disobeyed the rule to stay on their block. She had shrugged off their parents' attempts to control her. In his mind, he could still see her balancing on the roof of their house, tempting the fates. Walking the line. *Taste death live life*, she had written on her forearm in green Magic Marker. His sister, imperious and wild. He had never imagined it would lead to this.

Josh reached into his jeans pocket for the spiral notebook he always carried. "Just tell me," he told Pea. "Where is she?"

On the other end of the phone, there was silence.

"Hello? Hello? Pea?"

The line went dead.

"Goddamnit," he swore. She was playing him. He knew it. But what the hell was her endgame? None of it made sense. Josh swallowed his anger. First day at work, he reminded himself. He couldn't fuck this job up, or who knew what the next stop was on the one-way train to career suicide?

"Sorry, man. Family stuff," he began, expecting to see Samba around the corner, but there was no sign of his boss. Josh walked towards the front entrance, where he heard Samba's voice on the phone.

". . . each one. Got it. I can do that, yes, sir." The older man's voice was no longer the jolly tone of earlier; this was all business. Samba turned and raised a hand at Josh. "Yes. I've got help here, so I should be good. We will let you know when we've got something. Okay. Thank you."

"I'm glad you're here, Josh," Samba said before Josh could ask the question. "We've got a case."

CHAPTER ELEVEN

The bayou invaded Aurora's dreams that night.

She woke to the sound of a paddle being dipped and pulled through creamy swirls of earth-colored water. Aurora crooked a finger and pulled aside the gauzy white curtain by Papa's bed, revealing the violet swath of bayou outside her window. Mist hovered above the water, punctured by the knuckles of sunken cypress trees. A lone figure nudged a skiff in a wide arc around a sunken cluster of plants with leaves that reached skyward like upturned palms and then settled the boat against the opposite shoreline, resting the paddle across the bow of the boat. There was something unearthly about the landscape, especially at this time of the morning, so otherworldly that you could believe there was truth in those old bayou stories about ghost lights and mists that drew people deep into the patchwork of sloughs and never released them.

Aurora slid on shorts and a T-shirt and pulled on one of Papa's old baseball caps. The things she should do scrolled through her mind, a crisp and orderly list. Go through Papa's desk. File papers at the courthouse. Maybe put the house on the market. The real estate agent's glossy business card beckoned her from the desk. Renee Trosclair, the card proclaimed below a picture of a woman with an aggressively spiked blond haircut and a teeth-baring smile. *Look no further—you are home!!* There was something oddly disconcerting about the phrase.

The bedroom was blissfully free of the voodoo items filling the rest of the house. Here, framed pictures surrounded the oak bed covered with one of Nana's quilts. Aurora's mother and grandmother beamed at her, not from stiffly posed photographs but candid shots, their mouths open, their eyes shining, standing behind birthday cakes and reaching for each other across a sea of opened Christmas presents. All her life, Aurora had wished for something of her mother's: a talisman, a reminder that she had existed as more than a story, more than a forbidden topic of conversation. It was a request that she had never had the courage to make, too afraid of upsetting the careful equilibrium in her grandparents' home. And now here she was, surrounded by talismans, whether she liked it or not.

Between the frames were strewn souvenirs from places with names Aurora had never heard of: a thickly spotted seashell from Bayou Sauvage, a coffee mug with a faded logo that advertised a place called Baboon Jack's, an apron that bragged of the best barbecue in Hambone.

Aurora had expected neat stacks of paperwork, another version of Papa's office back home, legal pads and a tightly ordered file cabinet. She could handle paperwork; she did it every day. But Papa had left her with so much more than that. There were things here she needed to understand. If there were questions surrounding her mother's death, they needed to be answered. She wasn't ready to dismantle the house. Not today. Not yet.

A Mass card was fitted into the corner of one of Raylene's photographs, the faded image of a mournful saint on the front. *Internment, Ti Bon Ange Cemetery, 9* A.M. A thickness rose in Aurora's throat. Had she been allowed to attend the burial? Had Papa ever visited the grave?

The man in the skiff was moving again, floating past her house now, his oar laid across his lap, his head tipped back in the sunshine. She opened the front door, crossed the latticed porch, and made her way down to the boat ramp.

"Excuse me, sir?"

The man did not sit up but tilted his head in her direction. She was learning that nobody in this town did anything quickly, something that set her off balance after the frenzied rush of the emergency room. He wore a filthy T-shirt tucked into a pair of ragged cutoffs, one tanned bare foot dangling in the sun-dappled water.

"I was wondering if you could help me, sir," Aurora began, surprised at the timid note in her own voice. "I'm looking for Ti Bon Ange Cemetery."

This got the man's attention. He hoisted himself to a sitting position and shaded his eyes to give her a closer look. "You Hunter Broussard's granddaughter? Raylene's girl?"

"Yes." She was surprised at the hitch in her voice. She was part of something here; linked to this unfamiliar landscape in a way she did not yet understand. "Yes, I am."

He nodded. "Ernest Authement. Your grandfather, he used to buy shrimp from me. He was a fine gentleman." He crossed himself and pressed a thumb to his lips. "He buried in Ti Bon Ange? I know he was coming back to visit. Bayou gets a hold on you, it won't let go."

"No," she said. "My mother is."

"For true," he said. There was a warmth in his creased

eyes, a kindness that made her believe her family had meant something to him. "Well, you gonna need a boat to get there."

"It's an island?"

He laughed, a guttural chortle that morphed into a coughing fit, revealing a mouthful of graying teeth. "For true, you an out-of-towner. That cemetery's been half under water for years."

"Under *water*?" It seemed unimaginable that someone could let that happen.

The man shrugged. "A few years back they poured some concrete to hold it down. But that don't work forever. The bayou gonna rise—nothing they can do."

"So they just forgot about it?"

"Forgotten, maybe so," he said, extending a hand to her. "But not gone. Get in. I'll take you."

The dead lay all around Aurora, entombed aboveground in stone vaults choked with weeds and dying flowers. She stood on the soggy patch of land where Ernest Authement had dropped her off, promising to return in half an hour.

The bayou was wilder here, the water heaving past in an unrelenting torrent the color of strong tea, helpless to the pull of Laveau Bay and the ocean beyond. The line of vaults stretched ahead of her in crooked rows, the water's greedy fingers already seeping between the rows and lapping at their edges.

Aurora gripped the elbow of a submerged oak tree, scaled like an alligator's back, and began to scan the names. Was her mother's grave already gone? Or was she lucky enough to be one of the ones buried farther inland, facing the swamp?

She found it halfway down the second row, on a smooth headstone carved to look like a pillow. RAYLENE BROUSSARD ATCHISON. 1964–1989. AGED TWENTY-FIVE YEARS. HOW

MANY HOPES LIE BURIED HERE. Aurora traced the letters with her index finger and wished for a way to know what those hopes had been. She had carried Wade's name with her, even in death. Aurora wondered why Papa had not changed her own name back to Broussard. An eyeless angel perched on the edge of the tomb, a rusting locket shape embedded in the stone beneath it. Aurora nudged the tarnished cover aside to reveal a photograph of her mother. Raylene, bleached by the sun, peering over her shoulder. There was something so unencumbered, so free, in the smile she turned towards the camera.

Aurora slid the cover back and leaned against the grave, watching the glittering water make its inroads through the cemetery. How long would it take before this place was completely gone? Her mother's story would live on in the local anthology of tragedies. Raylene the person, the smiling woman in the pictures, was already being submerged. With Papa's death, Aurora was the last remaining vestige of Raylene. Aurora believed there were things that connected you that couldn't be explained in a neat spiral of DNA. Maybe it was the Southern part of her. She knelt in front of the grave, picking the headstone free of weeds. There was a kind of peace in it, like a small offering to her mother's memory. Tomorrow she would clip some of the lavender flowers in the front yard and bring them here.

The sound of someone approaching snapped Aurora to attention. Had it been half an hour already? She drew her hand across the carved letters, resolving to return, and made her way back towards the bayou, with one glance back at the grave.

"Better not do that," a voice said.

Aurora turned around so quickly she almost lost her footing. The owner of the voice was a woman, lounging against a tomb. She took a swig from a murky bottle of Bacardi and tipped in

Aurora's direction. She wore a blue knitted skullcap ringed with dangling seashells, improbably paired with blue jeans and a satin Bucs jacket missing most of its snaps.

"Excuse me?"

"Don't look back when you're leaving a graveyard," the woman said. She patted the tomb she sat on. "Or they gonna follow you."

"Thanks for the warning. I'm just waiting for my ride."

The woman shrugged. There was something unsettling about her manner. Aurora turned back towards the bayou. When she turned back, the woman was pouring the rum on the ground in a careful line, murmuring under her breath. She caught Aurora watching.

"You don't believe in this," the woman said, her tone accusatory.

"Believe in what?"

"*Voudon*," the woman said. She removed a tiny bag of what appeared to be bird bones from her jacket pocket and sprinkled them on the marshy ground.

"I guess I never thought about it," Aurora ventured, trying to be polite. Everybody mourns in a different way. She wondered whose grave this woman was here to visit.

"Ha!" The woman giggled. "Your *grandpère*, he thought about it."

"You knew my grandfather?" There was something disconcerting about the familiar way the woman spoke. It was a small town, she told herself. Everyone knows everyone else. Her arrival must have been more newsworthy than she imagined, and this woman had heard about it. That was all.

"Everybody knew him. The alligator man." The woman unzipped a dusty backpack and closed it over the rum bottle. Something hanging from the zipper glinted in the sunlight, catching Aurora's eye. A bag tied with string, like the ones in Papa's house. It was good luck, Luna had said. She wasn't sure why, in this woman's hands, it seemed to be something more ominous.

"Gris-gris, right? It's a good luck charm?" Aurora pointed to it.

The woman's lips curled back, half smirk and half sneer. "This ain't no good luck charm, beb." She lifted her chin. "It's protection."

Ernest stepped out of the reeds behind her. "You ready to go, Aurora?" He tugged his baseball cap down low, and his lips tightened. "Is Charlsie here giving you a problem?"

"*Mais non,*" the woman said in a singsong tone. "You need something from me, Ernest?"

"I'm a God-fearing man," Ernest replied. "I don't need none of that crap."

The woman laughed again, as though this were the funniest joke in the world. "Sooner or later, you'll be wanting something done," she said. "Just like the alligator man."

Ernest scoffed. "Hunter Broussard wanted nothing to do with you. Don't you be talking of a dead man that way."

"I know what I know," she said, her eyes moving from Ernest to Aurora. She zipped the backpack and swung it over one shoulder, retreating deeper into the graveyard.

Ernest shook his head and reached for Aurora's arm, guiding her over the sodden ground towards the skiff. "Don't listen to that crazy old bat," he said. "She makes her money selling spells to poor souls down the bayou who don't know any better. She never knew your grandfather."

Aurora nodded, but the woman's voice haunted her. *I know what I know.* Had Papa gone to that woman for advice? There were at least a hundred of those tiny bags in the house.

If they were for protection, what was he afraid of? He had convinced her that her father was no longer out there, that he could not hurt her. But what if that wasn't true?

Ernest drew the oars through the trembling surface of the water, steering them away from the graveyard.

Aurora made sure to look back.

CHAPTER TWELVE

There was a surplus of death in Cooper's Bayou this summer, just like the one twenty years ago. Long after the remains from the duffel bag had been packaged up and sent to the lab, James had stood in his office and thought about it. *We'll get to the bottom of it, Doc*, Rush had said at the scene, but a lingering uneasiness had followed him ever since, a sense that this was not the end of the story, but the beginning.

James prided himself on avoiding seeing patterns or relying on intuition. There was no place for it in his line of work. Life was terrifyingly random, and he acknowledged this while finding refuge in the clear confines of science. But there was something about this summer that he couldn't ignore, something about heading to these death scenes that felt like walking into a stiff wind. James rarely thought about his previous patients when he was working a case—you couldn't let the past cloud your judgment of the present—but now they clicked through his brain in a doomed catalogue, the same two people always pushing their way to the front of the line.

Soon the light would be gone, the nickel-colored sky above

the bayou succumbing to inky darkness. A single flashlight ringed by insects flickered inside the wheelhouse of the twenty-eight-foot Lafitte skiff he rode on. There were places out here the bayou claimed for its own, places the morgue van couldn't reach, so he'd hitched a ride with Ernest Authement, one of the local shrimpers.

"You want me to take you right on up to the dock at Tee Tim's?" Ernest hollered from the back of the boat, and beneath his cigarette-stained fingertips, the wheel twisted to the left.

James felt a stab of mild annoyance. If there were a way to drive the boat himself while working, he would have done it. There was a certain amount of focus and almost a kind of reverence required at death scenes, especially death scenes out here. It was something that was difficult for those outside of his line of work to understand.

"No," James called back to him in what he hoped was a curt tone that would discourage any further conversation. "Cut the engine and turn on the floodlight. They said they saw her floating right up around this next curve. She might be a couple hundred yards down by now."

"Yes, sir." Ernest gave him a salute from the brim of his filthy baseball cap. Ernest was from a family of shrimpers like James, but there was an uneasiness in their interaction. In Cooper's Bayou, there were people who lived up the bayou and people who lived down it, and those from up the bayou made sure you never forgot the distinction. The contrast between James's upbringing and his current profession placed him squarely in the borderland between the two groups, a unique and socially insurmountable situation that meant the men rode in silence, which was fine with James.

James gripped the railing and felt the spray across his knuckles. The rust-spattered boat was the same as the *Jeaner-*

ette, the boat he had grown up on with his father. Over his mother's protestations, his father had tied James to the winch as a toddler so he would be safe while the nets were being hauled. The memory of it stung and warmed him at the same time in the way that only grief could, both comforting and boundless. They had pulled Coleman Mason's boat intact from the bayou's depths the summer that James turned thirteen, his father's keys still in the ignition, the plastic googly-eyed shrimp charm James had given him for his birthday still on the keychain. How could these mundane things have survived while his father had not? The thought was incomprehensible, even now.

Ernest cut the engine, and the boat shimmied in the water, the copper-colored waves nudging it towards the shoreline choked with pitcher plants. The drowning had been reported an hour ago; a high school junior named Madison Leo had fallen overboard off a boat full of kids on Bayou Triste, out for a night of partying. Nobody had noticed her missing until it was too late. James had sent Glenn to handle the death investigation, the drunk kids, the devastated family. The living made James far more squeamish than the dead. He could not stand there and answer the family's questions the way Dr. Boudet had answered his mother's questions all those years ago. *How*, she'd asked then. Now James knew some of the answers, the ones he'd learned in medical school. He'd seen shooting victims, patients ravaged by disease, but drowning was still the worst kind of death that James could imagine.

Around the next curve, the aging knee of a bald cypress dripping with Spanish moss partially blocked their path, and James realized why his father had not been the sole occupant of his consciousness. This was the place where he had first met Raylene Atchison.

And not far from the place she had died.

"A little to the right, you can make it clear around," James instructed. All these years, and his eyes were still good, acclimating fast to the darkness. There was still life in the old man yet. Something moved in the shallows, and a line of obsidian-colored scales broke the surface, like a tiny mountain range, before submerging again, the water closing above it in a perfect seam. The gators were still in this spot, where Raylene had helped him. Of course they were. They'd been around for more than a hundred million years. Twenty-five years would be nothing to them, the blink of an eye.

James would always remember the case. It was back in the mid-eighties. An unexpected summer storm had come up strong and capsized a pontoon full of garden club members from Kervick County, its scattered contents drifting through the labyrinth of sloughs in the flooded forest. All but one of the passengers had swum safely to shore. The police chief had advised him to call the alligator nuisance man to help navigate the boat and accompany him for the body recovery of the one missing woman. James had resisted at first, but then dialed Hunter Broussard. When he'd arrived at the scene, he'd been met instead by the sight of a pregnant woman huddled inside an enormous jacket standing on the bow of an ancient-looking skiff.

"Mating season," Raylene had said by way of greeting and explanation. There had been a rash of gator-related incidents all across the county, and Hunter had sent his daughter out on this call. James remembered averting his eyes from her belly, her thundercloud of white-blond hair, and her wild, unabashed grin. He was used to being around women like his mother; soft-spoken in their strength, quiet in their manner. Raylene Broussard was neither of these things.

They'd navigated the waterways together. James could still remember that evening, the hush that fell over the bayou, so calm that the only evidence of the storm floated on its violet surface. They wound their way through the tangle of passages, he and Raylene, the alligators appearing every once in a while to remind him of their purpose for being together. He had never been a religious man—not then, and not now—but something about it felt supernatural, as though at just the right moment, his father's boat might come gliding across the water towards them, no time having passed at all.

Raylene talked to him nonstop, mistook his awkwardness for reticence, coaxed responses from him. A woman twenty years his junior, and yet she seemed more attuned to the bayou than most old people he'd met while keeping the sense of wonder that blesses only the very young. Raylene talked about being pregnant as though this were an incredible piece of good fortune visited upon her by a loving universe, not the result of a dalliance with Wade Atchison, the most talked-about petty criminal in town. Raylene asked him about being a doctor. Someday, she told him, she would be a nurse. She'd be great at it, he'd told her; she was strong and capable and had a good way with people. She'd grinned at him, genuinely touched at the compliment.

The two of them had skimmed the water's surface until they'd found Marie Guidry floating face up, her yellow raincoat folded around her face like damp petals. *See?* Raylene had told him proudly, her face shining. *The gators left her alone. They know.*

And even though James had seen many bodies before, there was something about this one that gripped him. There was something different, he told Raylene, about seeing a body at the scene instead of in the morgue, about realizing that she had so recently been in this world and now she was gone. It reminded him of his first cadaver in medical school. It wasn't that the person on the table had had green-gray skin or open eyes; it was that the cadaver had been wearing fingernail polish. It was the tiniest details that could blind you, overwhelm you, level you.

Raylene had nodded and agreed with him. She'd heard the ragged edges of his voice and understood. They'd pulled Marie aboard and for the entire way home, she'd told him about alligators. A group of them was called a congregation. They were naturally fearful of people. They could hold their breath for two hours.

He had clung to the bow of the boat and put his face in the wind and let these facts wash over him. By the time they'd reached the spot where his boat was tied up, he was able to handle it all again. That was the gift she'd given him, and the worst part was, all these years had gone by, and he still wasn't sure if he'd thanked her or not.

And a few years later, she was on his table, finger-shaped bruises around her neck. He'd owed it to her to do the best autopsy he could, to bring her justice—and then he had been robbed of that opportunity. This unsatisfying, unacceptable end to her story was all he had to offer her daughter.

"Up here. Up ahead." The sight of a raincoat jolted James back into the present. It was caught on a cypress branch, snapping in the wind.

"Got 'em," Ernest said.

James leaned out of the boat and reached for the other sleeve of the coat, which was still attached to its owner.

"Hang on, Madison," he told her. Ernest probably thought he was turning into a batty old man, but he didn't care. Doctors talked to patients who could not hear them all the time. He motioned Ernest over, and together they coaxed her body into the boat and fitted the nylon body bag around her, tucking her swollen limbs inside.

James tried not to look at the details; a silver anklet looped around her bare right foot, a partially scraped-off temporary tattoo heart on the inside of her wrist. In his mind he repeated the last alligator fact that Raylene Atchison had given him that night, something he did often when cases hit a little too close to home. He could still hear her honeyed voice forming the words: *Alligators have a third eyelid. It closes horizontally over the alligator's eye as it submerges, giving the alligator perfect vision underwater while still offering a layer of protection.*

In his mind, James closed his own third eyelid. He signaled to Ernest to head back home, where James's table waited for Madison Leo, and where Aurora Atchison waited somewhere, back in town after all these years. He thought about the bones in their plastic shrouds, on a gleaming lab table in another county, waiting to tell their story. James moved to a seat across from the body and looked out across the bayou, where a gator began its descent, its luminescent eye the last thing to disappear.

CHAPTER THIRTEEN

"You know, once upon a time, I wanted to be a cop," Samba reflected, watching Josh pull the last of the wilting cardboard boxes onto the evidence room's sturdiest table, a Day-Glo yellow Formica monstrosity that looked as though it had been a kitchen table forty years earlier.

"Oh, yeah?" Josh set the box down and wiped his face with his T-shirt. He was wondering how long Samba was going to wait before telling him what the case was about.

"Yeah. Can you imagine?" Samba snorted. "I mean, no offense. But out there"—he gestured through one of the dirt-streaked windows—"sure, that's where they think the action is. But the evidence room—this is where the magic happens. They might slap the cuffs on somebody, but this stuff is what catches the bad guys."

He stood back and patted the tops of the boxes, turning one to face Josh.

"Remember that one? Some yahoo truck driver, used to pick up kiddos and then dump them along the highway back in the eighties."

"Yeah, I remember. They caught the son of a bitch, right?"

Josh forced his tone to sound casual, even though he'd read up on the case.

"Yep. He got some hundred-year sentence." Samba shook his head. "It's a load of bull, if you ask me."

"Why?"

"I think," Samba said pointedly, "those kids' families should have the right to do whatever they want to the bastard." He issued this declaration through a mouthful of chocolate crumbs. "Being around all this long enough, seeing the things people do—well, it'll turn ya. I'd say I'm a peacenik in all other parts of life, but I'm pretty much a card-carrying fascist when it comes to criminals."

"Me too."

"They told me when I started, don't take nothing personal. Biggest load of bullshit you ever heard, excuse my French. The only woman I ever loved is in one of these boxes." He blinked, the tears searing his eyes the brightest blue Josh had ever seen.

"I'm sorry," Josh said, knowing how empty the words were.

"She was an angel on this earth," Samba said in a wobbled voice. "And I tell everybody who will listen, this job is personal. If it ain't under your skin, you ain't doing it right. We've all survived something. But you have to take that step back sometimes, let the evidence do its work so it can show you the right way." Samba crossed the space between them and put his hands on Josh's shoulders. "Do you understand?"

"Yes."

Samba kept one hand on Josh's shoulder. "The cops came to me this morning with a request to pull some evidence for an ID," he said. "Listen. I know you're a strong man, Josh. I see that. But if you don't want to be a part of this, I understand that too. I just want to give you the choice."

Josh reached across him and twisted one of the boxes so that the label was facing them.

Hudson, J.

His brother's box.

"Listen to me," Samba said. "They found some remains, over by Baboon Jack's, washed up on the beach in a duffel bag. Doc Mason sent them to some state lab, but word is they're those of a male child." Josh stared at the letters of his brother's name, Samba's voice fading in and out of his consciousness.

"Jesse."

"We don't know that yet," Samba said quietly. "I know how hard this is, Josh, believe me. They asked me to pull all the missing kids' files from the early nineties, and I knew your brother was one of 'em. I know all these kids. It's my job to know them. And if we do this right, this could be the end of their story. A real burial, answers for the family."

Josh thought about the splintered remains of his own family, his father in jail, his mother in the ground, Liana God knew where. There was nobody left but him. They knew Jesse was dead. The Shadow Man had given them that much as part of his plea deal to avoid the electric chair—but he'd never told them where, or how. Josh had told himself so many times that those details weren't important, the right man was in jail, the body was only the shell of the person Jesse had been. It was more important to focus on Liana, the person he could still save. Now Josh saw that Samba was right; that this might be a chance to end the story.

"I can help," Josh said. "I want to help."

Samba smiled. "Good," he said. "Whether it's your brother or not, we're going to help someone here."

Josh opened his mouth to reply and was interrupted by the bleat of the front door buzzer.

"Looks like we've got company," Samba said. "I'll take care of it." Dabbing at his face with his hopelessly damp handkerchief, he began to make his way to the front door.

A wave of paranoia rimmed with anger seized Josh. Was it someone coming to make the notification that the body in the bag might be Jesse? Why the hell hadn't someone from the station called him right away? He felt a surge of protectiveness for Samba. At least the old guy had the balls to say it to his face, to give him the chance to help.

All these thoughts propelled Josh to his feet and he barreled towards the doorway, overtaking Samba in the aisle.

Josh flung the door open, but instead of coming face-to-face with Rush or Boone, he found himself looking at a woman.

She was tall, almost six feet, and her hair was hastily shoved into a ponytail, but a few curls had escaped and tumbled around a little owlish face. She wore black athletic shorts and a white shirt, but she had the stance of a fighter, her green eyes friendly but also determined.

Only his detective instinct told him she was nervous; still half turned towards the door, her body was tense and coiled like a runner at the starting gates.

"Hi, I was hoping you could help me out. I was hoping to request some information about a case. I saw the emblem outside—I wasn't sure if this was the police station or not."

Josh struggled with a reply, the rational part of his brain rendered momentarily silent by the caveman side. Samba crowded next to him in the doorway. "You're in the wrong place," Samba said. "This isn't the police station. Although Josh here is a cop."

"Kind of," Josh mumbled.

"The police station is over on Cardamine Road," Samba

continued. "But it's hotter than hell out there. Why don't you come in for a second?"

She smiled. "Sure," she said. "That'd be great." She stepped past him into the entryway.

"We've got sweet tea, a couple of waters," Samba told her. "Got some of the hard stuff too, but it's under lock and key in the back."

"Sweet tea's fine," the woman said. "Thank you."

She sat on the edge of the orange paisley couch with the center cut out and stared at the hole in the foam.

"So if this isn't the police station," she asked, "what is it?"

"It's the evidence room," Josh explained. "All those rows back there, they're full of boxes of evidence—everything from bikes to guns to booze."

Something in her face changed. "Every case? How far back?"

"Older than me," Samba said, handing her the glass of iced tea. "Don't even hazard a guess."

She chuckled, at ease again.

"I'm Samba, by the way. And that's Josh. What's your name?"

For the first time, she hesitated. It was only for a beat, but Josh saw her consider her options before answering.

"Aurora Atchison." She almost whispered it. It took Josh a minute to process the name, roll it over in his head, figure out why something about it sounded familiar.

Samba didn't take as long. "Well, I'll be darned," he answered, removing his glasses and studying her. She looked towards the door and shifted uncomfortably when Samba spoke again, this time more gently.

"Are you here about your mother's case?"

She stood up so quickly that she almost upended the table.

"Yes. I can come back, though—I know it probably takes a while to pull the files. You guys are probably busy. Thanks for the tea. I—um, I've taken up enough of your time. I'm just going to go."

"I'm sorry," Samba said. "I shouldn't have said that."

"It's all right. Really." She bolted for the door. Josh followed her outside, his brain churning with the details of her case. Aurora Atchison. It was an old case that was almost a legend in Cooper's Bayou—part horror story, part cautionary tale. An abusive husband, a murdered wife, the baby daughter left at the mini-mart. So this was her—the little girl lost, now returned.

"Hey, listen," Josh called to her. "I get it. You don't want to talk about it—believe me, I get it." She paused on the bottom step and turned to face him, shading her eyes from the sun.

Josh dug around in his pocket and retrieved a folded white square. He scribbled a number on the back of it. "I mean, if you get lost, or whatever." That was ridiculous—the town was four streets wide—but she took the card.

"Thanks, Josh."

"I'm not really from here either, you know," he said. It was all he could think of to say. "I know what it's like to be new in town."

She smiled and nodded, and he watched her walk to her rental, a cherry-red subcompact. In his mind, he finished the sentence.

I know what it's like to return to the scene of the crime.

CHAPTER FOURTEEN

Aurora wanted a margarita.

She'd never been much of a drinker. Usually, she just ordered a Diet Coke at bars when she was out with friends. "I'm driving," she'd tell the bartender when he shot her a questioning look, even though they both knew nobody drove in New York City.

Control freak, Nicky teased her at work, but she was right. It was better than being out of control, wasn't it? "Tightly wound," her attending had called her, which made her think of the cheap gold watch he wore too snugly on his hairy wrist. It wasn't a completely bad quality. It made her a good friend and a fantastic nurse. It made her reliable and punctual.

It also made her a little bit boring.

Still, this trip to Florida was changing all of that.

She felt a strange comfort in the house on the bayou. She had even ventured into town a few times, to the grocery store, and then to the evidence room. Of course, she hadn't made any friends here yet, and she didn't feel like she could just stroll into a local bar and order a drink the way you could in New York. It was an odd sensation, being a stranger in town whom everyone knew. Papa had left her instructions about the house, but he hadn't told her who was trustworthy. All she knew was that he had been working on something, that some question remained about the night her mother died.

Aurora settled for a glass of iced tea and stepped out onto the porch. In the darkness, the waters of the bayou rose and fell in thick waves, like swirled cream. A boat laden with partygoers idled a mile offshore, music blaring.

They had all been on a boat ride the night of the murder. Aurora, her mother, and her father. She tried to conjure Raylene's image from the depths of her mind. She remembered climbing into her mother's lap on someone's porch, in front of a glass table rimmed in white. "You're too old to be held this way," her mother had said with a laugh, but she'd cradled her anyway, rocking her back and forth, Aurora's spindly legs draped over the chair's armrest. Aurora couldn't remember her face or anything she was wearing, or even whose porch it was, but somehow she remembered that grip. Loving. Intense.

Aurora stemmed the tide of emotions that were rising to the surface. There was no time to sit here and let the past engulf her. If Papa wanted her to continue the search for the truth about that night, she was up to the task, no matter how painful it was.

She shut the French doors behind her. Tonight she would tackle the files in the cherry-finish secretary desk in Papa's office. Royce Beaumont, the attorney, had told her about several documents she needed to bring to their first meeting in the morning. She was counting on the contents of the desk to be what she expected—papers, bills, checkbooks—but was afraid there would be something else there that she wasn't ready to see.

The sight of Papa's spindly handwriting on the file folders

brought an unexpected rush of tears to her eyes. Why had he left all of this for her to do? She could feel a throb between her eyes beginning to bloom into a headache. Well, it would only take a minute; Papa was organized, and everything was easy to find. The folder labeled HOUSE was tucked in the back. A manila folder was among the deed to the house and other legal papers. A folder labeled with a single word.

Raylene.

She was unfolding the contents even as her mind was screaming at her to stop, to let it be, to leave it alone. So he had done his research after all. She spread the pages out across Papa's desk. It was an old, blurred photocopy of the autopsy report and the police report. This was what Nana and Papa had been protecting her from all these years, and now she understood why. Aurora read the details, knowing they would never be erased from her memory. Death by asphyxiation. He had strangled her with his bare hands. There was evidence consistent with rape; she had been found half-naked on the shore of the bayou, less than a mile from where Aurora was sitting right now. Papa had circled and underlined words on the autopsy report. *Contusion, right knee. Defensive wounds. Broken fingernails.*

Aurora felt the weight of it all settling in her chest. She caught sight of herself in one of the antique mirrors hanging to the right of the desk. She resembled her mother, but she was Wade's daughter too. Was that why Papa could not share this? When he saw her, did he see his treasured daughter but also the man who had taken her away forever?

Clipped to the report was a letter from the police department, informing Papa that every effort was being made to bring Wade Atchison to justice. Her grandfather had circled her father's name and written a question mark above it. Was he questioning who had killed her mother? Wade was a criminal, a violent man, a jealous man. Who else could have possibly killed Raylene?

The rest of the file contained clippings from area papers. Aurora paged through them. She'd seen the local paper, *The Bayou Bumblebee,* for sale at a gas station she'd stopped at on the way into town. These papers mentioned places she didn't recognize: Starflower, Kervick, Papillon City. She expected accounts of the murder, but the articles were all about alligators; probably mixed in with some files for his job.

The house phone rang. Aurora had not even known it was connected. Probably Jefferson, checking on her. Reflexively, she picked it up.

"Hello?"

"Time to go home, beb," a singsong voice warned. She thought of the woman in the cemetery who had used that same word—what had Ernest said her name was? Charlie? This voice was different. Fuller, stronger, angrier. Male.

"Who is this?"

"Go back where you came from, Aurora. Or else you gonna be sorry," the voice hissed, "just like your mama."

She slammed the phone down, her heart galloping in her chest. They got calls like this at the hospital all the time, crazies saying vile things. Aurora and Nicky laughed about it, didn't give it a second thought. Something about being under the bright lights of the hospital made her feel safe, secure, indestructible.

But now she was in this house on the bayou.

By herself.

Get it together, she told herself. It was just some hillbilly kid with nothing else to do on a Friday night, looking to scare the new person in town. She checked the lock on the front door and resumed her seat at the desk, but the words on the paper seemed meaningless now; all she could hear was the voice from the phone.

You gonna be sorry just like your mama.

Outside, the wind picked up. The tree outside her bedroom window listed to one side, its branches heavy with Spanish moss that fell like a curtain across her view of the bayou. Maybe she should call Jefferson, let him know about the prank caller. But he was an older man; what could he possibly do? Or the police? She'd seen a cop at the coffee place this morning. But what could they do? Everyone in town knew who she was; they either addressed her by name or stared at her when they thought she wasn't looking. A late-night call to the cops would only fuel the gossip mill. There was nobody in town she could trust to stay quiet.

Go back where you came from.

"This is where I came from," she said out loud. There was no way some voice on the phone was going to stop her now. She settled back into the chair, thumbing through the rest of Papa's files. She was a New Yorker; she didn't scare easy. Aurora imagined recounting this story to Nicky. *Just me and the voodoo dolls, all alone in the house!* The two of them would laugh about it. Aurora smiled to herself and made a mental note to text Nicky in the morning.

And then the phone rang again.

CHAPTER FIFTEEN

Josh was breaking into his place of employment.

He realized it on the ride over, chuckling at the thought of how ridiculous his life had become. Was this latest adventure criminal? Probably. A bad idea? Certainly, but he was in the habit of stockpiling bad decisions. What was one more? Sleep was an impossibility. Hope had taken root inside Josh and would not let him rest. He hoped it was Jesse in that bag, and prayed it was not. People said it was always better to know, but ignorance looked real good sometimes.

Josh glanced at the clock. Almost eight. Back in his old life, he'd be doing surveillance on some slimeball crack dealer right now, parked in the shadows, poised to strike. Now he was coming back to the warehouse. All night he'd been thinking about Jesse, about the promise he'd made to his brother that he hadn't kept. And then he'd realized that his salvation had been surrounding him this whole time.

Evidence.

He needed to look at the boxes again, to learn the stories of the other missing boys, to know them as well as he knew his own story. It was more than a need: it was a raw compulsion. There was something in one of those boxes that would give him the clue he needed to identify the boy in the bag, whether it was his brother or not. Samba was right. He had a responsibility to all the people whose stories were in those boxes, not just his own kin.

Josh cut the engine and stepped into the velvety darkness. There was a charge in the air, a faint sizzle that warned of another thunderstorm creeping across the bayou. Someone had busted all the streetlamps on Spruce, so the only light was from the bone-white moon, draping the evidence room in a patchwork of shadows. The place was ominous in the daytime; at night, its hulking form was downright spooky. Josh closed the distance between his car and the warehouse in a few quick strides, ignoring the twist of apprehension in his gut.

Feeling around the sides of the building, Josh's fingers finally caught the sharp edges of broken wood where the door had given way after the last big storm. Samba had taped an ancient blue tarp over the hole, and it flexed and crackled in the slight breeze. The recent rain made it slimy to the touch, like a rotting banana peel. With little effort, Josh tugged one corner free and ducked inside.

"Hold it right there."

Josh froze in a squatting position on the floor, eyes scanning the dimly lit room for the source of the warning. The dusty end of what looked like an old-fashioned rifle was pointed at him. The owner of the weapon took a step towards him out of the darkness.

"Josh?" Samba lowered the weapon, wiping the brow with the hem of his tie-dyed shirt. "Christ on a bike, you scared me."

"I scared *you*?" Josh slowly stood up, his heart still slamming against his ribs. "I thought you were going to shoot me with . . . what the hell is that thing?"

Samba admired the rusted weapon, turning it over in his hands like a new present. "I just grabbed it from the weapons aisle when I heard scuffling outside." He thrust it towards Josh in a careless arc. "She's a beauty, isn't she?"

Josh put a protective hand on the barrel and slowly lowered it. "Samba, is that thing loaded?"

"Who knows?" Samba shrugged. "It scared you, didn't it?" He beamed at Josh. "Anyway, I'm glad you're here! I always love company." He walked to his desk and grabbed a yellowing stack of takeout menus from one of the piles and thrust them in Josh's direction. "Do you think the El Cap still delivers this late?"

Josh looked at Samba, bewildered. "What are you doing here this late?"

Samba chuckled. "That young lady, the one who was here earlier. She called me, told me she'd spoken to you about requesting some information on her mother's case. Isn't that why you're here?"

Josh had logged the request in his notebook when Aurora had called, figuring he'd get to it in the morning. How could there be something so urgent about a case twenty years cold?

"Sure," he said. "I wasn't doing anything else, so I figured I'd come down." Samba had probably guessed at the real reason, but Josh wasn't going to let him know that he was right.

"Same here," Samba echoed. "She seemed like a nice gal, too. Reminds me of my wife. I always had a thing for tall brunettes."

He led Josh towards the middle of the room, where a white cardboard box sat alone in the center of the metal folding table. It looked just like the boxes Josh opened every day at work, except this one wouldn't contain fallout from an anonymous crime; this one held the broken pieces of Aurora's past. Earlier today he had opened his own box, held the plastic container that had a coil of his brother's DNA. The thought of strangers opening this box, of reducing him from a person Josh loved to a series of tags and numbers, sickened him. And now he stood ready to unseal the horrors of what had happened to Aurora, throwing light on all the darkness she had survived, violating the memory of her mother. There was something sacrilegious about it, and he hesitated in front of the box, his fingers instead brushing the edge of the table.

"I don't know, Samba," Josh said. "This is—I don't know. Private. Maybe we should wait for her."

"She asked us to, Josh. It's our job to help."

He lifted out the first file folder.

Inside was a single eight-by-ten photograph, one of those posed portraits that families get for their annual Christmas card, everyone standing stiffly in front of a cheap blue-sky background. Aurora's father, Wade, clearly not at ease in a collared shirt, stood behind her mother, Raylene, a sweet-faced woman with puffy white-blond bangs and pink-frosted lips. And in front of Raylene, snug in the circle of her arms, a little girl with pigtails and one of those unabashed kid smiles a mile wide. Aurora.

Samba held a corner of the picture and whistled under his breath. "Geez. She was just a baby," he said, shaking his head. He flipped through the police report underneath. "Four years old."

A kid, just like he had been. Josh swallowed. Aurora had been a small child, helpless and innocent, while Josh had been a few years older. Old enough to understand what was going on.

Old enough to have done something about it, and yet, he hadn't.

For the next hour, Josh and Samba stood at the table, thumbing through the pages in the file folders. Samba squinted over his glasses, reading parts of the police report out loud.

"This guy Wade was a real prince," he muttered. "He takes Aurora and her mom out on the water for an evening on the bayou. Late that night, the cops find Aurora at the mini-mart by herself and her mom laid out on the shore, strangled. The dad took off." He shook his head. "I gotta tell you, I'm not sure what she's looking to find here, other than a real sad story."

"So they never found her father? He never tried to find her or contact anyone or anything?"

"Nope. I guess he's still out there."

Josh thought of Aurora, tall and lean, wound tight like a runner on the starting blocks. She could run; she was strong. Her father must haunt her, the way the Shadow Man haunted him. But the Shadow Man was behind bars; Wade Atchison could be anywhere. He imagined Wade, living on the run all these years. By now he could be anything—a homeless man melting into a doorway, an office guy in a suit waiting for a knock on the door. Josh wondered if Wade ever thought about finding Aurora. The idea brought a chill with it. Wade had spared her life that night on the bayou. Would she be so lucky if they met again?

Samba put down the stack of papers and let out a dramatic sigh. "I don't know about you, Josh, but I'm sta-ar-ving," he said, stretching the word out as far as it would go. "I'm going to give the El Cap a ring-a-ling, see if they're still open. You up for a fried grouper sandwich?"

"Absolutely."

"You know what, maybe we can swing by Aurora's too, bring her copies of the file."

"So the evidence room delivers?"

"Sure, why not?" Samba said with a shrug. "You wanna give her a call?"

Aurora answered on the first ring, something breathless in her voice.

"Hey, Aurora. Hope I'm not bothering you—it's Josh Hudson. Samba and I were wondering if you wanted us to deliver the copies of your file. If it's too late, we can definitely come tomorrow or whatever works for you."

"No, tonight's great," she said. There was relief in her voice. Well, Josh couldn't blame her for wanting company out at the Broussard place. It had to be creepy as hell, coming from a big city to a lone house on the edge of the bayou.

"Great," Josh said. "We're on our way."

CHAPTER SIXTEEN

"Have you ever saved somebody's life?"

Samba twisted in the passenger seat, his question hitting Josh's right temple as sure as a bullet. In the semidarkness, Samba's quizzical face glowed like a round moon. Josh propelled the Jeep, trembling and shimmying, down the causeway and through the slinging sheets of gray rain. All around them, the bayou churned, greedy fingers of water reaching over the guard-rails and grabbing at their tires. It was a matter of time before they closed the road. People around here knew you couldn't hold back the bayou for long.

"Well? Have you?" Samba persisted.

"Never," Josh replied. Samba's question summoned a memory of Jesse, of a closed stall door, a moment for courage that could never come again. "Why, you think this is a life-saving situation? You think she's in danger?"

"I don't know, but I bet she's scared to be back in town. I mean, her pop let her go all those years ago when she was a kid. Maybe she's afraid Wade'll come back."

"After this long? What for? That doesn't make sense."

"I don't know. It doesn't have to make sense. Fear doesn't

make sense. She's probably been looking over her shoulder her whole life, know what I mean?"

Josh knew. He eased down on the accelerator. It was getting harder and harder to see through the rain; the road in front of him was now reduced to a scramble of shimmering dots. Josh searched for landmarks. A smear of bright blinking yellow on their right had to be Crabby Jim's, a fried-fish restaurant known for its seven-dollar buffet. That meant the turnoff was around the next curve.

"Anyway, I think your answer is a bunch of baloney," Samba said.

"Excuse me?"

"You heard me. Baloney. I'm sure you've saved somebody's life before. You probably just don't know it."

"I think I'd remember something like that." The back end of the Jeep glided into a slow fishtail, and Josh gripped the steering wheel, bringing the car back under his control. "Why, have you?"

Samba shrugged, his tone casual. "A few times."

"A few times? So in addition to being a singer, guitar player—"

"Ukulele player," Samba corrected.

"Sorry, a ukulele player, and a tamer of feral cats, you're also—what, an EMT? Volunteer firefighter?"

"There's more than one way of saving a person, Josh." Samba patted Josh's hand on the steering wheel. He gestured towards the turn. "This is it."

Josh swung the Jeep onto the dirt road. The abandoned houses down here were so choked with kudzu it looked as though they were floating in a fuzzy green sea. Aurora's house sat at the bayou's edge, twinkling in the darkness.

She opened the door when they pulled up the drive, backlit

by the living room. She wore the same shorts and T-shirt that she'd had on earlier, but something about her looked more vulnerable now; childlike even.

"Hi, guys." Samba was right—she did look glad to see them. She ushered them into an immaculate sitting room, where she had laid out coffee.

"Hey, Aurora!" Samba held the greasy sandwich bag aloft. "Bet you haven't tried a fried grouper sandwich yet."

"You're right about that."

"Well, you are in for a treat. It's from the El Cap, this place downtown. Real spicy, but I bet you can handle it. It's like being kicked in the face, but, you know, in a good way."

Aurora and Josh exchanged a smile. "Come on in," she said.

Josh had never been inside the Broussard home, but everybody knew the alligator man's house, with the magnolia trees and the yard that dipped towards the bayou. Inside, the place was tidy, as though someone had scrubbed every surface. It smelled of gardenia and lemon leaves.

"Everything okay, Aurora?"

"Sure. I mean, sort of. I just got this creepy phone call. It was probably just kids being stupid, but it just kind of threw me off balance. Let me get some plates for the sandwiches." She headed back to the kitchen.

Josh followed. "What did the caller say?"

"Go back to where you came from, or you'll be sorry, just like your mama." It had rattled her, that was for sure.

"Kids, probably," Josh said. "There's not much to do out here except get into trouble." He wasn't convinced, but he hoped she could not hear that in his voice.

"Hey, check this out," Samba said. A felt doll leaned against the windowsill behind the couch, covered in gold pins and tied with an orange ribbon. "Aurora, you know what this is, doncha?"

Aurora and Josh emerged from the kitchen with the plates. "I'm not really sure," Aurora frowned. "My grandpa had some—strange stuff like that around here."

"It's a juju," Samba explained. "Lucky, for protection. People like stuff like that around here. I have some. Crucifixes too. You never know what works, so I guess I'm just hedging my bets."

Something in Aurora's face told Josh to change the subject, so he held up the files. "So, we've got the file here," Josh told her. "Police reports, evidence log, the whole thing."

"Thank you so much," she said.

Samba patted her knee. "Sometimes it's tough," he said, "seeing everything again. Just take things one at a time. Go slow. Maybe we can even sort through things for you. Is there something you were looking to find? You said it was important."

She hesitated, looking between Josh and Samba, sizing them up. "I have some questions. I should probably take them to the police—but I just don't know."

"Atta girl," Samba said. "You can't always trust the cops. It's best to stick with the evidence, plain and true."

"What are your questions?" Josh could see that she wanted to tell them, could see the story rising through her. She opened a drawer in the stately varnished desk in one corner of the room and brought out a file.

"It looks like my grandfather was starting to look into the case on his own," she said. "There's some stuff here in the house, but it seems pretty incomplete. I don't really know what to make of it."

"Did they ever run the samples for DNA?" Josh thought

about the backlog, the rows and rows of sample kits. Back in 1989, it was still a relatively new thing.

Aurora shook her head. "It looks like my grandfather requested it when he asked them to reopen the case, but they denied it. Said the sample was too degraded because it hadn't been preserved properly so there was no chance anyway."

Samba made a humphing sound. "Well, that's a bunch of hogwash," he said. "I'm a stickler for preserving things the right way. And I log every request. Nobody has asked about those samples. I'd remember."

"Can you look at this stuff? I mean, are you authorized or whatever?"

Samba chuckled. "I'm not law enforcement, not technically. To work in the evidence room, you've just got to have a GED and pass a background check. But I've seen a lot in my time there. And I can tell you, Aurora, that cops make mistakes. People jump to conclusions sometimes, instead of looking for the truth."

Josh watched the color drain from Aurora's face, like someone was pulling a white curtain across her features. He was willing to bet she'd always been running from this moment, the same way he was. Sometimes Josh thought he was destined to meet a bad end, that he was just running out a length of rope, and one day he'd reach the end and be snapped back to the day of the attack, some kind of evil waiting there for him to finish what the Shadow Man had started. There were certain things you couldn't outrun.

"I think I know someone who can help us," Josh said. Doc Mason at the morgue would help them put the pieces together. He'd have autopsy records that the evidence room didn't have.

"Thank you. I really appreciate it."

"Sure. We can head over there in the morning, if you want." Josh's phone buzzed in his pocket.

"You know what, guys, I'm gonna take a walk around the outside of the house, make sure everything's secure. Can't hurt, right?"

He pushed open the door and stepped out onto the porch. Outside, the rain had given way to a cloudless night, and below him the bayou sparkled, barely a ripple on its creamy surface, no hint of the choppy water of less than an hour before. He answered the phone.

"Pea?"

"*Bonjour,* Josh," she trilled, the Southern accent still crowding out the French one.

Josh steadied himself against the railing. "Did you get any more information? About Liana?" He was willing to pay drug dealers, play ball with anyone. Whatever it took.

Pea laughed, a velvety sound. "Well, of course. I always follow through on my promises. I just need some funds."

"How much?"

"Well, now, I don't like to talk about money right away," Pea purred. "I was raised better than that. I was just making sure you hadn't changed your mind. You didn't call me back after we last spoke. I was feeling a little—rejected."

Josh turned away from the bayou. Through Aurora's front window, he could see Samba and Aurora sharing the remains of the sandwich, their two heads close together. He ached to be like them, to be able to confide in them about who he was, about Liana, about Jesse, about how the attack had made him a stranger in his own life. He wanted to tell Samba that he was right; there was more than one way of saving a person's life, but there was also more than one way of taking it.

"Josh? Hello?" Pea spoke again, the lushness in her voice replaced by impatience.

"I'm sure," he said. "Just text me what you need." He hung up.

Josh flicked on the outside light, illuminating the pale rows of hibiscus that stretched across the yard. There was no place to hide a car out here; if you wanted to sneak up to the house, you'd have to pick your way through the tall grass that obscured the path down to the bayou.

He completed a perimeter sweep of the house and was reaching for the light when he saw them.

Footprints.

They were fresh. Someone had trampled a few of the flowers in their hurry to get down to the bayou. Something orange glimmered on the outside sill. Josh moved to get a closer look. A small flannel bag was overturned, and a fine orange powder was spread across the sill. Josh bent closer. He would have known the smell anywhere; it was part of his mother's chicken marinade. Cayenne pepper.

Josh heard the sound of it then; the whisper of a rope being unwound, a skiff slipping onto the water.

"Hey! Wait!" He skidded down the path. The exterior lights shone only as far as the edge of the yard, and beyond that was only the black maw of the bayou. He could hear paddling, but he couldn't see a damn thing. There was no way to catch them.

Josh turned back to the house. He could hear the sound of laughter, of Samba putting Aurora at ease. Now he was going to be the one to have to tell her.

Someone was out here.

Someone was watching.

CHAPTER SEVENTEEN

Charlsie the voodoo woman was also the proprietor of the local pharmacy.

Aurora was learning not to be surprised at this kind of information; after all, in Cooper's Bayou, everyone seemed to have more than one job. She wondered what Josh Hudson's other job was, since he'd told her he wasn't a cop. She'd wanted to ask him more about this, but something in his face had stopped the question. Everyone was allowed to have secrets, she reminded herself. She thought about Mike. He'd texted her a few times since her trip down south. They were sweet little missives like *Everything okay?* It wasn't the kind of question that could be answered over text; she could not even imagine what she would write back to him. *Insane family—voodoo and murder! Drinks next week?*

She was supposed to be in the attorney, Royce Beaumont's, office right now, but she had decided that could wait. It was something about the voodoo woman's voice. She'd known Papa, known something about what he was doing. He had confided in her for some reason, and Aurora was going to find out why.

The entrance to the pharmacy was almost completely obscured by a wooden statue of an American Indian grasping a sword, his lips pulled into a leering smile. A cheap dish towel adorned with a map of the state of Florida was tied around his hips in an attempt at modesty. Glass jars, opaque with age, lined the sides of the room, labeled in spindly purple handwriting and filled with seeds and grains of all shapes and colors with magical-sounding names that suggested strains of psychedelic drugs rather than ordinary houseplants. *Mustard spinach tendergreens,* Aurora read, *Squash crookneck blues, Pepper California wonder.*

"Need some help?"

It sounded like more of an accusation than a question. The speaker was a woman in her seventies, her hair piled high and secured with a paisley scarf on her head. Her eyebrows were penciled in thick violet eyeliner and curved upward at a spectacular angle.

"I'm looking for Charlsie. Is she here?"

"In back," the woman said, and turned away. Aurora followed the woman down the aisle. Half-melted votive candles flickered on every available surface, illuminating rows of bottles and canisters. Next to the cash register, a black felt doll with two gold fleur-de-lis pins for eyes hung from a coat hook, a knitting needle protruding from its crotch. A tiny charm hung around its neck and Aurora recognized the palm with shooting stars that she had seen in Luna Riley's office engraved on the front.

The woman followed her gaze. "To scare shoplifters," she said matter-of-factly, and then pointed behind a beaded curtain. "She's back there. You got an appointment?"

"No. I just—I'm a friend."

"Friends, neighbors, enemies, they all gotta pay," the

woman shrugged, regarding Aurora with pity. "Ain't nothing in this world for free."

Aurora dug in her pocket and unfurled a twenty-dollar bill.

"Charlsie," the woman sang out in a bright tone, "your ten thirty's here."

Behind the beaded curtain, Charlsie appeared to be in a trancelike state, her eyes focused on the wall in front of her. It took Aurora a moment to realize that she was watching a small television in the corner. On the screen, Diane Keaton, in round sunglasses and a white power suit, was berating a balding man in a restaurant.

"Romantic comedies," Charlsie muttered. "Love them." She aimed the remote at the screen and powered it off, pointing a ringed finger at a chair across from her, a flimsy lawn chair draped in a thick curtain. Aurora sat.

"I knew you'd be coming to see me, beb," Charlsie said. Her fingers worked a set of cards, softened and yellowed with age.

"Oh, that's all right," Aurora protested. "I don't need a reading. I just have some questions."

"We all got questions, as long as we brave enough to hear the answers. I'm glad you came here, beb. I'm gonna tell you what you want to know."

"My grandfather."

"Your grandfather," Charlsie echoed, "the alligator man. A good man." She placed a shiny green pebble the size of a cough drop on top of the card. "He help people in need, he never judge anybody too hard. That's why I helped him when he was in trouble, you understand?"

"Trouble? I didn't know he was in trouble. I thought he came to you to try to reach my mother. What kind of trouble was he in?"

Charlsie ignored the question and instead fiddled with her necklaces, then held out a simple gold chain with a browned tooth on the end. "You know anything about alligators? He teach you?"

Aurora shook her head and for the thousandth time wished that she could remember being a kid here, sitting in the plastic pool with the baby gators, anything before the house in Connecticut. Some mornings she'd look out onto the bayou, the sun slicing through the sunken cypress, and a memory of her mother would grip her so fiercely she had to sit in the woven chair on the porch and rock back and forth until it subsided. Back home, her mother had existed only in objects; a photograph, a piece of jewelry. But here on the bayou, she was as real as anything alive, so real that Aurora felt the boundlessness of her loss in a way she had never before experienced.

"They been here millions of years, them gators," Charlsie continued. "This tooth, your grandpapa gave me this tooth. It brings strength. And the head, it means wisdom, power. My people, we respect those creatures, like your grandfather did. But not everyone respects them."

Charlsie clicked her tongue. "Your father saw some bad men out on the bayou, hurting the alligators. Killing them to take their heads."

"Bad men?"

"Men who twist *voudon,* who turn it into something ugly."

Aurora thought about the felt doll next to the cash register. "So it's not about putting spells on people, or talking to people who have passed on?"

Charlsie chuckled. "Ah, no, *chère.* I don't put spells on people. I don't do nothing that endangers my soul or my Social

Security benefits. I help people, do good when I can. But there are some who work with both hands."

"What did you do for him?"

"When he came to me all those years ago," Charlsie murmured, "he was already sick. His complexion was darkening, his faith was shaken. I did everything I could to help." Aurora's mind was already racing to a diagnosis. Her grandfather was unhappy with his daughter's boyfriend, Wade. He was dealing with alligator poachers. He was depressed. He'd always had problems with arthritis. The *voudon* explanation was ridiculous.

"So you cured him." Aurora played along. This woman was a crook or an idiot. Or both. But maybe she knew something.

"I did everything I could," Charlsie said. "But it was not enough. Two weeks later, he lost his daughter. Your *maman*." She reached across the table and squeezed Aurora's hand. "We can call upon the orisha to do things for us. They can throw stones in our path or make them clear. All we can do is ask."

Aurora dipped a hand inside her purse and pulled out one of the gris-gris bags. "I found these all over the house. He must have kept them. Are these what you gave him?"

Charlsie unwound the small flannel bag and dumped the contents on the table, drawing a finger through them. A strong aroma, a mix between cinnamon and cough drops, rose from the small pile of dirt and sticks.

"Dried toadstool top," Charlsie murmured. "Piece of High John the Conqueror root. This is from me, for true. I gave this to him when he came to see me a few months back."

"A few months ago?" The fishing trip, the last one before he'd gone into the hospital. He had been in Cooper's Bayou.

He had been here. "Why did he come to see you then? For luck?"

Charlsie shook her head. "This gris-gris is not for luck. It's a powerful one, for protection from danger. Whatever your grandfather was afraid of, it was still here."

CHAPTER EIGHTEEN

"Stop it! That tickles and it's way too cold. You gotta warm it up next time."

This wisp of conversation floated through the beveled glass doors of the medical examiner's office, where Josh hesitated on the cracked concrete steps. Doc Mason would have access to Raylene Atchison's complete file. Josh wondered what Aurora hoped the information might lead to. Exoneration of her deadbeat father? Not likely. Closure? It didn't exist, as far as Josh was concerned. Being here was a gamble anyway. The only thing Doc Mason hated more than an alternate theory about a case was anything that questioned his judgment.

"Hello?" Josh pressed the buzzer and peered through the door, but all he could see was a distorted image of the lobby, with its plastic ficus plants and shiny paisley chairs. This misguided attempt to make the place inviting had only made it more creepy. It was like they were trying to distract you from the fact that it was the gateway to infinity and that most people came in through the back entrance on a stretcher.

Josh gave up on the intercom and pushed on the door. It swung open under his fingers.

Ruby, Dr. Mason's receptionist, was reclining in her swivel chair, her head tipped back, the cloud of her curls tumbling over onto the desk. A husky guy in his twenties, with an unruly mass of cashew-colored hair, knelt, head bowed, at her feet.

"Sorry to interrupt," Josh said, unsure what he was witnessing. Ruby Contreras had something of a reputation in Cooper's Bayou. A Cuban-born bombshell of indeterminate age, she was beautiful in an almost terrifying way, a woman who brandished her power over the opposite sex like a weapon, who wore her man-eater title with pride. There wasn't much that happened in Cooper's Bayou without Ruby knowing about it. Josh had gone to her for info on cases a few times, and she'd never disappointed him.

Ruby laughed, and the blond kid scrambled to his feet, swaying like a cornstalk. He looked like some hick linebacker who'd gotten lost on the way to football practice. "Ruby's helping me study," he mumbled. "Anatomy exams."

"I'm sure she's an excellent teacher."

"No, you don't understand," the guy stammered. "Ruby's letting me write the names of the major arteries and veins on her body so I can learn them for my exam." He held up a glitter felt-tip pen. "See? But my pen was on top of the blood fridge, so it was too cold, and she made me stop."

Ruby lifted a shapely, caramel-colored leg onto her desk and wiggled her peach painted toes at Josh.

"Arcuate artery," he read on her foot.

"Glenn's got a couple more to go," she said. "Enough for now, though. You'd better get back to work."

"Yes, ma'am," Glenn replied, scurrying back into the autopsy suite.

Josh racked his brain for some medical knowledge. "Great saphenous vein?"

Ruby grinned. "Nobody's labeling that one until they buy me a drink. So tell me, Detective Hudson, how've you been?"

"Well, I'm sure you've heard, I've been put on a bit of a mandatory vacation by the PD."

She frowned. "I did hear about that. I heard the reason why, too."

"My sister."

She nodded, a fierce look coming over her face. "I'm really sorry about that, Josh. I know what it's like to miss somebody like that."

"I wish you didn't."

"Well, we're all carrying something, ain't we."

Josh thought about Aurora, about Samba's question. *Are you here about your mother's case?*

"That's true," he said.

"So they gonna let you back anytime soon?"

"In a while," Josh said, even though he had no idea. "For now I'm working in the evidence room."

"No shit," she said. "You tell Samba that I said hello. I love that crazy old man. He's like you, a true Southern gentleman. And believe me, y'all are a dying breed."

"That means a lot to me coming from a fine woman like you."

Ruby snorted. "Well, I know you didn't come down here to stand there and pay me compliments, as much as I'd like to think so. So what's your business here, Detective Hudson?"

"I need to see Doc Mason. It's important."

"Huh. Well, I guess you don't listen to your scanner no more, or you'd know there was a big pileup on the causeway this morning. We've got a full house back there. And let me tell you, Doc had four cups of coffee this morning, and he's still got his nose out of joint."

"Please. Can you just try for me?"

Ruby put a hand on the phone. "All right, I'll buzz him, because I like you. But if he fires me, I'm moving in with you, Hudson, you understand? And a woman like me—I am *not* low maintenance."

She picked up the phone and hit a button, and in a professional voice that sounded to Josh like it came from someone else, spoke clearly into the phone. "Detective Josh Hudson here to see you urgently, Dr. Mason." Josh barely detected a reply, and then she hung up.

"Go on back." Ruby beamed at him.

Josh was incredulous. "He said he would see me?"

"Yeah, he did. You must be one of his special favorites. Don't forget to suit up."

"You're the best," Josh told her. He grabbed a paper face mask and blue smock off the wall and pushed through the swinging door to the autopsy suite.

Behind the glass in the autopsy suite, Dr. Mason was leaning over a body. Josh figured that he had once been somewhat tall, but age was pulling his body towards the horizontal, so that he had the appearance of always being on the verge of taking a bow. He stared at Josh from behind goggles that made his stern eyes look comic-book huge and held up a finger.

Josh had always gotten along with Mason. He wasn't warm and fuzzy, but he'd give you the straight story, and he was thorough. Josh had complete faith in his opinion of the Atchison case. Still, even though Josh had built up some measure of goodwill over the years, he knew he was probably one poorly phrased remark from being kicked out of the autopsy suite.

"Detective Hudson. I figured I'd be seeing you today," Mason said, peeling off his gloves. He was accompanied by the smell of the autopsy suite, a minty stink with undertones of something darker. Mason reached behind Josh and pulled a plastic bag from the drawer.

It was not the greeting Josh had expected. He chuckled and gestured towards the row of steel drawers. "Really? That's not good."

Mason paused, and Josh saw for the first time the bag he was holding, with its clear plastic cylinders and white swabs, already labeled with his name, just like his brother's box in the evidence room. *Hudson, J.* And then he understood without asking.

Jesse.

"I'm so sorry, Detective Hudson," Mason was saying. "I just assumed . . . someone from the station had contacted you."

"It's all right. I understand." He avoided Mason's gaze.

Across the room, feet stuck out from one of the stainless-steel drawers. Women's feet. Josh moved closer, unable to stop his mind. Would he recognize Liana's feet, after all this time? And where were the bones? Would he know by seeing them that they belonged to his brother?

"Where are—the remains?"

He saw the relief in Mason's face; here was a question he could answer. "They've been sent to the forensic anthropologist up in Kervick County. Dr. Fontaine."

Josh imagined a laboratory, a woman with a paper face mask running a gloved hand over the bones. He remembered a case a few months before, when caskets from the old part of Ti Bon Ange Cemetery had floated away in the storm, how he and Boone had pried them back from the bayou's fingers, how he'd heard the bones rattling inside when they'd pulled them onto the shore.

"I don't have anything with me. Of Jesse's." The box of his

brother's things was in his coat closet, sealed up since the day of his mother's death, an old wound waiting to be split open. "I could get something, though. If you needed me to."

Mason shook his head. "It's for you. Mitochondrial DNA, passed through your mother. We can extract it from the bones and then compare it to a sample from a family member."

Josh opened his mouth and Mason swirled the cotton swab inside his cheek.

"So if you weren't here to ask about your brother, what brought you here?"

"I'm here to ask for some information as a personal favor." It was as good a time as any to ask about Aurora.

"I'm listening."

Josh took a deep breath. "Homicide, back in 1989."

"Unidentified vic?" He had Mason's full attention now.

"No, no. The case was closed."

"So you're here to question my report?" Mason frowned. "I'd like to think you had better things to do with your time, Detective Hudson.

"That's the thing, Doc. It wasn't you. The name on the autopsy report was a Dr. Gentry."

Josh had done his research. He knew that Doc Mason had worked alongside Gentry in the eighties. He was also willing to bet that Dr. Mason wasn't a fan of the other medical examiner and preferred working solo.

"Oh, Dr. Gentry. Well, he didn't last long," Mason sniffed. "Not everybody has what it takes to do this job. I wouldn't be surprised if the report is a mess. Gentry was sloppy. But I can't just review a closed case, Josh. Not without a court order. Those are the rules."

"I'm not asking you to reopen the case," Josh said, "just to take a look at the file. She really wants to see it."

"She?"

"Aurora Atchison. She's the surviving daughter of the vic."

Mason inhaled sharply and steadied himself, but not before Josh saw the look that crossed his face. He had some connection to this, to Aurora. Josh was sure of it. He pressed on.

"Listen, Doc. She deserves to know everything. I just want to be able to give her the right information, some kind of peace."

Mason exhaled, the silence thick between them.

Josh saw something shift in his expression. "I'm familiar with the case. Let me see what I can do."

"Thanks, Doc. How soon will I know—about the bones, I mean. How long will it take them to find out if it's Jesse?"

The expression on Doc's face was oddly tender, and he looked past Josh to the bayou out the window behind him. Josh vaguely remembered hearing about some tragedy in Mason's own past. *Everybody's carrying something.*

"Not long," Doc said. He cleared his throat. "I am familiar with your brother's case. I'm so sorry for what you went through. For what you survived."

Josh nodded. He was lucky to have survived, to have been returned home to his family, to have been spared by the Shadow Man. He should have been grateful, he should have spun his life into something noble, something memorable, some homage to Jesse. Instead he was still chasing ghosts, his own and now Aurora's. He'd survived, sure, but he hadn't escaped.

"Thanks, Doc," he said. "Let me know what you find."

CHAPTER NINETEEN

Raylene Atchison's sightless eyes, luminous and transparent, stared at James from the autopsy photo clipped to the light board.

Dr. Gentry had taken the case the first time around, worked the autopsy unassisted the morning after Aurora had left. James remembered standing in his office that morning, the full weight of what had happened bearing down on him. Raylene was dead. *This is going to be a big case*, Gentry had said by way of explanation, and shut the door in James's face.

James paged through the investigator's report. Wade Atchison had disappeared that night, a manhunt across four counties coming up empty. *I see the good in people, sometimes when it ain't even there.* How had she seen goodness in Wade Atchison?

Outside, bruise-colored clouds hung low over the blackberry water of the bayou. Ruby's seashell wind chimes began to tremble and sing against his office window, signaling the approaching storm. James closed his eyes and leaned back in his swivel chair. In another hour, the parade of people he didn't want to deal with would begin their tiresome daily march into his office. The day was unfurling, and there wasn't a thing that James could do to slow it down.

On the desk, his cell phone began to shriek.

"Hello?"

"Five-car accident with car fire on the causeway," Ruby shouted in his ear. "Just passing by on my way into work. Two flambéed on their way to you once they cut them out of the car. You want a chocolate donut or coconut?"

It was a cavalier way to talk about death, but it was the way Ruby handled her job. "Chocolate," James said.

"Why are you there so early?"

"Oh, you know. Just reading through a few things." Ruby had a finely tuned bullshit radar, and James winced as he said it.

"Atchison case, huh. Well, don't wear yourself out. It's gonna be a long day."

James ended the call and glanced at Raylene, backlit, staring at everything and nothing. Violet finger marks ringed the snowy expanse of her throat. Wade had strangled her. It was a brutal way to die, like drowning on dry land. Brutal and personal. Raylene was young and strong, a person with a lot to live for—a mother. She wouldn't have gone down without a fight.

He opened the report and, within a few pages, felt the anger begin to buzz in his ribs like a trapped wasp. It was beyond incomplete—it was ass-backwards. According to the paperwork, the autopsy had taken only two hours, an absurdly short amount of time. James frowned at the loopy, ostentatious signature at the bottom of the final page. It confirmed what he already knew: Gentry was an idiot. James conjured up an image of Gentry in his mind: a tall, sneering man with a caved-in pompadour who thrived on a steady diet of attention.

James pushed the image to the back of his mind and focused again on the report. He had always prided himself on being methodical; he would not sign a report until everything had been double-checked. He never would have signed off on this one. He paged through the police case file, attached to the back of the report.

Wade Atchison had earned his spot as the prime suspect in Raylene's death. The man's criminal history stretched back all the way to his early teens. By his early twenties, he'd racked up charges on every misdemeanor out there. Petty theft; vandalism; destruction of property; trespassing. The beginnings of a life as a career criminal. Nothing violent.

And then Raylene had changed all that. The domestic disturbance reports were almost two inches thick. Time and time again, police were called out to the Atchison address. Every time, Raylene refused to have Wade arrested. And then the calls abruptly stopped, two months before the murder. It was a pattern James had seen in files before, a calm before some horrifying conclusion.

James flipped the pages to reveal the man himself in a series of booking photos. Wade Atchison was the personification of the bad-boy stereotype. Tall, lean, and good-looking, he smirked at the camera in every picture, his gaze challenging and taunting James, daring him. He held the placard with his booking numbers on it at a jaunty angle, the weight of it in his left hand.

A detail. A small one, but those were always the most important, weren't they? He tore back through the other photos, each time looking at the right hand. In every picture he held it at an awkward angle, as though hiding an injury.

A familiar looking injury.

James was willing to bet that Wade Atchison was a

shrimper, and the report confirmed this suspicion. Now there was only one more question to ask.

James scrambled to his feet and grabbed his cell. Shrimpers were up early.

"Mornin', Doc," Ernest Authement said.

"Ernest, I was wondering if you could help me out with something. You remember Wade Atchison working on your crew all those years ago?"

"For true," Ernest said. "Can't forget that son of a bitch."

"Do you remember anything about him getting hurt?"

"Sure do. His hand got tied up in the winch, as I recall. Lost a couple of fingers. Couldn't work too good after that." It was a common injury among shrimpers; it had happened to James's father. The winch mechanism would draw in your arm, crushing your fingers, rendering your arm half as strong as it used to be. After his accident, James's dad could barely lift a fork.

"Thanks, Ernest," James said. With a trembling hand, he held Raylene's autopsy photo aloft and counted the half-moon finger marks on her neck.

A perfect ten.

Wade Atchison had been a thief, a wife beater, a no-good son of a bitch.

But he wasn't a murderer.

CHAPTER TWENTY

Sooner or later, all criminal investigations in Cooper's Bayou led to the Crumplers.

Josh and Samba stood on the scorched riverbank and stared up at the *Sweet Camellia,* a paddle wheeler turned casino riverboat and probably the only place in town creepier than the evidence room. For as long as he could remember, the Crumplers had been running the place. It was listed as Wade Atchison's last known place of employment.

It was almost unimaginable that the vessel was once seaworthy. With her white layers of lattice railings and a chipped gold smokestack on top, she looked like an enormous melting ice cream cake. She leaned away from the dock, as if one day she might break free of her moorings and collapse, exhausted, into the syrupy brown river.

"At the nickel slots," Samba explained, "they bring you free drinks just for sitting there. Of course, I always tip 'em. I used to be a waiter, you know. Thankless job."

"You waited tables in this place?"

"A waiter, a crusader for peace, a musician. It was the sixties, Josh. You had to be there."

Josh grinned and followed him up the splintered wooden gangplank.

"Were the Crumplers running it back then?"

"Oh, for true. There was all kinds of stuff going on behind the scenes, but I just kept my head down and focused on the bourbon. Jeremiah Crumpler was in charge back then, but he passed the torch to Burdette after that."

In a flash of memory, Josh saw Burdette Crumpler and his own father hauling out of the front yard of their summer place in Cooper's Bayou in a sun-battered pickup, Josh's mother yelling in their wake. They were drinking buddies, and he wasn't sure where the association ended after that.

The girl at the front desk wore a skin-tight tank top that read ASK ME ABOUT THE PLAYERS CLUB. Her glittering eyeshadow had been applied with such fervor that stray sparkles illuminated her cheeks and strands of the hair around her face. There was no way she was eighteen yet. He'd call it in, let Rush know.

After they found out what they needed.

"Good morning, miss," Josh began. "We need to speak with Burdette Crumpler, please."

"He's a busy man." She turned from them and began to dump change into plastic buckets with the Sweet Camellia logo on the outside.

"Well, I'm sure he'll make time for us. We're old friends."

"Is that right," she drawled. "Didn't know Burdy had any friends."

Josh freed a twenty from his back pocket. "We'd be much obliged, ma'am."

She took it from him, no change in her bored expression. "He stays for the beginning of the show, but after that, you'll find him on deck out back."

Samba leaned in. "Show?"

"Yeah, some psychic medium. Main ballroom, that way."

"Thank you, ma'am."

She shrugged and looked past them to the next customer.

Josh followed Samba up the grand staircase to the ballroom, the carpet, thick with ground-out cigarette butts, crunching underfoot. Signs around them advertised Dewitt Vick, psychic medium. In the pictures, a man with slicked-back hair in a shiny gray suit leaned against a tombstone. YOUR LOVED ONES ARE STILL HERE—the ad promised—AND THEY HAVE A MESSAGE FOR YOU! Josh's mother had gone to one of these people after Jesse's death, a woman with hair-sprayed curls who sat at their kitchen table and told her that Jesse was at peace, that he was watching them. Doc Mason's plastic bag would be at the state lab by now, some technician putting it into a machine that would spin what they had taken from Josh's cheek into a thousand pieces.

"We missed the early show," Samba called back to him, a note of disappointment in his voice.

"Please don't tell me you believe in this bullshit."

"Do I think there's things we can't understand? Absolutely. Do I think that Dewitt Vick has the key to those things? Absolutely not," Samba said.

They reached the top of the stairs. The ballroom was almost full; they'd lined up cheap folding chairs on every available inch of space, for maximum profit. Josh tried to conjure up an image of Burdette in his head; a blurry portrait of someone with red hair and missing teeth.

"Burdy, we gonna close the doors soon," someone shouted.

"Yep," came the reply, and Burdette Crumpler came into view, propelling a wheelchair up the aisle with two muscled arms sleeved in tattoos. He began a slow glide behind the back row of the audience and disappeared out an exit at the back.

"Let's go around," Josh said.

Out on the deck, Burdy smoked with his back to them. His long, red hair was pulled into a ponytail, and stray wisps of it littered his shoulders like tumbleweed.

"Burdette?"

He wheeled around to face them. "Hey, I know you."

Samba grinned. "Yeah, I used to work here for your pop, a few years back."

"No, not you." Burdette pointed at Josh. "You're Doyle's kid, right? I loved that guy. He took me fishing, got me drunk the first time. How the hell is he doing?"

So Josh's dad hadn't just been drinking and committing crimes; he'd been playing father of the year to someone else's kid. Unbelievable. "He's up at Craw Lake."

"No shit," Burdette said, but he didn't look surprised. "Didn't know he was still locked up. You tell him to come see me when he gets out. I'll get him a job, get him set up."

"That's nice of you. So you're running things around here now?"

"Sure am," Burdette said. "It ain't hard." He gestured towards the ballroom. "This shit is a real moneymaker, I'll tell you that. I just get info from the crowd, listen in on conversations so Dewitt can do his thing."

Samba piped in. "So it's a trick?"

"Well, sure."

"Dewitt's not a soothsayer?"

"A what? He's an ex-con from Birmingham." He glared at Josh. "So you're the cop, right? You here about Dewitt? Because it ain't illegal, you know. It's like a magic trick. Entertainment."

"We're not worried about that, Burdy," Josh said. "Just looking into an old case and hoping you could help us out."

"What case?"

"The disappearance of Wade Atchison."

Burdy laughed. "Disappearance, huh? They still call you disappeared when nobody's looking for you? Who wants to find that asshole?"

"So you worked with him, right?"

"My daddy, Lord rest him, he did. Wade worked the shrimp boats, then he messed up his hand and couldn't work no more. My daddy gave him a job."

"Working the casino?"

"Hell, no," Burdy said. "Wade worked in one of my daddy's other businesses, out in the swamp. Something that was a better fit for Wade's, um, talents."

"What business was that?"

"Hunting gators."

"That's illegal," Samba said.

Burdy shrugged. "Like I said, it was a better fit."

Wade's father-in-law had been the alligator nuisance man. Hunter Broussard had been a well-liked member of the community, by all accounts a stand-up guy. Had Wade involved him in something shady?

"So you haven't heard anything about Wade since then?"

Burdy shook his head. "Nope. Don't know if he's alive or dead, but I'm hoping for dead."

"Why is that?'

"Everybody around here knows he done it." The tone of his voice changed, and he looked away from them, out at the swamp. "Raylene, she was a nice girl. Always sweet to everybody. She didn't deserve what happened to her. That son of a bitch Wade, he used to beat the hell out of her all the time, for no reason."

"So you think he's capable of murder?"

"How do you think I got in this chair?" Burdy slapped the armrests of the wheelchair. "After all my family done for him, he pushed me out of the truck while we were riding down the highway towards Hambone. He done it just for fun."

He flicked the ashes from the cigarette and watched their descent to the river below. "I think he's capable of anything."

CHAPTER TWENTY-ONE

"Are you sure you want to do this?"

Aurora nodded and wiped the veil of sweat from her cheeks, where a fresh coat immediately replaced it. She'd been in Cooper's Bayou a week, and she already knew she was never going to get used to the humidity.

"I'm fine."

"Everything okay at the house?"

He'd been checking on the place in the evenings, a gesture that she appreciated more than she let on. *I'm sure it was nothing*, she kept telling Josh, as though her determined tone of voice might make her believe it. Something else was going on; she knew it, and so did he.

"Sure, it's great." After the visit to Charlsie, she'd taken the gris-gris bags that she'd stuffed away in the closet and put them back where Papa had left them, but he didn't need to know that. God help her, she was becoming a superstitious Southerner. "Tell me about what happened with the Crumplers." She'd wanted to go along that morning, but the Realtor had accosted her at the mini-mart to discuss when she might be putting the house on the market. "Anything there?"

Josh turned to face her. "The Crumplers have been raising hell around here for years. Your daddy was involved in some of their side businesses."

"Drugs?"

Josh pointed to the swamp. "Alligator hunting. Poaching is the more accurate term. It's been illegal for years, but there's money in it."

"And Papa was the alligator man." She thought about Charlsie and the bad men she had mentioned. "I think Papa was afraid of the guys who were poaching—the Crumplers."

"Everyone in Cooper County's been afraid of them at one time or another," Josh said, "and with good reason. They've been raising hell around here for decades."

"And you think they had something to do with my mom's murder?" There it was again in Aurora's chest, a thread of grief, a link to her mother that was being strengthened with every day she spent in Cooper's Bayou.

He ran a hand through his hair. "I don't know about that. But when something bad happens in town, the Crumplers are either behind it or they know about it. I think we might be on the right track."

"Then let's bring them in for questioning. Find out what they know."

Josh grinned. "Easy there, New York City. We don't have any authority to do that yet. We have to keep on following the evidence."

Ahead of her, Josh motioned towards a row of houses on stilts. The whole row of them looked abandoned, with their wilting porches and broken screen doors, kudzu curling out of every open window. In front of them, the bayou appeared stagnant, but Aurora could feel the water thumping beneath their feet, pulling the ground below them lumpy and uneven. The house closest to them bowed towards the water, a sole cracked plastic lawn chair half submerged in front of it. A porch light coated in bugs dangled above a rotting doorway. A gaping hole in the roof was ringed with a cluster of yellow songbirds.

Aurora had been born in one of these houses.

She focused on the back of Josh's T-shirt, which was sticking to his shoulder blades. The dog glanced back at her and then resumed trotting at his side. Aurora wasn't sure why he had agreed to help her with this case. All the years in New York had made her a cynic—no, a realist, she told herself. Why would he spend time on her case? What did he want?

"This is it," he announced from what had been a front yard. Two planks of wood formed an X across a splintering yellow door, and the yard had succumbed to weeds and trash. Beau darted around the side of the house to explore the tall grass. Aurora took a seat on the top step and Josh sat beside her.

"Do you remember it at all?"

She'd expected some kind of revelation, some moment of clarity, but looking up at the house, all she felt was a suffocating sadness, an unexpressed grief for the people who had once lived here.

"That night," she said. "They questioned me."

He stared across the bayou. "Yes."

"There must be a record of it somewhere. Did I say anything important? Was it in the file?"

"We didn't find anything," he said. "Do you remember it?"

The question took her back twenty years, to the police station. Detective Rossi. He'd picked her up at the morgue, brought her to a windowless room in the station. She'd sat on two phone books to reach the table, waiting for Nana and Papa to pick her up. Detective Rossi had rolled out a stream of paper and handed Aurora a bouquet of Magic Markers.

Draw what you remember, sweetheart.

What had she drawn? It was a blank spot in her memory, something scrubbed clean by time or by some protective mechanism in her brain.

"I don't think I gave them anything helpful," she stammered, unable to keep the emotion out of her voice.

"Hey," he said, putting a hand on her back. "You were just a kid. Nobody would expect you to remember anything. You did exactly what you were supposed to do—you survived. That's all we can do."

She knew it was a speech the police probably gave every victim, but it didn't feel like empty platitudes coming from Josh Hudson.

"Thanks," she said. She stood and cupped her hands to peer inside the doorway behind them. "So who owns this place now? I'm the last surviving Atchison, right? How come the Realtor didn't ask me about this house? Looks like a prime slice of waterfront real estate." She tried to smile, but the expression on Josh's face stopped her.

"Your dad."

Her dad. Alive or dead, Wade Atchison had always loomed over her life, a shadowy presence, the person who had killed her mother but let her live; an act of violence paired with an act of mercy. What did it mean? She thought about the question mark that Papa had drawn above her father's name on the letter in his office.

"Do you think he's still out there?"

"I think," he said, "there's a lot about this case that we don't know yet."

That was the understatement of the year. "I think you're right." Everything she thought she'd known about Papa, about her past, it was all unraveling, and she was determined to keep up.

"Aurora." Josh was standing now, pointing to a spot a few feet away from the front yard where they stood. "Look, right there."

An eye surrounded by scales broke the mossy surface of the water.

"Oh, my God."

Josh grinned. "Your first gator sighting in the wild since you've been back." The gator slipped beneath the surface.

"I probably should have seen it first, being the grand-daughter of the alligator man and all," she said with a laugh.

"Maybe you're just a little out of practice."

"Maybe," she agreed. Together they watched the place where the alligator had been, but the surface remained smooth and unbroken. There was something otherworldly about the gators, and she understood why Papa had been so captivated by them. And Wade had been hired to kill them, take away the very thing Papa had worked so hard to protect. "I didn't real-ize how huge they were."

"Some can be nine feet long," Josh said. "My dad used to say they didn't get that way by being nice."

His cell phone began to beep.

"Doc Mason," he told her, holding up a finger. The medi-cal examiner. Aurora had a flash of memory of a stainless-steel table, a man with glasses who helped her. Nana and Papa had shushed her every time she'd mentioned it later, but the memory of the morgue still popped to the surface. Twenty years later, what did Doc Mason remember?

"Great," Josh was saying into the phone. "She's with me right now. We can head on over." He ended the call.

"Doc's got something for us, from the autopsy," he told her, the excitement rising in his voice. "He wouldn't tell me over the phone." He whistled for Beau. "You ready?"

"Sure."

He began to trudge back down the path, but Aurora hesitated a moment on the step, looking back at the house.

"Thank you," she said to Josh's back.

"What?" He stopped and turned around.

"For helping me," she said. "You don't have to do this. I know that. I just really appreciate it."

"It's not a big deal."

"This detective stuff—is this what you did before you worked in the evidence room with Samba?" She caught up with him, avoiding a pile of litter at the bottom of the steps.

"No, I worked narcotics. Undercover drug busts, that kind of stuff."

"Sounds exciting."

"I guess."

"So you're an undercover cop turned evidence expert who alligator wrestles on the side," she joked. "What else don't I know about you, Josh Hudson?"

It was a lame joke, but Aurora saw immediately that she had crossed a boundary, taken a step into forbidden territory. It was engraved on his face, written in the tense way he was now holding his shoulders.

"Not much to tell." The tightness was in his voice as well, the flirty banter was over. He snapped a branch off a tree leaning into the path and tossed it in the direction of the water. "I'm just like you, born here but grew up somewhere else, then made my way back to the bayou." They reached the car and he held the door open for her. "We'd better hurry over to Doc

Mason's before he gets called out on a case," he said, a false brightness in his tone.

She wanted to apologize to him, but for what? What had made him bristle, act so strangely? His words haunted her.

You survived. That's all we can do.

What had he survived?

CHAPTER TWENTY-TWO

The last autopsy of the day always made James hungry.

It sounded gruesome, but it was really no different than a businessman looking forward to coming home to a cooked dinner. In James's world, there was no homemade meal, but there *was* a slightly wilted Cuban sandwich Ruby had picked up for him waiting in the fridge. Now that the last autopsy of the day was complete, nothing was standing in the way of his dinner.

Except Glenn.

"You're going to eat? Now?" Glenn lolled against the open refrigerator in the break room, his round face pink and shiny as a boiled ham. He was like an unwieldy piece of furniture that James was always stubbing his toe on. A brand-new tech fresh from school in Utah, Glenn straddled the border between eager and downright annoying. James ignored him and reached for the sandwich.

"Detective Hudson and his guest are on his way here, Glenn," James said. "Let's clean up around here a little bit."

The truth was, James wasn't even sure if Josh would bring

Aurora. He wanted to see her, to be able to somehow convey what her mother had been like, fearless and compassionate. There was so much he wanted to say; he wanted to tell her how the memory of their meeting had echoed in every child that had been on his table since then. Nobody ever warned you in medical school about the kids, about what it was like to see them laid out on your table, baby teeth and friendship bracelets and socks with little ruffled edges. In every one of those patients, James had seen Aurora, wondered where she was, hoped that someone was keeping her safe. He wanted to tell her this. But James was no good at these kinds of things, and so of course he would say nothing.

"Yes?" Glenn was still standing there, a questioning expression on his face.

"Ruby wanted me to give you a phone message from earlier," Glenn stuttered. "Captain Rush at the PD returning your call. Also, I have the report from our earlier patient, Jasmine Doe? It's on your desk."

One of their earlier intakes had been a prostitute, killed by blunt force trauma, her body a testament to a life of pain and struggle. James had let Glenn take the lead on the exam, watching as he'd combed the limp strands of her hair, collecting evidence. He'd cradled her head like a baby. Glenn wasn't so bad, James decided. Annoying, sure, but at least he cared about his job.

"Thanks. Nice work today, Glenn." The tech grinned and gave him an emphatic thumbs-up.

In the quiet of his office, James hesitated before picking up the receiver, running his hands over Raylene Atchison's file. Asking the police to open a closed case was risky; criticizing the work of another medical examiner was unheard of. And when that medical examiner was Davis Gentry, who was now a bigwig in the state capital, it was tantamount to career suicide. But Raylene had seen something good in James; she hadn't been wrong about that.

Rush answered on the first ring. "Cooper's Bayou PD, Captain Rush speaking." James had never liked Rush. It was one thing to take your job seriously, but Rush had elevated his position at the PD to the level of a royal birthright.

"Doc Mason here," James said, trying to sound jovial.

"Doc! Great to hear from you. What can I do for you today?"

"I have some questions about an old case." James would leave Josh's name out of the conversation; it seemed Josh had enough troubles of his own.

"Sure."

"The Atchison homicide," James said. "I was going through the file, and there are some problems here with the report."

"Hold on, Doc. You're talking about Raylene Atchison? That case was closed decades ago. Wade Atchison was guilty as sin. Everybody knows that."

"I'm not so sure. Looking at these pictures—and given some of the evidence, I think there are some real questions about his guilt."

There was a long silence at the other end of the phone. "Doc, this case is closed. Leave it alone."

"What?"

"You heard me. Leave this one alone. Now, if you're look-ing for something to do, we've still got some cases on the docket here."

"Captain, with all due respect, I think you need to reopen this case. I'm not criticizing the police work on this mat-ter"—James glanced at the file, half the size it should have been—"but we have some real issues here. Wade Atchison may be innocent."

"Well, it's not like he's in jail, right? Wade's probably whooping it up someplace in California or, hell, working a margarita stand in Mexico. No harm, no foul, Doc. I ain't authorizing a reopening of this one. Leave this one be."

The cavalier tone of his voice rattled James. Wasn't anyone concerned about justice?

"I'm afraid I can't do that, Captain Rush," James said. "I'm bound by my ethical obligations to raise a question when there is a discrepancy in the autopsy report."

Rush laughed. "Well, good luck with that at the DA's office. A twenty-year-old murder? Some girl from down the bayou? They're gonna laugh you all the way out of your job, Doc Mason. I'm telling you, the case is closed. Now, I have some paperwork to get to, and I'm sure you do as well. Good afternoon."

James sank, stunned, into his desk chair. *Leave this one be.* Maybe Rush was just lazy. *Some girl from down the bayou.* The careless way he said it enraged James, and not just because he was from down the bayou himself. James looked through the glass separating his office from the autopsy bay. In death, they shed all the trappings of their life with their garments, each one deserving the same justice, the same dignity from his office and from the police. James didn't believe in God, but he knew it wasn't for him to judge, and it sure as hell wasn't up to Clarence Rush, either.

Someone knocked softly at the door.

"Just give me a second here, Glenn."

"I'm sorry—Dr. Mason?"

A young woman edged into his vision. Brown curls, a

cherub face. She was taller, she was older, but James would have known her anywhere. There was so much of Raylene in the set of her jaw, the quiet strength in her eyes. Her little bow mouth was set in the same stubborn line that it had been all those years ago.

"Aurora," he said. Before he could stop himself, he was on his feet and doing what he had done that July evening so many years before, putting his arms around her in a hug. She squeezed back, resting her head on his shoulder.

"It's good to meet you," she said, "again. Josh said you might be able to help us?"

"I'm going to do everything I can," he said, looking over her at Josh Hudson, standing in the doorway. She ran a finger over the open file, the picture of Raylene on the riverbank.

"I'm sorry," James said quickly. "Looking at these—I can't imagine." He flipped over the photograph to reveal the one of Raylene in life, standing in the front of a pontoon boat. "I knew your mother a little bit."

"You did?"

"I did. She was extraordinary."

In the doorway, Josh broke the spell. "Doc, you mentioned that you might have some new information?"

"Right, right. Come through here to the autopsy suite for a second." He hesitated in the doorway. "Aurora, I'm not sure how you feel about seeing these pictures of your mother this way."

"It's all right, Doc," Aurora assured him. "I need to know."

Something in her voice told him not to argue. "All right, then."

He led them through and fitted the picture of Raylene up to the light board, then hit the switch so that darkness enveloped them. He pointed to the bruising on her chest, and Josh leaned in to get a closer look. "Can you see that?"

"Finger marks," Josh said.

"Exactly. Marks from fingers Wade Atchison didn't have. His hand was mangled in a shrimping injury."

"So there's no way he did this," Josh said.

James snapped the light back on. "Absolutely not. He could have been involved, sure. But he's not the one who killed Raylene Atchison. Those are someone else's hands."

"Maybe he had help," Josh mused.

"Maybe. I brought my findings to the police department, but they're calling it a closed case."

"That's what they told Papa," Aurora said. "He had questions too. He asked them to retest some of the old samples, and they refused. So what do we do?"

"There is another option," James said. "Sometimes, in the case of an unexplained death, families send evidence out to an independent lab. I have details on a few independent places we've used before. I'd just need your permission to release it to them for testing, Aurora."

"Really? It's that easy? Just tell me where to sign."

"Ruby has those forms—you can get them from her. How is the rest of the investigation going?"

Josh was inspecting the toe tag on Jasmine Doe, the prostitute from the earlier intake.

"Doc—do you mind?"

"Sure," James said, confused about who Josh could be looking for. Was he working another case? "She was brought in this morning. Blunt-force trauma. No ID on her yet." He watched Josh slide the drawer out, curl back the sheet and stare into the remains of her face, then replace the sheet. "You want me to keep you posted?"

"No, that's fine. What were you saying about forms?"

"Ruby has them up front."

"Thanks, Doc. We'll get out of your way. Really appreciate your help on this one." He shook James's hand, and Aurora followed him out the doorway, then turned to face James.

"Thank you," she said.

"Don't thank me yet." He leaned against the stainless-steel table. "There's an old saying about medical examiners—we have all the answers when it's already too late. But I'll do everything I can on this case."

She grasped his hand, threading her fingers through his own, the flat of their palms pressed together. The tenderness of the gesture startled him. It was as though she saw something in him, the way Raylene had.

"I know," she said. "And I have a feeling it's not too late."

CHAPTER TWENTY-THREE

From inside Praise The Lord Donuts, Jesus Christ was watching Josh.

Not just one of Him, but more than Josh could count. On statuettes and candles, and from a lofty perch atop a cake made entirely of chocolate glazed donuts, the bearded man with the crown of thorns regarded him with a sorrowful gaze. Josh hoped that if there really was someone on high running this shit-show, he would look more like Buddha, a laughing fat guy reminding you that life was great. That was a God Josh could get behind, not some emaciated guy reminding you that he was strapped to a cross and it was completely your fault.

Raylene Atchison had worked here, alongside Bobbie Sharpless, her best friend, who still owned the place. There was no statement from Bobbie in the police report, but Josh was willing to bet she had some good information, had shared some kind of silent camaraderie with Raylene the way women did with their friends. It wasn't much of a lead, but he had to work every possible angle.

There was something familiar about the bluetick hound that blocked the doorway to the shop. He eyed Josh briefly and

then resumed chewing a catfish head with slow, lazy bites. Josh
gave him a scratch behind the ears before gently easing him
aside to open the screen door.

"Miss Bobbie?"

She was behind the counter, her arms elbow-deep in a
sink jammed full of soaking dirty baking trays, her apron
shiny with streaks of grease. Her homecoming days were long
past, but beauty still clung fiercely to Bobbie Sharpless. Her
bottle-blond hair was swept into a cheerleader's high ponytail,
with a few strands pulled loose around her delicate face. Sweat
from the heat of the ovens had rendered her pale pink sun-
dress translucent, revealing the creamy skin of her chest. Bobbie smiled at Josh, the tired smile of a person who wishes she
were somewhere else.

"Josh Hudson," she said, her voice fluttery in a girlish
way. "And why is the law coming to visit me today?" Under
the bakery's fluorescent lights, she looked otherworldly, incandescent. Bobbie shook her hands dry and pulled a cruller
free of a congealing pyramid behind the counter using pink
tongs. "How 'bout a Lamb of God Lemon Crème, Josh? Fresh
today."

"A policeman can't say no to a donut. Thank you, ma'am,"
he said, pulling it free of the tongs with a napkin and taking a
bite before wrapping it up. "I just had a few questions for you
about Raylene Atchison."

"Raylene." Bobbie crossed herself and sank into an orange
plastic chair behind the counter. "Now, there's a name I ain't
heard in years. I heard that her little girl is back in town. I've
been meaning to come by, bring her some goodies. I guess she
ain't little no more."

"No, ma'am," Josh said. "I'm sure she'd love to meet you."

"You think so?" Bobbie leaned back in the chair. "She was

the most precious child. Raylene and Wade just could not get enough of her. I told them, that baby's never gonna learn to walk if y'all don't put her down. They carried her everywhere, just like a little queen." She sat back up. "And why are you asking questions now?"

"We have reason to believe that Wade might not have been the one who took her life."

She covered her mouth with a hand. "Jesus, Mary, and Joseph," she said. "I always thought the story didn't make sense."

"What do you mean?"

"I knew Wade," she said. "We were sweethearts before he met Raylene. Nothing serious—we were just kids. But he was a good man."

Josh thought about the police report. "I saw a lot of domestic violence reports in the file," he said quietly.

"I ain't saying he was perfect. They fought, for true. Raylene wasn't no shrinking violet, either. But when they had Aurora—it changed him. Wade came in here, he stood right where you were standing, and he told me, 'That little girl is the reason I was put on this earth. I'd die protecting her.'" She dabbed at her eyes with a corner of the dish towel. "A man doesn't say those things lightly, Detective Hudson. Do you understand that?"

Josh thought about Jesse. "I understand," he said.

"I wanted to take her," Bobbie said, and the pain in her voice sliced through Josh. "I wanted to raise Aurora like my own child. That little girl, all by herself."

Josh reached for her hand across the counter. Behind her, outside the window, rain began to shatter the bayou's silken surface. "You can still help her, Miss Bobbie. Tell me something that might help us solve this case. Anything."

"Raylene was afraid," she said.

Above them, the lights in the store hissed and flickered, and outside a trembling finger of lightning split the bayou in half.

"Who was she afraid of?"

"She wouldn't tell me. We used to talk about everything. My ex, Tim, he'd go out to his daddy's fishing camp with Wade, and Raylene and I would stay on the boat. We talked about our husbands all the time. Wade wasn't the problem."

Josh thought about the file, the litany of domestic violence calls. "Bobbie, the police were out there at the house a lot. You have to understand why people think Wade's the one who done this."

"He wasn't the problem," she repeated. "I know what you're saying about him, and you're right. He was an asshole when he drank. But I'm telling you, Josh, that little girl changed him. Being around Hunter changed him. He was doing better."

"So who do you think it was that Raylene was afraid of?"

"I don't know. She didn't like the people Wade was working for. You know the Crumplers. You can't trust any of their kin. I know Raylene was mad about them cutting up those gators. She loved those damn animals."

"How do you know she was afraid?"

Bobbie walked over to the screen door, and the hound wriggled in, shaking his mottled fur free of raindrops before settling at Josh's feet. Bobbie smiled. "Looks like Cyrus remembers you," she said. "We lost him last year. He got spooked and ran behind the boat rental place. And you're the one who brought him back."

So that was why the dog looked familiar. The memory clicked into focus: Josh crashing through the underbrush, the dog crouched in a tangle of dying flowers, terrified. It was Josh's first year as a patrolman in Cooper's Bayou.

"Yes, ma'am, I do remember."

"You're a good man." Her words vibrated through him, as though someone had plucked a single string deep inside. It wasn't true, but he saw in her face that she believed it.

"I'm just trying to help out a friend," he said.

Bobbie fingered the tiny gold cross that rested in the hollow of her throat. "She knew something was coming, Josh. She saw it. And it wasn't that bayou voodoo, neither. She told me someone was following her. Threatening her. God help me, I don't know if I could have done something to help her."

Josh's mind lit up with the possibilities. Was someone angry with Raylene for protecting the alligators? It was big business on the bayou; people had been killed for less. He was going to have to go back to the Crumplers for answers.

"You are helping her now, Miss Bobbie." Her face was shiny with grief, the weight of a long-carried burden etched in the skin underneath her eyes.

The bell above the door jangled, and Boone filled the doorway.

"Good afternoon, Miss Bobbie. Detective Hudson." What was he doing here? Josh felt a sickening jolt to the gut. The game was up; Rush had found out about his little investigation, and now he was going to be fired.

"It's sure been nice chatting with you, Miss Bobbie," Josh said. "I do hope I'll see you soon."

"Y'all take care," Bobbie said, collecting herself and hurrying back behind the counter.

Outside they stood under the awning, the silence heavy between them.

"So you following me around now, or what?" Josh attempted a joke, but Boone's mouth remained set in a straight line.

"Josh, I have some news. Your dad is a free man. I wanted to be the one to tell you."

"How long ago?" He hadn't thought the parole board would be dumb enough to recommend release, but if anyone could sell bullshit, it was Doyle Hudson. This was going to make the search for Liana more complicated.

The storm was picking up steam now. The Jesus statues rattled like chattering teeth against the window behind them.

"This morning." Boone laid a hand on Josh's shoulder. "I tried to have the guys keep tabs on him, but he's in the wind. I'm sorry, Josh."

Josh looked out over the bayou, over the tops of the cypress trees to the towns beyond, where somewhere his sister waited, probably unaware that her father was out there, free. There wasn't a damn thing Josh could do about it. He would try Pea, but what good would that do now?

"Thanks, man," he mumbled to Boone, and pulled his collar up against the rain.

"I know what you're up to," Boone said. "This Atchison thing."

Josh stared at him.

"Relax. I'm not going to turn you in, buddy." They descended the stairs together.

"So what's your take on it? The Atchison case?"

Boone frowned. "It's a long time ago. These cold cases, I mean, I don't know. Some stuff just never gets figured out, you know? Nobody's got a one hundred percent solve rate."

"Damn," Josh swore. "Boone, your work ethic is just blowing me away right now."

"Seriously, man."

"Just because something happened a long time ago doesn't mean it stops being important," Josh told him. He thought about the boxes, stacked high in the evidence room. "You can't just give up."

"You're right. Absolutely. Just be careful."

"Yeah. See ya." Josh pulled up his hood and faced the rain.

"Josh. Wait a second." Boone reached into his waistband and handed Josh a gun. "It's my personal one," he said. "Until you get yours back," he explained. "Keep it on you. I have a feeling you might need it."

CHAPTER TWENTY-FOUR

Royce Beaumont, the attorney whom Luna Riley had recommended, worked out of an office above a kiddie playland called Baboon Jack's.

Aurora stood in the blistering heat next to a man in a frog costume who was chain smoking on the front steps.

"Excuse me," she said. "Do I go around back to get to Royce Beaumont's office?"

The frog man shrugged off the felt green hood of his costume and glanced up at her with mild interest. "Only way out is through," he said, pointing to the kiddie park. "They just got done with the glitter ponies carnival. Watch your step."

"Thanks." The guy wasn't kidding. Inside, glitter and streamers surrounded one traumatized-looking pony standing in the middle of the room. Aurora made her way down the main hallway to the staircase at the back. On all sides, children shrieked and darted among arcade games and pits filled with brightly colored plastic balls. In the corner, a pink stereo blared a tune that sounded like it was being played at twice the normal speed. Everything shimmered with glitter. She wondered if she had ever come here as a kid.

Aurora wound her way up the back steps to an office door and pressed a buzzer. It was amazing that anyone could hear with the insistent thump of the music below, but miraculously someone pulled the door open.

A woman in her forties with feathered bangs and cat's eye glasses smiled at Aurora and beckoned her inside. "Aurora Atchison. I can't believe it's you." Aurora was getting used to the stares she got around town, but this was something more.

"I have an appointment with Mr. Beaumont."

The woman took both of Aurora's hands in her own. "Oh, sugar. You're just as pretty as your mama. You don't remember me, do you? Miss Pearline?"

She was too young to have been one of Raylene's friends, not much older than Aurora. A childhood playmate? Aurora smiled. "I'm so sorry, I don't remember."

"Well of course you don't! Oh honey, I prayed for you so many times. I'm the one that found you that night your mama went to be with the Lord. At Margie Belle's."

This was the woman who had called the police. Her rescuer. Aurora reached back into her memory of that night, but there was only Doc Mason and the morgue, and before that a terrible blank space. This woman could not have been more than a teenager that night; she must have been terrified. Aurora squeezed her hands.

"Thank you," she said, the words painfully inadequate. "For what you did, for helping me that night."

"Oh, honey," Pearline began, but she was interrupted by the screech of the phone. She tottered back around the desk.

"Mr. Beaumont's just finishing up a conference call." She pointed to a shiny leather couch. "Y'all make yourself comfortable. This phone's been ringing off the damn hook all day!"

Aurora took a seat by the window next to an older woman reading the newspaper. Above the bayou, clouds were beginning to gather in gray spirals. From here, the mini-mart and boat dock were barely visible through the fog. She imagined her father carrying her there, leaving her on the steps to be found. Why had he spared her? And if Doc Mason was right, was he completely innocent? She'd spent her entire life coming to terms with the fact that her father was a murderer, fitting this horrendous fact into the confines of her life, and now it was possible that he wasn't. More questions cropped up at every turn. She could feel a headache coming on, something in her brain beginning to pulse along with the beat of the music from Baboon Jack's. Aurora leaned back on the couch and glanced upward, where a framed row of records decorated the walls.

"He was real famous, you know."

"Excuse me?"

"Mr. Beaumont," the woman said in a half-whisper, peeking around the newspaper. "You ain't never heard his song 'Where I'm Bound'? It went to number seventy-one on the country music charts. He went to the Grand Ole Opry and everything when he was just an itty bitty thing. That man had a voice sweeter than honey when he was a little boy."

"Now, Pearline, you've got to stop bragging on me," a male voice said. "You're going to scare away all my clients."

Royce Beaumont was what Nicky would have called a silver fox. A tall man in his fifties, he wore a brown cowboy hat and a large belt buckle. He could have played the role of a cowboy if they needed an extra at Baboon Jack's.

"Royce Beaumont," he said, pumping her hand with enthusiasm, his voice deep and manicured. "And you must be

Miss Atchison. Forgive me for staring, ma'am. You are just as lovely as your mother."

"Thank you," Aurora said. She would never get used to hearing this compliment, and she would savor it every single time. "Congratulations on those records."

"Oh, that was a long time ago," he joked, but he beamed at her, obviously enjoying the praise. "Please come in, away from all that racket."

Aurora sat across from him in a red wingback chair. "It's not the best location for an office," he continued, "but it's better than my old spot above Tee Tim's bar. Especially on quarter beer night."

"Different crowd here," Aurora agreed.

"You'd be surprised at the amount of overlap," Royce said with a smile. "Now, you're here about your grandfather's estate, correct?"

Aurora rummaged in her bag. "Yes. Luna Riley gave me your name. She said you could help me, file the will and all of that."

He reached for the papers. "Well, sure. Luna's kin are from Kervick County, and I met her down here at a conference. She's a great lady. I'll take a look at all this paperwork. I'm not surprised Hunter knew what he was doing when it came to this stuff. Smart man, your grandpa. I'm so very sorry for your loss."

"Thank you," Aurora gave the stock response and felt the familiar burn of her grief rising up in her throat.

"And what about this property? Spotted Beebalm Drive?"

"I spoke with a few Realtors, and I decided to go with Renee Trosclair. She's going to help me sell it."

Royce laughed. "Renee's been wanting to sink her teeth

into that property for months. I'm sure she won't have any trouble. Have you been staying over there? It's a beautiful house."

Except for the person threatening me. "It is," she agreed. "I wish I could stay."

"Careful what you wish for," Royce said. "I've tried to leave this place a bunch of times. Something about the bayou, it always brings you back."

"Are you from here?"

"Born and raised up the bayou," he said. "Went out to Nashville for law school and opened up shop here. Just can't get enough of this place."

He clipped the papers and wrote something on a sticky note. "I should be able to get these filed tomorrow, then we can go from there." He stood up and reached for her hand. "It was really a pleasure, Miss Atchison. I'll be in touch as soon as this gets taken care of."

"I appreciate it, Mr. Beaumont."

"Please. Royce."

She hesitated at the doorway. "Royce, can I ask you something?"

"Anything at all, Miss Atchison."

"You knew my mother—and did you know my father too?" It was the first time she had asked anyone about Wade. Everyone in this town had information that might help as long as she was bold enough to ask.

Royce nodded. "I knew them both. Your mother was a real Southern belle—she was the prettiest girl in the room, but she could shoot and haul shrimp nets too. She was something else."

"And my dad?"

He paused, as though searching for the right words. "If you'll excuse my language, Miss Atchison, I hope that son of a bitch is dead for what he did to her. He was a piece of garbage."

The venom in his voice surprised her, and it looked as though Royce noticed. He straightened up to his full height. "I hope you'll excuse my manners, Miss Atchison. All these years later, and—well, I don't have to tell you. A lot of people around here still miss her."

"That means a lot to me," Aurora said, and it was true.

He walked her to the door.

"There's an emergency exit around back," he said. "In case you got enough of Baboon Jack's the first time around."

"Thanks for the tip."

She opened the door into the sunshine and found herself a few steps away from the bayou, now almost completely shrouded in mist, the view of the boat dock obscured. She had settled the will; the house was about to be sold. She had taken care of what she needed to do here. There was no reason not to return to New York on the next flight.

She took a few steps down the bank and stretched her feet down to the earth-colored water. Royce Beaumont was right, the bayou did draw you back. She'd started asking questions, and she wasn't leaving until she had the answers.

She started her car and began to drive towards the morgue.

CHAPTER TWENTY-FIVE

"I need to know Doyle Hudson's room number."

The man behind the glassed-in front desk at the Sweet Salvation Motel ignored Josh and dug the earbuds further into his ears. Two miles east of town, the Sal had been the place Doyle holed up with his mistress during the summers when they came to Cooper's Bayou. A flamingo pink atrocity that attracted the seedier element, the city council had been trying to shut down the Sal for years, but Josh knew half of those guys had been here with a woman at some point in their lives, and so the place persisted. Blackmail was almost as powerful as voodoo around these parts.

Josh remembered his dad bringing him and Liana and Jesse here as kids, rolling down the windows of the Oldsmobile and telling them to play in the car while he went to a "business meeting." Back then, the place had seemed almost glamorous to Josh, with its waterslide and luminescent soda machine. Liana had known what their father was doing but hadn't let on, telling Josh and Jesse that the car was a spaceship, making up stories about the people who walked by, peering in the windows. The Sal had always been one of his father's favorites. He was here, Josh was sure of it.

"Hey. Wake up. I'm a *cop*." He slammed his police ID up against the protective glass, and the man sat up straight. "Where's Doyle?"

"Never heard of him," he smirked, his eyes glued to the screen of his cell phone.

"You know, I think I saw a couple of hookers, couple of drug deals going down in the parking lot out there. Why don't I just make a call? I can have this place swarming with uniforms in five minutes flat. That should be great for business, right?"

"All right, all right, man. Let me check our guest registry." He ran a finger down the seam of a coffee-stained ledger. "Hudson. Room 203."

"Great."

He took the stairs. His father had had nothing but time in prison, time to find Liana, the person who had put him there. What if Josh was too late?

"Doyle, open the door." Josh smacked the door with his open palm. "Open the goddamn door."

When there was no response, he tried the handle, and the door creaked open to reveal an empty room, the bedside lamp illuminating rumpled sheets. The place smelled like Josh's childhood: last night's whiskey and the tang of the kind of cologne you could get from dispensers in the men's room at a bar. Various vending machine snacks and papers were scattered across the bed, as though he'd been sitting there reading something. Josh rifled through them. Most were copies of release forms, lists of places that hired Craw Lake alums.

"Josh Hudson. Didn't expect to see you here." Burdette Crumpler filled the doorway.

"Burdette." Josh stood.

"Well, did I miss the family reunion?" Burdette wheeled himself inside and parked next to the bed. His face was coated in a sheen of sweat, and there were deep hollows underneath his eyes. Pills, Josh guessed.

"Doyle's not here. Why do you need him?"

"I told you before, me and your daddy was friends. I was gonna get him a job on the boat. You know, help him get back on his feet."

"Well, that's very kind. Y'all must be the last people in town Doyle doesn't owe money."

Burdette snorted. "I wouldn't say that."

"So you talked to him today? Did he say where he was going?" Josh was standing over him now. "Did he say anything about my sister?"

"No, man," Burdette shrugged. "He left me a message, told me he was staying here. I don't know nothing about your sister."

Josh pointed to Burdette's backpack. "Well, let's see what you got in there."

"C'mon, man. I ain't bothering nobody."

"Let's go." Josh snapped his fingers, and Burdette tossed him the backpack.

Josh unzipped it. A lighter, a pack of cigarettes, a prescription bottle full of oxy with someone else's name on it. At the bottom, a plastic bag slouched to one side, heavy with powder and secured with a sticky note.

"Well, I don't need Dewitt the steamboat psychic to tell me what this shit is," Josh said. "So are y'all making your own crank out there, or what?" Josh pulled the bag out and folded open the note.

Spotted Beebalm Drive.

Aurora's address. Josh opened the bag and held it under the light. Orange powder. Cayenne pepper.

He crossed the room in two strides and grabbed Burdette's collar, half lifting him out of the chair.

"Is this what you and your shithead brothers are doing for fun? Scaring a woman who's alone?"

Burdette widened his eyes. "Josh, I swear on my mama's grave," he said. "It wasn't me. Look at me. How the fuck am I going to do that?"

"You'd better tell me everything you know, Burdette. Right now." Josh pointed to the backpack. "You tell me right now, or hillbilly heroin is gonna be the least of your goddamn problems."

"I told Lionel not to do it, I swear," Burdette held his hands up.

Lionel was the youngest Crumpler, not yet eighteen but already making a name for himself in town for all the wrong reasons.

"What did Lionel do?" Josh let go of Burdette's collar and sat on the bed across from him, watching his face darken with fear.

"He told me he got a call from this guy, told him he'd give him five hundred bucks to scare Miss Aurora. You know, crank call her, scare her a little bit."

"Is that why you had the powder?"

"He was afraid," Burdette said. "He's just a kid, Josh. He got out there to her house and started to spread the powder around, and he said someone else was at the house, so he ran off."

"What was the powder for?"

Burdette shrugged. "Some voodoo thing. He was scared

he didn't do it right and the guy would be pissed, but he paid up anyway."

"And you got no idea who this guy is."

Burdette wiped a hand across his forehead, and for a moment, Josh was afraid he was going to pass out. "I only found out who it was today, I swear," he said. "I told him our kin ain't got no business with him and that the cops were looking for his sorry ass."

"Who is it?"

"The devil himself," Burdette said in a half whisper. "Wade Atchison."

CHAPTER TWENTY-SIX

When you try to understand the universe, it will knock you on your ass every time.

James's father had spoken those words many times. A shrimper by trade, but a philosopher too. The words echoed through his brain, and he raised his eyes to the bayou outside, where a single shrimp boat cut through the water, a veil of nets trailing behind. How strange, he thought. After all these years, he could still feel the grief pulling a cord tight in his chest. How strange that he could step back from all the other tragedies he had seen over these last twenty years, but the Atchison case had marked him for life, and now he held the answer in his hands.

The dark parallel bands of the DNA profile covered the entire first sheet of the documentation from the independent lab. They had been able to get a sample from skin cells underneath Raylene Atchison's fingernails. It wasn't necessarily a direct link to her killer, but it was a start.

James was a firm believer in answers. It was better to know. This was what Aurora wanted, he reminded himself. Still, this case had robbed him of his greatest attribute, his ability to be neutral. He did not know how to prepare for the information held in the dark and light strips on the paper before him, and even less how to relay this information to Aurora. For the thousandth time since he'd opened the file, he'd gotten the sense that this was just the beginning, that there was much more to uncover. Aurora would have to learn the truth of what happened, no matter how dark. He wished for peace for her, for stillness, not for the pain these revelations would bring.

James had worked in the medical examiner's office long enough to know there was no such thing as closure, no joy in knowing the brutal details of a loved one's last moments. There was a reason people closed caskets, sanitized the story for their relatives and friends and the obituaries. James wished that he were not alone in the autopsy suite at this moment, the only noise the hush of the fan overhead.

James trusted Malachi; he was the independent lab's best tech, someone who knew what he was doing, and someone without the horrifying self-righteousness that characterized the younger generation. Malachi did not make mistakes.

Database hit, Malachi had scrawled at the bottom of the profile, and then, even more ominous, *Call me*.

The database he was referring to was CODIS, James guessed. A link had been made, Raylene's case matched to a criminal, known or unknown, in the nationwide catalogue. There were a million possibilities, but the meaning of a CODIS hit was clear; Raylene Atchison's murder had not been the murderer's only known crime.

Malachi answered on the first ring.

"Doc Mason. How are you?"

"Doing fine, thank you." James's voice was barely recognizable to himself—too loud, too eager. "About those results on the Atchison case."

"Sure, sure. We got a hit, as I mentioned. I can send you the link."

James tapped his computer mouse, and the screen shuddered to life.

"Thanks." James was no good with computers; he usually left these things to Ruby. "Sorry, it's just been a while since I've been on CODIS. Is it pretty easy to navigate, or—"

"It's not CODIS."

Malachi's voice filled the phone just as James clicked on the link and the screen was enveloped in black.

"NamUs," James said. It was the National Missing and Unidentified Persons System.

A dead man.

It should have been comforting, but instead he felt that familiar twinge, the sense of something cracking wide open inside him. He hung up the phone with a numb thank-you and turned his attention to the screen.

He was familiar with NamUs and its galleries of death photographs and reconstructed faces. It was one of the things that had astonished him in his first year as a medical examiner, the number of people who could remain nameless for so long, discovered along highways, in ditches, stuffed in discarded refrigerators or wrapped in trash bags. Some of them had died accidentally. James remembered a case last year where he'd entered the information of a transient, the Bird Lady, who had been walking alongside the interstate when she was hit by a car. Everyone in Cooper's Bayou knew her by sight, but in the end, she had belonged to nobody, a woman without an identity. Unclaimed.

Others were crime victims, lives reduced to a bunch of numbers and a picture of a filthy sweatshirt or a faded shapeless back-alley tattoo. It was amazing, the things they found in

the unidentified victims' pockets; little bits of fallout from someone's life. Bus vouchers, fifteen dollars in Canadian money, a
bracelet in the shape of a dolphin, a signet ring with "Valerie
Forever" inscribed on the inside. They were the kind of personal details that you'd think would lead to immediate identification, but somehow weren't quite enough.

He clicked through the profile. The unidentified decedent
had been found in Sweetwater Bayou, August 1989, a month
after the murders, but the information had not been entered
into the database until last year. Gotta love bureaucracy, James
thought, moving at the speed of molasses. There was no picture of the victim, just a blurry snapshot of a torn navy work
shirt. The body condition was listed as "not recognizable/pu-
trefaction." That was the swamp for you, unforgiving and
cruel. His eyes were missing. He had two dollars in his pocket
and a voucher for a soup kitchen, along with a tiny sachet
initially thought to be drugs, but later discovered to be a mix-
ture of herbs. Gris-gris, James almost said out loud. The guy
had all the signs of a vagrant. Wearing all the clothes he owned,
no ID, no missing persons report.

He clicked through to the next page. The man had died
from blunt-force trauma to the head.

James sank to a seated position, absorbing this new information. Was it possible that this man was the killer? The DNA
under Raylene's fingernails meant that they had been in close
contact, but what was Raylene Atchison doing with an unidentified drifter who'd ended up dead himself a month later? James
had been around long enough to know that there was no such
thing as a random crime—not in Cooper's Bayou, anyway. Was
the drifter someone Wade had hired to do the job?

He thought about the Hudson case, the man who sat in jail
for murdering Josh's brother, an innocent child, who'd never

even had the decency to tell them where the body was. Evil was out there, even in an ordinary town like Cooper's Bayou.

Outside someone rang the buzzer, the sound sending a shock through James's veins, reverberating in the cave of his chest. He pressed the intercom button.

"Yes, may I help you?"

"Sorry to bother you, Doc—it's me, Aurora."

"Not a bother at all. Come on back." With a supreme effort, James stood and steadied himself on the edge of the table. So much of him wanted to tell her that everything was all right, that he could close her case.

She appeared in the doorway, the resemblance to Raylene so striking in the half-light that it knocked him off balance, made him question again what he was about to ask, but then his resolve returned and he gestured towards one of the work stools.

"I'm glad you're here, Aurora," he said, and it was true. "I need your help."

CHAPTER TWENTY-SEVEN

"This guy in the database could be the one who killed my mother, but we have no idea who he is?"

Aurora sprawled next to Josh on the bank of the bayou and kicked off her shoes, letting the full meaning of what Doc had said wash over her. She'd called Josh from the morgue, and he'd picked her up without a question and taken her for something to eat at Possum Pete's. The conversation had been easy between them, music and sports and the difference between New York and Florida, neither of them paying attention to the new knowledge that hung heavy between them. And then Aurora had requested that he bring her here, to the exact spot where her mother had breathed her last, a lush shore blanketed in spotted beebalm.

"That's what we need to figure out," Josh agreed, tilting his head back to the sky. "The important thing is, we've got eyes on the Crumplers. My partner Boone's been tracking them. They make a move towards you, or try to contact your dad, we're all over it."

"I just can't believe he's alive. I mean, he's still out there." The shock of it was giving way to terror. Her grandparents had been wrong. Wade Atchison wasn't in a ditch somewhere. He was alive.

And he knew where she was.

"We're going to get him," Josh said.

She wanted to believe him, but Wade had eluded authorities for twenty years; he knew what he was doing.

"So maybe he hired this guy in the grave to help him kill my mother. Or he did it himself. Either way, he's a criminal." She had always known it, but had also wondered which part of Wade Atchison was bound up in her bones, deep in the recesses of her heart? She imagined some dark spot, some latent evil waiting to spring to life.

"Welcome to the club," Josh said.

"Your dad too?" It was the first time he had spoken about his past. She was guessing the bourbon at dinner had loosened something inside him.

"Doyle Hudson," Josh announced, with a grand gesture of his arms. "Petty theft, fraud, forgery, embezzlement. You name it, he's done it. Biggest con in three counties and proud of it." He tossed a pebble at the bayou, where it skipped twice before disappearing beneath the surface. "He was paroled a couple days ago, then got picked up again within the week."

"Did he leave your mom?"

"Not before he took everything she had. She still didn't turn him in, though, even after all of that. In the end, it was my sister who did that."

"Where is she now?"

Josh stretched his bare feet down the bank, and Aurora watched tendrils of earth-colored water fill in the spaces between his toes.

"She's missing, I guess. I don't know what else to call it."

"What do you mean?"

He tilted his head back towards the sky. "She left by choice. When I was a kid, my brother was abducted. When something like that happens, it fucks up your family, makes it something unrecognizable. You know what I mean?"

"Yes," she said, and she did.

He turned to her, as if hearing her voice for the first time. "I was there," he said. "When Jesse was taken. Liana was there too. After a while, she couldn't deal with it anymore, watching my mom and dad destroy each other. She took off when she was eighteen. Legally, she was an adult, so nobody was looking for her."

"Except you."

"Except me," he agreed.

They lapsed back into silence.

On the far bank, tiki torches winked at them, and Aurora could hear the faint tinkle of country music. Someone was celebrating at the Bayou Breeze; a wedding, or a birthday party. Aurora watched the guests, clutching at each other, dancing barefoot in the grass, making lazy circles that edged closer and closer to the opposite shoreline. She strained to hear the words to the song.

"Patsy Cline," Josh said. "She was my mother's favorite."

"Mine too," Aurora echoed. It was one of the few facts about Raylene that she knew, and so she kept it stored up inside like a treasure. There was a longing in Patsy's voice, something raw and painful that cut right through to your soul.

"*You don't know the heartache, or the laughter you'll forego, until you've lost that one love, then you'll know,*" Josh sang along, unabashedly, the way you'd sing alone in your car.

Behind him, the hillside was choked with kudzu, curling around the skeleton of an abandoned pickup truck. Beyond that, a grove of cypress trees twisted toward the violet sky.

These were the last things her mother had seen before she'd died here. *It was quick,* Doc Mason had told her, but Aurora knew better. It took a long time to strangle someone, and strength too, strength that Wade Atchison didn't have. Had he stood there and watched as the stranger had helped?

Across the water, a tiny light snapped on.

"What's that?"

"The mini-mart," Josh replied.

"That's where they found me."

"Yes, it is." He sounded spent, his voice hushed.

"Do they know anything? The people who work there, I mean. Someone found me there, right?"

"They left you on the steps. The place was closed, and when one of the girls came in for her shift, she found you."

Aurora leaned back, digging her elbows into the soft earth. "So my father—or the killer—dropped me off there to be rescued."

Josh rolled over to face her. "That's why everyone thought it was your father. Nobody else would've—" He trailed off.

"Nobody else would have left a witness," she finished. It was chilling, but it was true.

"Do we have any idea who this other person could be?"

Josh nodded. "Miss Bobbie in town, she said someone was bothering your mother. A man. I think he might be the key to this whole thing."

"So my dad was probably involved, and he's still out there, watching me." She shivered. "What if he knows, Josh? He knows we're looking into this—what if he finds out we're getting close to the truth?"

He put a warm hand over her own. "We're gonna find him, Aurora. I promise you. Nobody's going to hurt you."

His voice had a quiet power in the dark. Her back ached,

and she wanted to lean into the touch, to let this man comfort her. But he had done so much for her already; she couldn't ask more of him.

"Are we ever going to know what happened that night?"

As if in answer to this question, there was a movement in the undergrowth behind them. Aurora hoped it was another gator, but something told her it wasn't. Josh was on his feet instantly, grasping the gun in his waistband, inching towards the noise. He gestured to her to stay put, and she stood and followed him.

Silence.

A single sliver of light pierced the mossy blackness a distance in front of them. Aurora watched as the light flickered and then became brighter, illuminating a row of stones, candles, and a dark figure crouched between two of them.

A graveyard?

Josh raised the gun.

"Cooper's Bayou Police! Make yourself known!"

The figure jerked upright and Josh saw for the first time that it was a woman in a hooded blue sweatshirt, backlit by a lantern, wielding a carved wooden cross like a vengeful angel.

An angel with a familiar face.

"You fucking make *yourself* known! This is holy ground," Ruby howled, hurtling towards them, arms extended like a furious bird of prey. She shined the light directly in their faces and stopped a few feet short of them, brandishing the cross like a dagger. "Holy shit, is that you, Josh?"

"Ruby? Jesus, I'm sorry," Josh apologized. "Aurora and I were just out here, and—"

"Didn't mean to scare ya," she said, extending a hand to Aurora. "Ruby Contreras." Behind her, Josh swept his flashlight across the clearing at the neat rows of headstones, each one with its own circle of wildflowers, stubs of candles, and piles of what looked like bird bones and torn pieces of paper.

"Is this a graveyard?" Aurora asked.

Ruby leaned against one of the stones. "Yes. This is a voodoo cemetery, one of the last in Cooper County."

"Ah, yes. Aurora's been introduced to Charlsie Trosclair."

Ruby humphed. "I'm talking about *voudon*. The religion. From Haiti. Not that Cajun crap for tourists. No offense, Aurora."

Josh read the name on the stone she leaned against. "Billy Bob Contreras," he said. "He a relative of yours?"

Ruby laughed and spread her arms in a sweeping motion. "All these people are my relatives. Josh, you remember BB, right? He was that homeless guy that used to walk along the bayou in his tighty whities, hooting at the moon. Bet you didn't know he was also a Vietnam vet. Died last May. I just give everyone my name. Cubans got big families, people don't ask questions."

There was a silence between the three of them, like three ghosts in the graveyard, remembering lives lost. Aurora was the first to break the spell.

"But it's nothing bad? Nothing evil?"

"No, not at all. Even hacks like Charlsie, they don't mean no harm."

"Still, you got to be careful out here this late," Josh told her.

"I got my gun. And what about you? What are you doing out here this late?" She rummaged through her bag and emerged with a bottle of rum. "My holy water," she explained, taking a swig and passing it to Aurora.

Aurora sipped the rum, letting the burning sweetness settle on her tongue while Josh answered Ruby's question.

"Investigating."

"Don't you bullshit me, Detective Hudson."

Josh grinned. "Flailing. Trying to figure out what the hell is going on with this case."

Ruby nodded. "He's a good man, *chère*," she told Aurora.

"Thanks for the vote of confidence."

"Anytime," Ruby said. "I heard Doc say he found a possible perp in NamUs. You know where he's buried?"

"No idea, but I'm guessing the potter's field."

Aurora thought about the man in some mass grave, among a group of faceless criminals.

Ruby whistled. "I hate that place. You ever been out to Weir Island?" Her voice softened. "Six people to a grave over there, no flowers, no nothing." She straightened up. "Well, not on my fucking watch. Nobody's been sent there since I started working at the morgue. All of them come here."

"I had no idea," Josh said.

"Well, don't be telling your little cop friends."

Josh held up his hands in surrender. "I'm not going to tell anybody, I promise. I don't want to get on your bad side."

Ruby held out a bag towards Aurora so that she could see the contents: tiny bird bones and dirt. "This is what voodoo does," she explained. "It keeps a place safe." She reached down and released her feet from her tangerine sandals. "So," she said, lifting the hem of her dress like a child to step through the grass. "If your killer is out there on Weir Island, why don't you dig him up and get some answers?"

The meaning of what she was saying churned in Aurora's stomach. If they could unmask the man in the grave, they would have the key to this whole thing.

"You're right," Aurora said. "I bet that if Doc could look at the body, he might be able to find something to identify him."

Josh chuckled. "It's not that simple."

"What if it is?" Ruby stood up, defiant. "I bury people all the time, so why can't you dig him up?"

"I don't know. The law?"

Ruby snorted. "Come on, Josh. You are the law. That ain't never stopped you before."

"I mean, we could petition for an exhumation—"

"I'll sign whatever paperwork they need," Aurora chimed in.

Ruby laughed. "And who are you going to ask, the county commissioner? You met that guy, Josh? He doesn't give two shits about the medical examiner's office, or cold cases. He's a fat cat who cares about getting reelected. They haven't approved a budget increase for Doc in ten years."

She yanked a cluster of white candles out of her bag and turned away to light them. "The way I see it, you want something done, you have to do it your goddamn self."

Aurora and Josh exchanged a glance, and she could see he was thinking the same thing. They needed answers, and so they were going to dig them up.

Ruby knelt in front of a stone labeled JASMINE CONTRERAS and leaned in close, as though she were trying to persuade the person below to linger just a little longer with the living. She rocked back and forth, chanting in a language that bore little resemblance to anything spoken on earth.

As if in response to her words, the trees around them began to shudder in the wind. Clouds had begun to hover just above the water, and the gilded surface of the bayou split into thousands of tiny copper waves.

"So, Ruby," Josh said, "you got any digging tools in that bag of yours?"

She turned to face them and grinned. "Well, well, Josh Hudson," she said. "Aurora, I told you he was a good man." She nodded at Josh. "I always knew you had a pair under there. I've got a shovel in my car if you need it. You be careful now."

CHAPTER TWENTY-EIGHT

On the morning of their scheduled grave-robbing adventure, Josh found himself parked in front of the mini-mart, his conversation with Aurora the previous evening ringing in his ears. Someone had dropped her off here to keep her safe.

But who?

Pearline Suggs, the cashier who had found Aurora, had been interviewed several times, her story never wavering. She had arrived early for her shift, found Aurora on the steps, and had called the police immediately. She had been sixteen and terrified. Now she was a receptionist at a law office in town. There had been no other witnesses. Josh didn't know what he was hoping to learn, but in a town like Cooper's Bayou, you never knew who might know something.

The manager of the Margie Belle Grocery was supposed to be mean or crazy, depending on whom you asked. Josh was hoping for crazy.

Inside, an ancient metal fan churned the hot air and spit it out again, along with a cloud of small brown bugs. The peeling shelves were stocked high with junk food. A boy of about five stood on tiptoe to reach a puffy red bag of potato chips. Patsy Cline's distinctive warble floated out of a dusty old radio with a crooked antenna, and someone was singing along. Josh followed the sound of the voice.

"I miss yer lovin', yer kisses too," the voice sang. Josh found himself staring at the rather large rump of the singer, who was a few aisles down and two steps up a ladder, wrestling with a box in the tobacco section of the store.

"Ain't nothing on earth, I wouldn't do for you," Josh finished the last line in his tenor, which wasn't very good.

"Gracious light!" The woman turned to look at Josh. She had to be at least eighty, with a kind face that was as smooth as a freshly fluffed pillow. She wore an orange housedress that gave her the unfortunate appearance of a pumpkin. Her silver hair was set in enormous pink rollers with a large, shiny piece of tinfoil tucked carefully over each of them.

"Let me help you with that," Josh offered.

"Well! Ain't you just an angel sent straight from hay-ven," she drawled. She placed a meaty pink hand in Josh's and stepped down from the ladder with a surprising grace.

"Nobody sings like Patsy," Josh remarked, tugging the box of cigarettes free from the top shelf.

"Well, now, that's the truth," she agreed. "You just set that box right there." He could feel her studying the side of his face. "I know you. You're Doyle's boy."

"Yes, ma'am," he said. "Please don't hold that against me."

She shook her head. "Your mama used to come in here with your sister. Your mama was just as sweet as can be." For a moment, Josh stood there, basking in the warmth of this observation. "Your sister too."

"Liana," he said, as though it was important that she

know her name. He took a deep breath. "I don't know where she is." He'd wired money to Pea this morning, against his better judgment. *You won't be sorry*, she'd told him.

She took this comment in stride. "Well," she said, "people have a way of coming back home. You did, didn't you?"

"I did," he said.

"And where'd y'all live? Somewhere up North?"

"Tennessee," Josh said. "My mama's folks are there."

She looked pleased. "Tennessee folks are good folks. Well, I'm pleased that you're here, Josh Hudson. I'm Miss Margie Belle." Her sweet expression darkened when she saw the little boy clutching the bag of Ruffles near the counter. She hiked up her dress and began hotfooting it to the front of the store.

"Hey! You gonna pay for them chayda pips? If not, you better hightail it out of here!" She lunged in his direction, and the boy dropped the bag and tore out the front door.

"Some people," she said, disgusted, "they just wanna come in here and enjoy the air-conditionin'. Well, ain't nothing in this life comes for free." Josh wondered what air-conditioning she could possibly be referring to. "Now, sugarplum, you tell me what I can help you with."

Josh realized that he was definitely going to have to buy something. He looked around for a big-ticket item that would make her happy and settled on a dubious-looking ham sandwich, an oversized cookie, and a Coke. Margie Belle seemed satisfied with these choices.

"Miss Margie, I'm guessing there's not a lot that happens around here without you knowing something about it," Josh said.

"You'd be right about that."

"So were you working here back in 1989, ma'am?"

Margie Belle looked indignant. "Well, of course I was.

Long before that, too. Way before you were a twinkle in your mama's eye."

The charm came easily to Josh, like slipping on a favorite pair of pants. "Huh, 1989. . . . Let's see, what were you then—about twenty?"

Margie Belle laughed, a hearty, throaty laugh that ended in a bout of coughing. She touched her hand to one cheek, where a circle of pink began to bloom on the surface. "You go on, now, with that foolishness," she said.

"So you knew Aurora Atchison," he continued.

Margie Belle placed a doughy hand on her heart. "Bless her little heart, you know I did. Someone left her right outside on those steps." She pointed in the direction of the door.

"Did you know her parents?"

Margie Belle opened her mouth to speak and then thought better of it. "You ain't a friend of her kin, now, are you?"

"No, ma'am."

"Well. Her mama was Hunter Broussard's girl, you know, the alligator man? Her name was Raylene. She was a little wild, but always respectful. She was so essited when she got pregnant with Aurora."

"What about her daddy?"

"He was one sorry fella, if you don't mind my saying so. Sorry as a two-dollar watch. Raylene was too good to take up with him." She lowered her voice. "Those two ate supper before they said grace, if you understand what I'm saying. That precious little Aurora was almost two when they got married. Yes, sir. Although Raylene's other boyfriend wasn't no prize, neither."

Josh tried to hide his surprise. "Boyfriend?"

Margie Belle made a humphing sound, which led to another fit of coughing. "Oh, yes," she said, relishing this last hidden piece of gossip. "He was one of those boys, got a big head. Thinks the sun come up just to hear him crow." She shook her head, and one of her curlers fell out, hitting the linoleum with a click. She bent over to retrieve it.

"Do you remember his name?"

Margie Belle scoffed at this, regarding Josh like he was crazy. "Not sure I do. Some name not found in the Bible. I know she left him to be with Wade."

Josh felt a surge of energy course through him. Maybe this old boyfriend was important.

He thought about what Bobbie had said about Raylene, how she was on edge in the weeks before the murder. *She told me someone was following her.*

"Thank you very much for your time today, ma'am," he said. "I do appreciate it."

"Oh, I'm sure I didn't do nothing," she said.

"That's not true, ma'am," he said. "You helped me tremendously."

CHAPTER TWENTY-NINE

The idea was completely crazy. Still, Josh had to admit, there was a kind of simple beauty in it too. They wanted answers, so they were going to dig them up.

Literally.

Josh rolled down the windows to let the evening breeze cool the sizzling interior of the Jeep. Next to him, Beau gingerly poked first his nose and then his whole head out the passenger window. For the entire ride to Samba's house, the dog remained that way, content to let the breeze tickle his nose, his tongue a long pink flag flapping in the wind.

They stopped at the turnoff to Cooper's Harbor and watched a young couple cross the street with a wolf-sized fluffy white dog. The woman cooed adoringly at the animal while the man produced a red Frisbee from his bag, offering it to the dog, which began a cheerful sprint towards the park across the street.

Beau gave a soft whine, and Josh patted him vigorously on the neck. "Don't be jealous of that big cotton ball. He doesn't get to go on secret investigations like you do." In reply, Beau sniffed and pawed at the backseat, where Josh had stowed a bag containing provisions from Two Ton Toby's BBQ for the night's mission. Josh laughed. Beau could not distinguish drugs from baby powder, but the pup still could identify a pulled pork sandwich a mile away. Josh reached back into the bag and offered Beau one of the bones Toby'd given him.

Samba's house was the last one before the street yawned into a large dirt trail towards the bayou. The house itself, a dilapidated white cottage, was almost completely obscured by a lush curtain of palm fronds. The yellowing front yard was littered with plastic and ceramic lawn ornaments of every imaginable variety, from orange and white polka-dot toadstools to a small gray-haired wizard in a purple robe that bore an uncanny resemblance to Samba himself. At least a week's worth of newspapers struggled to break free from their plastic wrappers on the sagging steps. A green sign proclaimed in flowery lettering ALL ARE WELCOME.

Josh was wondering if an oddly shaped wind chime made entirely of pink crystals was in fact the doorbell when a clearly exhilarated Samba appeared at the screen door. He wore a bright tie-dye T-shirt that had probably fit better a few years ago and a faded brown baseball cap with what looked like part of a flashlight affixed to the front with duct tape.

Not exactly the ideal getup for a covert operation, but this was as understated as Samba got. Josh appreciated the effort.

"Ready?"

"Showtime!" Samba gave Josh a thumbs-up and followed him to the Jeep. With some difficulty, Samba wedged himself into the front seat. Beau welcomed the intrusion, jumping into the back. Samba gave Beau an affectionate scratch behind the ears. From his pocket, Samba produced a yellow bandanna, which he proceeded to tie around his head, further securing the flashlight. He lowered his voice to a dramatic whisper.

"So what's the plan?"

This question reminded Josh of his dad, who had always told him and his brother and sister that you needed three plans: a plan, a backup plan, and an emergency plan. Probably a good rule of thumb when you were running a criminal enterprise, but Josh decided early on that, for him, that was three plans too many. Tonight was really no different. He had basic digging tools, flashlights, and a vague idea of where the potter's field was located. They were probably in trouble.

"Once we get out there," Josh informed Samba, "we'll just look for the right number and start digging."

Samba turned and stared at him. "What do you mean?"

"We've got the vic's ID number from the system." Josh indicated a crumpled piece of notebook paper stuffed into one of the drink holders between the two front seats. "They've got to have it organized somehow."

Samba let out a laugh punctuated by a snort. "It ain't the supermarket," he said. "You see how organized the evidence division is. And that's stuff that's supposed to be important!"

Josh reddened. Samba had a point. There weren't going to be red arrows steering them towards the correct gravesite. Still, he reasoned, it was a limited amount of space, so it had to be somewhat organized.

Didn't it?

Samba noticed his reaction and put a comforting hand on his shoulder. "We'll figure it out. It's gonna be great! It's been a long time since I've done something like this."

Josh wondered how a do-it-yourself exhumation compared with Samba's other escapades and decided not to ask.

The sun had long set by the time Josh eased the Jeep off the causeway and the headlights swept over Aurora standing next to her rental car on the shoreline. He felt a little rush at the sight of her; they were in this together. Coming here was crazy, but seeing her, he was convinced that it had been the right decision.

Josh got out of the car.

"Hey, Aurora." He joined her, and together they looked down at the concrete slip. Tiny waves licked the shoreline, but farther out in the bay, the obsidian water stretched smooth as cream.

"So we're ready to go?" She stood there expectantly.

"Yep." Josh removed the folded map from his back pocket and pointed in the direction of where Weir Island was supposed to be. A dim yellow light winked back at him from the dock. "It's right out there. Should be an easy trip. Time to hit the water," Josh announced, opening the door. Samba and Aurora both gave Josh a similar apprehensive look.

Josh crossed his arms and pulled his T-shirt over his head in one smooth motion, relishing the surprised stares.

"What, you're both born on the bayou," Josh teased. "Don't tell me you don't know how to swim."

Samba looked at him in abject terror, and Aurora laughed. "You've got to be kidding," she said.

"Yeah, yeah, I've got a dinghy in the back." Josh popped the trunk and watched as Samba's expression melted into a relieved smile.

"You had me going there, Josh."

Josh grinned and hooked the pump up to the dinghy. With each burst of air, the white lettering on the boat's side came more into focus. Samba peered at it above his glasses.

"Police," he read. "Did you steal this?"

Josh shrugged. "Borrowed it. You're telling me you never nabbed any office supplies from work?"

Samba, honest to a fault, probably hadn't.

"Don't worry, Samba. I promise I'll return it when we're done." Samba shook his head, and he helped Josh and Aurora drag the inflated boat down to the water.

"Hop in," Josh invited, extending a hand to Aurora.

"Hang on, guys," Samba said. "If we're bringing back—um—a friend from Weir Island, this boat's gonna be too heavy."

"He's right," Aurora agreed. "I can stay behind. I'll keep an eye on the water, let you know if anybody's coming." She must have seen the trepidation on Josh's face, because she touched his arm. "Really. It's fine."

"Okay. Be safe."

She helped them push off, and Josh watched her slip back into the shadows.

The crossing to Weir Island seemed to take forever, and Josh's arms ached from rowing by the time they reached the splintered old dock.

Josh helped Samba out of the boat and secured the dinghy, unable to shake the feeling that they were being watched. There was no cool breeze; the air was stagnant and thick with insects. There was none of the peacefulness found at a churchyard here. Weeds strangled and smothered every stone surface. Nobody had bothered to clear a path to where the rows of white markers began. The markers poked out of the ground at unnatural angles. Even though it was already late spring, nothing was budding or blooming. It was like a human landfill.

Samba took a step towards the first row of markers and squatted down, pushing his glasses up on his forehead to stare at the numbers.

"Well, what do you know," he remarked. "It is like the supermarket! They've got the numbers right on there." He moved farther down the row. "They're in order! I can't believe it."

Trying to share Samba's enthusiasm, Josh followed him, Beau trotting close behind. Josh was still unsettled by the careless upkeep of the place. The graveyard by the state prison was manicured and well-kept, but these people—people whose greatest crime was dying anonymously—were spending eternity in an overgrown dump. Unbelievable. Josh gazed down the rows that stretched all the way to the other shore of the island. He was seized by the urge to dig up every coffin, unravel every story, send every person home.

They had walked up and down rows for what seemed like hours, following the numbers.

Josh's eyes smarted from peering at the tiny numbers in the darkness. Samba skipped a few rows and gave a low whistle.

"Jackpot!"

In his haste to get to the spot, Josh almost tripped over his own feet. Wiping sweat from his eyes, he stared down at a marker that read JOHN DOE, #82-659709.

Everything in Josh's body told him this was it, the missing piece. One of Raylene's ex-boyfriends, or a hit man Wade had hired. He was going to find out who.

"Let's get you out of here," Josh muttered as he produced the shovel and sank it into the marshy earth.

He paused for a second. Josh was certainly not religious, but something tugged at him. It wasn't right, disturbing the dead like this. Josh looked up at the sky and hoped that if there was a God, he understood that they were doing this for a bigger purpose.

Samba noticed Josh's hesitation and awkwardly made the sign of the cross over the grave. Josh looked at him. Glasses askew, tie-dye shirt riding up over his belly, gray ringlets heavy with sweat, with Beau looking up at him adoringly, he looked like some absurd hippie preacher. Samba nodded, as though he had received permission from some higher authority.

And then Josh began to dig.

CHAPTER THIRTY

She was the lookout.

Aurora wasn't sure what that meant for her criminal liability, but she was too involved to worry about that now. She stood on the edge of the boat slip, holding a flashlight in each hand, casting a ghostlike glow over the black silken water.

She could see the dinghy about two hundred yards out, dipping and twisting its way towards her. Part of her had wanted to be there for the actual exhumation, the curiosity overwhelming her. Whose body was it in the ground?

And how was he connected to her father? She remembered fishing with her dad, sitting next to him at the camp, giggling at the tiny worms squirming on the line. He'd always carried a little bag of herbs tied together with a ribbon. His lucky charm. She remembered his fishing hat. She had gotten a sticker at a birthday party—could it have been at Baboon Jack's? Her dad had put the sticker on his hat even though it looked goofy. It was a tiny gesture, but all these years later, she still remembered.

It's done. Josh's text lit up her phone. They had dug him up. All this time, could it be that Mother's killer had been tucked underground in a nameless grave? She should have felt relief, but she was still gripped by dread. This man was dead, but her father was still alive.

The boat was getting closer; she could hear the cough of the engine. Josh had said this was the only way, and she believed him. The court order for an exhumation would take months, and they needed answers now.

She only hoped they could convince Dr. Mason.

"Hey, Aurora!" Samba waved to her, his round eyeglasses two glinting orbs in the darkness, some kind of flashlight affixed to his head. Beau splashed out of the boat and galloped towards her, almost knocking her down with his enthusiastic greeting.

"How'd it go?" She caught the rope Josh tossed her and helped pull them ashore, trying not to notice the chipped wooden box resting in the bottom of the boat.

Josh exited the boat in one leap, as surefooted as a sea captain. His white T-shirt was drenched and covered in dirt, and his sneakers made a squelching noise when he landed. Her fellow criminal. Ruby was right; he was a good man.

"We found him," he said. He fished the keys to the Jeep out of his pocket and put them in her palm, holding her hand in his own for an extra moment. "It's hot as hell out here, Aurora. Why don't you and Beau wait in the car, and we'll get loaded up."

Aurora nodded and whistled for Beau, who trotted towards her. Together they approached the Jeep. Aurora opened the trunk and then clambered into the backseat, Beau beside her. She stroked his fur, comforted by the dog's warm hulk. She'd come back for the rental car later.

Aurora glanced in the rearview mirror and saw Josh and Samba trudging up the embankment, the box on their shoulders. She thought of the contents. What could possibly be left? Science had come a long way since the eighties, she reminded herself. The tiniest strand of hair could help them identify this person.

"All roads lead to the morgue," Samba said, as Josh turned the key in the ignition. He said it with his usual cheer, but the words were somehow sinister. Samba twirled one of the buttons on the radio, and a country singer's melancholy voice filled the car, singing about something being just beyond his reach.

"We'll get this figured out." There was confidence in his voice, a quiet strength that she needed to hear. When they pulled into the morgue lot, she was ready.

Aurora wasn't surprised to see the lights on, but once inside, she was shocked to see that Ruby was behind the reception desk, casually flipping through a magazine as though it was two in the afternoon instead of two in the morning.

Ruby bounced out of the chair when the three of them entered the room, her eyes expectant. "Well? How did it go? Can't believe I missed all the fun."

"We did it," Samba said, holding up his hands in victory.

"Wow," she said, "I wasn't sure you had it in you, but you proved me wrong. And now I'm guessing you want to see Doc. Head on back. But he's in some mood tonight, let me tell you. Don't say I didn't warn you." She pressed a buzzer under her desk, and the door to the back swung open for them to go inside.

Doc Mason was bent over the crumpled body of a man, his face twisted into a scowl. He brightened when he saw Aurora.

"Hey, look who it is," he said. "I'm glad you're here. We got the full report on the John Doe. The next step is requesting an exhumation. It won't be easy, but since Aurora is a family member of the victim and we have the DNA link . . ." Mason stopped midsentence and looked at each of them. "All right, what's going on here? Is there something I need to know about?" He was like the questioning parent confronting his three disobedient children.

Samba broke first. "We did it already," he blurted out.

Mason looked puzzled. "You did what already?"

"We went through, um . . . unofficial channels," Josh explained. "We were able to . . . umm . . . to recover the remains ourselves. Actually, we have them with us if you'd like to take a look."

Mason looked at Aurora, then Samba, then Josh, his mouth set in a scowl. "Are you telling me what I think you're telling me? You three went to Weir Island, dug up an unidentified body, put it in your car, and drove it over here for me to take a look?"

Aurora and Josh were shamed into silence, but of course Samba was unfazed. "Sometimes you have to go outside the law," he confided to Dr. Mason.

To Aurora's surprise, Doc Mason's mouth widened into a broad smile, and he erupted into a fit of laughter. "Bless your hearts." There was something else in his expression, something that looked to Aurora very much like admiration. "Well, I guess you'd better bring our friend in the back entrance, so I can take a look."

"I'll pull the car around," Josh said quickly, as if trying to escape before Mason changed his mind. He hightailed it out of the room, leaving Samba and Aurora frozen in surprise.

Mason put an arm around Aurora. "Looks like we're on our way to getting some answers for you," he said. She nodded and followed him to the rear entry, where Josh had backed the car all the way up to the door so they could unload their cargo.

Aurora watched as Dr. Mason, surprisingly strong, wielded what looked like a tire iron. With one pull, he pried off the coffin's lid. Aurora braced herself for the sight, but when she looked down, there was nothing but a black abyss. Mason reached into the coffin and pulled out a sweatshirt wrapped in a black trash bag.

"Well," he said, rising to his feet and looking squarely at Josh. "Looks like somebody beat you to it."

CHAPTER THIRTY-ONE

They stood in silence, a familiar chill in Josh's side. They had been right; someone else was out there, someone who didn't want them to find this body.

But who?

Samba broke the spell by removing the sweatshirt and rags with gloved hands and placing them in evidence bags. Doc had gone back into the autopsy suite, leaving them standing there around the empty coffin.

"You never know, there could still be something here," Samba said, his voice full of false enthusiasm. "Evidence has a funny way of sticking around, even when you try to hide it. There can be trace on the coffin, even something in the smallest little crack in the wood." He put an arm around Aurora, whose eyes glazed over. Josh had no idea what to say to her. Where did they go from here?

In his pocket, Josh's cell phone began to buzz. Boone.

"Sorry, I've got to take this." Outside the filmy moon was barely visible behind the shredded clouds, the bayou's surface a dark mirror.

"Hey, Boone."

"Josh, where are you? I can come pick you up. We gotta talk."

Josh leaned against the building. Had someone seen them paddling out to Weir Island? He would take the fall for all of them.

"What's this about, Boone?"

"I'll tell you when I see you."

Liana. It was always the first place his mind went. If she was hurt, if she was dead, he would know. That was what he told himself; there would be some blip in his consciousness, some flash of terrible knowledge at what happened. After all this time, there was still a connection between them.

"I'm at the morgue."

"Okay." There was a question in Boone's voice. "I'll be there in five minutes."

Josh ducked back inside, where the rest of them looked at him expectantly, still gathered around the empty coffin. For some reason, this angered Josh. Why had they trusted him to be able to solve this case, when he couldn't even solve his own?

"I need to take care of something," he mumbled. "Family." Without giving them a chance to respond, he stepped back outside.

"Josh."

Aurora was behind him, backlit in the doorway, her hair loose around her shoulders.

"I can come with you," she offered.

Some crazy part of Josh wanted to accept. She was holding open the door, giving him a way out of his grief.

But he didn't deserve it. He couldn't do it. Not yet.

He turned to face the car so she would not see his face; he was not sure if it would betray him.

"I'll be fine," he said. "I'll catch up with you later."

•   •   •

In the half-light of the police cruiser's interior, Boone's face was pulled into a grimace.

"What's going on Boone? Just say it." Josh slid into the passenger seat.

"It's about your father."

"I thought this was about my sister!" Josh slammed a hand on the dashboard. "Whatever Doyle's doing, it can wait. I've got better things to do."

"Hey!" Boone slammed on the brakes and the car bumped on to the shoulder. "I have done nothing but cover for your ass since you've been away, Hudson. So now you're going to listen to me."

He had never heard Boone raise his voice, not even once. Josh sank back into the seat and listened.

"Your father was picked up on some drug charges, made bond this morning. Ten grand. I asked myself, who on God's green earth would bail out Doyle Hudson when he's burned every bridge in this town? So I went down there for you, and I checked it out."

Josh felt his insides turn to liquid, then stone. The money he'd wired to Pea.

"And do you know who posted bond? That would be Pernaria Vincent. How do you think a drug dealer who turned on her crew finds that kind of money, huh, Josh?"

Pea and his father were closer than he had thought. She'd been working with Doyle this whole time, dangling Liana in front of him, and he'd taken the bait. The pieces began to slide together in Josh's mind, the realization of what he had done washing over him.

"Shit."

"Yep, that was my reaction too, buddy."

"Boone, I—"

Boone held up a hand. "There's no time," he said. "I understand why you did what you did, Josh. Something happened to my kin, Lord have mercy, I'd do whatever it took. But you gotta stop this now, Josh. You know I'll do whatever I can to help you find your sister. These people—people like Pernaria Vincent—they're not the way."

"I know," Josh said. It was a lesson he kept on learning, over and over. The curse of Doyle Hudson. His birthright. "I'm sorry about all this, Boone. I really am. I owe you, buddy. I know that."

"Don't worry, I'll collect on it someday." The edge of Boone's mouth curled in a reluctant half smile. "Also, I tried to drive up to the Crumpler place, see what's going on. You been up there lately? They got that shit locked up tighter'n Fort Knox. I got eyes out for that Crumpler kid, though. You let me know if he comes near Aurora again."

"I appreciate it, Boone. I'll probably head on up there myself at some point."

"You got a death wish or something, Josh? Because even your Tennessee charm ain't gonna work on those people."

Josh grinned. "Worth a try, though."

Boone shook his head. "Laura Jane's not expecting me for an hour or so. You want to grab a bite to eat?"

It was the second generous offer of the evening, and for the second time, Josh refused. "Another time," Josh said.

Everywhere he turned, there were more questions than answers. The trace on the sweatshirt from the grave would take forever to process. He knew Mason put his faith in science, but there were answers in other places, in details long forgotten, in overstuffed cardboard boxes.

"Hey," he said to Boone, "do you mind dropping me off at the evidence room? I can catch a ride home after that."

Boone raised an eyebrow. "Overtime? You trying to get back on Rush's good side? Don't get me wrong, you got a long way to go. But I think he'd respond better to Bucs tickets and a bottle of Maker's Mark."

Josh laughed. "Just something I'm working on."

"So that's how it's gonna be, huh? Josh Hudson, covert operations. All right. Well, you tell me if you need help." Boone tipped his hat, and Josh got out at the curb.

He felt an unexpected swell of emotion at the sight of the evidence room in the dark. He and Samba had done a good job the previous week cutting back the hedge so that the place looked less haunted. He'd start with the interviews from the night of the Atchison homicide and work his way back through missing persons, trying to find a match for the guy in the potter's field. Maybe have some possibilities for Samba in the morning.

Something shifted in the bushes behind him, and Josh reached for his gun. He took a step and someone hit him from behind, a cheap shot cuffing him and sending him to the ground. A man's face loomed above him in the darkness, something familiar about the sneer, the way the eyes pulled down at the corners.

"What the hell do you want?" Josh heard himself say the words, heard the man's low laugh in reply.

"The train that's comin' for you, boy? You got no idea," the man said, and hit him again before the words dissolved into something he could not understand, and then everything collapsed into blackness.

CHAPTER THIRTY-TWO

The air above the bayou crackled, ready to burst with the secret of the approaching storm. Inside the house on Cooper's Bayou, Aurora sat with the locked safety deposit box on her lap.

Royce Beaumont had given her a box full of indexed binders, with a list of all of her grandfather's assets, but the safety deposit box had not been mentioned, although she had seen it catalogued in her grandfather's diaries. Papa must have forgotten to include it in the list he'd given Luna Riley. She'd headed to the bank, and after a pleasant exchange with the teller, returned home with the box.

It didn't seem right to open it without Josh.

She had not heard from him since the previous evening when he'd left them at the morgue. She wondered if it was something to do with his family. Father in jail, sister missing—had one of them turned up somewhere? She'd felt like an idiot, asking to go with him, knowing he would turn her down. But he had hesitated; she'd seen it. All the time since, she'd occupied herself around the house, the thought of him tugging at the back of her consciousness. She'd stopped by the evidence room after the bank, but Samba had no news either. Tomorrow morning, she would call him and make sure everything was all right, and then she would open the box.

Aurora decided against switching on the grand ceiling fan in her bedroom. While it was beautiful to look at, the air it generated was hot anyway, and the noise it produced was akin to a jetliner preparing for takeoff.

She sprawled on top of the sheets, pressing her eyes closed. She would try to sleep for ten minutes, and then if she was still awake, she would do something constructive. Make a list of goals. Floss. Do yoga poses.

Thump.

The first noise could have been an animal. God only knew what critters were out there, with the house practically spilling into the bayou.

Thump.

Aurora fumbled for the tiny silver can of pepper spray that she had brought with her from New York. She'd carried it for years but never used it. It looked almost comically small in her hand. Everyone down South had a firearm. How much time would it really buy her?

Thump.

The Crumplers? Her father?

She was going to have to face this one on her own.

Aurora approached the door slowly, her sweating bare feet sticking to the wood floors. She pressed her eye to the peephole and then slid the deadbolt and threw open the door.

"I'm sorry," Josh said.

He was almost unrecognizable, peering out from under a stained gray hoodie. His left eye was almost completely swollen shut, the rest of his face cut and bruised. She pulled him into the room.

"Sit on the couch," she said, her heart still pounding from the fear of opening the door. "First things first. Let's take care of your face." She pulled a first-aid kit from under the couch. "I always have one of these around. Habit, I guess. Now hold still."

"Okay." He lifted his face to hers, obediently, like a child, and she dabbed at the cuts.

"I'm sorry," he repeated.

"You got nothing to be sorry for," she said.

"I wish you'd come with me. But it's probably better that you didn't."

She focused on the cut above his right eye, trying not to let her face betray how stunned she was at this sentence, at the genuine way the words sounded.

"What happened? Who did this? We need to call the police."

He closed his eyes as she held the gauze pad against the cut. "No police."

"Josh."

"I can't tell them," he said. "Boone—my partner—I can't drag him into this." He was protecting someone again, she could see that. Someone important.

"Is this about Liana?"

He looked up at her in surprise, as though he had forgotten he'd told her the name. "That's what I thought at first," he said. "I paid a drug dealer to find her, and the dealer took off with the money. She conned me, and I played right into her hands."

"You did what you had to do," she said, surprising herself with this assessment. Dealing with criminals wouldn't have been her choice, but Josh was the type of person to do anything for his sister, whatever the cost. She could see that now. He would do anything to find someone who was missing.

"So it wasn't a drug dealer who did this?"

He shook his head. "There was something familiar about the guy, though."

"Where did it happen?"

"The evidence room," he said.

"Why did you go back there?"

"I wanted to work on the case. Your case."

"Why are you doing this, Josh?" The words came out more accusatory than she'd intended, but she had to know.

He turned back to face her, something raw in his expression. "What do you mean?"

"Why are you helping me?" It was the question that had been haunting her since the first day in the evidence room. Everybody wanted something, everybody had an angle, but what could he possibly be gaining from helping her?

"I'm helping you because you can still be helped," Josh said simply. Aurora added the postscript in her head, *and I can't.* She remembered waking up that first morning in Connecticut at Papa's house, the unfamiliar bedroom, the low murmur of their voices downstairs. *There's nothing we can do except go on*, Papa had said, and so Aurora had done just that. And Josh was doing the same thing.

"Thank you," she said. "For—you know, for all of this."

"No need for thanks," he said, but she saw the beginnings of a smile before he turned back to the window. "What's this?"

"Safety deposit box," Aurora said, grateful for something else to talk about. She retrieved it from across the room. "The funny thing is, my grandfather didn't list it on the information he gave the lawyers, but I found the key here at the house."

"What's inside?"

"I was waiting for you." She removed the gold key from the top drawer in the desk.

"Well, here I am." The smile was back.

Aurora fitted the key into the lock and slid the cover off the box to reveal the contents: two black videotapes sheathed in plastic.

They stood in silence for a moment.

"Any ideas?"

Aurora shook her head.

"Seems like a weird place to store home movies." Josh frowned. "Well, let's fire up the VCR."

"There's no television in the house," Aurora said. "And why would Papa have videotapes?"

"No idea." Josh ran a finger down the list on the desk, the ledger of Papa's assets, recorded in his perfect handwriting. "Your grandpa was a perfectionist. Recorded everything. So it's strange that he would leave this off the sheet, yet give you the key."

"Like he wanted me to find it."

"Exactly. We can head to the evidence room. There are tons of VCRs there."

"Wait a second, Josh." Aurora peeled the backing from a Band-Aid and smoothed it across the cut. "Do you think what happened to you tonight has something to do with me? With my case?"

"I don't know." His eyes fell on the open sheaf of papers from Papa's filing cabinet. "Did you go through all this? Anything there?"

"Just a bunch of articles about alligator laws, that kind of stuff."

Josh pulled out one of the newspaper clippings, an article

about the lifting of the ban on alligator hunting in 1989. Splayed across it was a picture of a man in overalls holding a gator by the nose. *Local fisherman Niney Crumpler admires his kill*, the caption read.

"That crooked nose," Josh mumbled. "His nose."

"What do you mean?"

"The man who hit me. He had to be related to Niney. Had to be a Crumpler. One of the younger ones." He grabbed both her arms. "This is good, Aurora. This is really good. Do you know what this means?"

"We should go to the police?"

"No," he said. "It means we're on the right track."

CHAPTER THIRTY-THREE

"Wish I had a dollar for every unmarked videotape I have in here," Samba mused, tugging an ancient VCR-TV combo on a dusty cart into the center of the evidence room. "Family vacations, dance recitals, sex tapes. You name it, I've catalogued it."

Somewhere in this warehouse, the surveillance tape from the day of Jesse's murder was tucked away in a box. Josh had seen it once, watched images of the three of them at the men's bathroom entrance. Josh and Jesse, hand in hand, walking in silent slow motion through the door while Liana stood just out of frame and watched them go, unaware of what was behind the door waiting for them.

"You ready for this?" Samba hesitated, one hand on the VCR. Josh snapped back to the present, but the question was directed at Aurora. She was the case that mattered right now.

"Roll it," Aurora said in a firm voice that trailed off at the end. She had to be nervous. Josh sat next to her on the couch.

Samba pressed play and the screen turned a pearlescent blue, then dissolved into zigzag lines that formed a familiar image.

The Cooper's Bayou Police Department. A time stamp flickered at the bottom of the screen: July 17, 1989. It was amazing how little it had changed. There was the interrogation room that doubled as a break room, an earlier incarnation of a cheap refrigerator nestled in the corner, a warped metal table pushed into the center of the room. A man with a seventies-style mustache and sideburns edged into the frame, adjusted something on the camera. Josh recognized him. Detective Floyd Rossi. He'd played third base on their softball team. Nice guy. He'd retired last year; Boone had thrown the farewell barbecue at his house. Rossi moved out of state, lived near his grandkids by some lake in Alabama.

The image shimmered and then another figure came into focus, sitting at the metal table, and Josh realized what it was they were watching.

A little girl.

Aurora.

"We don't have to do this now," Josh said, turning to face her. She sat straight upright, her expression betraying nothing.

She held a hand up to Josh. "No," she said in a low voice. "I want to see it. We need to see it."

The girl on the screen was bent low to the table, coloring a picture in furious strokes with a crayon. Rossi appeared uncomfortable, as though he didn't know how to approach her. Josh couldn't blame him. Kids were the worst to interview, not because they couldn't sit still, but because they always told the truth, no matter how much it broke your heart.

"Hi, Aurora," Rossi began. "Can I talk to you about what happened last night?"

The little girl gave no sign that she'd heard the question, but continued to draw the crayon across the page in careful lines.

"Aurora? Sweetheart? Can you draw what you remember, sweetheart?"

Aurora lifted her head and pushed the crayons aside. "I was on the boat with Mama and Daddy."

Next to him, Aurora gasped at the sound of her own voice. Josh put a hand on her shoulder. "We can stop anytime you want."

"No," she said.

"Great," Rossi was saying. "And what happened when you were on the boat with Mama and Daddy?"

"Daddy showed me the fishes."

"That's great, Aurora."

"I can catch them too. He teached me how."

"And then what happened after that?"

"Somebody hurt Mama." The little voice trembled and then broke. "Somebody hurt Mama and then the lady took me to the steps."

"Did you see who it was who hurt Mama?"

She nodded. "A monster."

"What did the monster look like, sweetheart?"

Aurora did not answer.

"Sugar, I need you to think real hard for me. Can you remember what the monster looked like?"

"I want to go home," the little girl murmured, pushing the crayons away.

"Just a little longer, sweetheart. Was the monster old or young? Tall or short? Black or white?"

"I want to go home," the little girl repeated, her lower lip quivering. "I want Mama and Daddy." She bit her lip. "I want Mama and Daddy now." Her voice trembled, and she put her head in her hands and began to wail.

There was a loud noise offscreen, and a man in a canvas

jacket burst into the frame, scooping up Aurora in his arms, Josh recognized him from all the pictures in the house on Spotted Beebalm Drive. It was a younger Hunter Broussard. He murmured something in the child's ear and glared at Rossi.

"You're done here," he said.

"Hunter, please—she saw something. She can help us find out who's responsible. Our investigation—"

"She's a kid, Floyd," Hunter said. "Not now, for God's sake. Now, go out there and find out who did this." He turned away, so that Aurora's face was visible tucked against his neck, and then he left the room.

For a long moment, Rossi stood in the empty room. The face he turned to the camera was full of shame and concern.

He reached out and the screen went blank.

Samba gave a low whistle. "Jesus."

"Aurora? Are you okay?" Josh moved his hand to her back. She was still staring straight ahead at the empty screen.

"They tried, you know," she murmured. "After that. A doctor, a policewoman. They all tried. And I just kept repeating the same story about a monster. I don't know why that's all I said. I don't know why I couldn't help."

The relentless questions, the thinly disguised irritation of the investigators, the syrupy tone of the in-house psychologists, all of them circling her. He knew what they sounded like. They had circled him too.

"You were a kid," Josh told her. "It wasn't your job to remember." She leaned into him and he put his arms around her.

He looked across at Samba and saw his own thoughts reflected in Samba's expression.

A monster, Aurora had said.

Not Daddy.

She had seen the killer.

In the circle of his arms, Aurora lifted her head. "Why do you think Papa wanted me to see that? Because I didn't mention my dad?"

"You didn't mention your dad," Josh said. "But you talked about a lady. Who do you think that could be?"

Samba reached for the remains of the file. "Pearline Suggs was the cashier who found Aurora at the mini-mart. Says here she'd arrived early for her shift. She was a kid, a teenager."

"But Aurora said the lady *took* me to the steps, not *found* me. What does it say in her statement, Samba?"

Samba adjusted his glasses. "*I got there early because I was opening that day, and Miss Margie Belle likes everything all neat and tidy. The little girl was curled up on the steps asleep. I made sure she was all right, then I ran inside and called the cops and brought her inside with me until y'all got there. She didn't say nothing.*"

Had Pearline seen more than she was telling? She was just a terrified teenager back then. "So the way she tells it, she didn't move Aurora, she just came upon her. It doesn't make sense."

"You think Pearline is lying? But why?"

Aurora sat up. "Maybe she saw the killer, and she was scared. Maybe she was too scared to do something."

Josh thought about the bathroom at Fun World, the way the Shadow Man had approached them, pulling the heavy restroom door shut behind him, pushing Josh into a stall. *Lock the door. Be a good boy.* Josh had slid the latch across, stood there terrified while he listened to the Shadow Man destroy his brother, his only view of the monster the enormous oversized shadow reflected on the peeling yellow restroom wall.

"It's possible," he said. "Hang on a second." He paged through the file and pulled out a thick sheaf of paper held together with a heavy gold staple. "Phone records from Margie Belle's store."

He drew a finger down the page. "What time was it when the call came in to the police station?"

Aurora leaned across Samba to see the report. "3:45 A.M."

"And Pearline said she got there early to open the mini-mart, correct? And she found Aurora there, on the steps as she was about to open up?"

"Yup, that was her statement," Samba confirmed.

Josh found the call. 3:45 A.M., an outgoing call to the police station. But there was a call above it.

"Someone used the phone at the mini-mart earlier that morning," he said. "At 2:59. It's a local call."

"Maybe someone else was at the mini-mart?" Samba asked.

"Or Pearline lied," Aurora said.

"Either way," Josh said, "whoever made that call saw what happened."

CHAPTER THIRTY-FOUR

He was too close to this one.

James opened the letter from the Medical Examiners Association, a warning letter that he was overstepping his bounds. *It is imperative that all procedures are followed properly.* They knew he'd been asking questions about a closed case, and they weren't happy about it. A month ago, he would have dissolved into a full panic, the thought of his career on the line obliterating any other concern. He had always put faith in the rules, until he saw how spectacularly they had failed Raylene Atchison. It was his responsibility now to do whatever it took to fix it, whether it was approved by the Medical Examiners Association or not.

James tossed the letter aside and picked up the phone.

Malachi answered on the first ring.

"I'm sending you another sample," James told him, sealing the evidence bag with the sweatshirt from the grave tucked inside, along with samples of the coffin. "I need an ID on an unidentified vic." He was going to find out who it was.

On the other end of the line, Malachi exhaled. "You sure about this, Doc? Somebody gets wind of this, and—"

"You get any crap about it, you tell them it was my call."

"I'm not worried about that."

"Good."

"It's just—I just want to know, what is it about this case, Doc? What's so important? It's the first time—the only time—you've called in a favor like this. What is it about the Atchison case?"

James turned from the phone to the doorway where Raylene Atchison had stood all those years ago, brimming with light. To his right was the office where he had kept Aurora safe after her mother's murder. How could it be that so many years had passed since then? It seemed impossible.

"It's somebody I knew a long time ago," James said. "Just make sure you take your time with it, Malachi. The first time around, the file was a mess because Gentry was careless. I don't want any more mistakes."

"Sure thing, Doc."

"And, Malachi?"

"Yes?"

"Have you heard anything about those unidentified remains from a few weeks ago?"

"You mean Bayou John Doe?"

"Yes."

"Nothing yet."

"Thanks."

He wondered what news Josh was hoping for. Having his brother's remains would mean an end to the search, but it was an ending that seemed hollow. James remembered the sight of his father in his coffin, the way the pain and disbelief collided in his chest before splintering into a thousand pieces. How did that compare to the pain of surviving what Josh had?

There was a serious undertone in Ruby's voice on the intercom, something rare for her.

"Josh Hudson here to see you."

James stepped out of the autopsy suite. He wished he had news for Josh. "Send him on back, Ruby."

Josh Hudson had never been what James would call clean-cut, but he looked even more disheveled than usual. He wore the same torn gray hooded sweatshirt from the other night, and appeared to have been on the losing end of a fight, a cut swelling beneath a bandage above his left eye.

James tried to hide the alarm in his voice. "How are you, Josh?"

"Been better."

"I'm afraid I don't have any news for you about Jesse. They work at a glacial pace over at the state lab. The minute I know something, I—"

"I'm not here about Jesse," Josh said. "I'm here about Aurora's case."

"Oh, of course!" James opened the door to his office. "Here, let's sit in here."

"Thanks, Doc."

"So, what did you find out?"

Josh ignored the question. "Do you remember that morning? The morning Aurora was brought here?"

The events were scorched into his memory, the mundane and the profound.

"Absolutely. It had been a busy week. I was under a lot of stress. "

"Were you in the office that whole shift?"

"No. There was a bad wreck on the causeway that night. Teenagers out joyriding flipped their pickup. Four fatalities. It took them almost two hours to cut them out. I was on scene that night up until three."

There was something like relief on Josh's face.

"Why are you asking me this, Detective Hudson?" James said, puzzled.

"I'm sorry," Josh said. "It's just—take a look at this, Doc." He unfolded a piece of paper, a printout of a phone bill. "This is from the mini-mart, from when Aurora was found." He pointed to a line just above one highlighted in neon marker.

James recognized the morgue's phone number.

"I don't understand," he said.

"Doc, someone called here at three that morning. Before the police were called." He slid his finger across the page. "Four times, ten seconds each. Calling and hanging up."

"That doesn't make sense. I wasn't here. There was nobody here." There were no techs here that night. Just James.

"Well, was there anybody who had a key?"

James remembered his assistant from the pre-Ruby days, a fortyish woman named Dorothy who wore gray jumpsuits and subsisted exclusively on Tab and Wheat Thins. Dorothy, whose aggressive brand of cheerfulness irritated him to no end, Dorothy who lifted pink weights on her lunch break and had a Sandy Duncan haircut—could such a person really be involved in a murder? It seemed impossible.

"Maybe a past employee or something," Josh prompted.

And then James thought of it. Of course. It made perfect sense now. The careless autopsy report, the way he'd been shut out of the case. Malachi's voice on the phone. *Somebody gets wind of this, and . . .*

"Davis Gentry," he said.

CHAPTER THIRTY-FIVE

Aurora returned from Royce Beaumont's closed office to find a woman waiting on her front porch, fussing with the bark of the flowering pink tree in the front yard. People in Cooper's Bayou didn't seem shy about showing up at the alligator man's house unbidden. Aurora was getting used to it.

"Hello?"

"Aurora," the woman breathed. She was in her forties, blond bangs framing a sweet face. "I'm Bobbie Sharpless. I was a friend of your mom's." She sucked in a breath and reached a long-fingered hand to cup Aurora's face. "Oh, honey. I thought about you so many times. God never blessed me with a daughter. I called your grandpapa and nana, and they thought it was best for you not to have any contact with this place. But I wanted you to visit, Aurora, to stay with me."

Aurora curled her hand around Bobbie's. "I appreciate that," she said, and she did.

"She loved these trees," Bobbie continued, releasing her grip on Aurora to wipe a tear making its way down her tanned cheek. "Crape myrtles. I always loved them too. You know, they come all the way from China? But when they brought them to England, they didn't grow. It wasn't until the British brought them to the South that they bloomed for the first time, like they'd finally found their place." She plucked one of the audacious pink spikes.

"I never knew that. Bobbie, can you come in for a sec?" Aurora led her up the steps and into the house.

Bobbie paused in the doorway. "Your grandpapa, he kept this place up real nice. Beautiful." Bobbie set the bag that was tucked under her arm on the table. "Fresh donuts."

"Thank you." Aurora poured them both glasses of lemonade from the batch cooling in the fridge, and they sat on the porch with the sweating glasses, watching the bayou through the delicate lace of the trees.

"How did you know I was here?"

Bobbie laughed. "It's a small town. It's funny, Raylene and I used to talk about how we were going to get out of here as soon as we turned eighteen. We were so sure of ourselves back then, and look at us now. We'll both be here for all eternity, I expect."

"You were her best friend."

"She was the sister I never had," Bobbie said, something fierce in her voice. "You know, when you were little, you called me Auntie. There was something about your mother, honey. When I was with her, it was like—anything was possible. She could make you believe that you could do anything." There was such unfettered pain in her voice that Aurora reached across the table between them and touched her arm. "I'm just so sorry, Aurora. For your loss. I'm so, so sorry."

Aurora felt the familiar tightness in her throat, the grief fast becoming eclipsed by a new emotion: anger. It should be her mother sitting with her on this porch, watching the last slice of sunlight slip beneath the bayou's surface. Aurora had spent her entire life longing for a person she could barely remember, a person who had affected so many people in Cooper's Bayou. Doc, Jefferson Gibbs, Royce Beaumont, and now here was another person before her, weeping at the memory of someone who had been dead for twenty years, while Aurora, her flesh and blood, clung to a few scraps of memories that were becoming more shapeless with each passing day. It wasn't fair.

Aurora's eyes drifted to the embankment, heavy with pink blossoms. How long had her mother been there alone on that shore before someone found her?

"I'm going to find out what happened to her, Bobbie. I finished up all of Papa's affairs, but I'm not going to leave. Not until I find out who took her away from us." She was surprised at the timbre of her own voice, the nurse's voice, the one that told people who was in charge.

"I know you are, sugar," Bobbie drawled, patting her cheeks with a wadded-up tissue. "Josh won't give up on y'all, neither. I know he won't."

Josh. Aurora remembered the expression on his face when they'd watched the video of her interview, his warm hand on her back. *We don't have to do this now.* As much as he wanted answers, he wanted to protect her at the same time.

"Josh is a good man," Bobbie continued. "Easy on the eyes, too. You got a boyfriend up in New York?"

"No." She thought about the date with Mike, the softball game, the meeting with Luna Riley. All of it seemed like another lifetime ago. "Josh is sweet."

"He's been through enough, Lord knows. He'd have the right to be an asshole." Bobbie shook her head.

"What do you mean?"

"You don't know about the Fun World thing?"

Fun World. Aurora remembered the sign on the way into town, a peeling monstrosity with a clown's head dangling from the top edge, lips pulled back in a leering grin.

"I saw the sign on the interstate. Some kind of amusement park?"

"It was. We all went there when we were kids. Rides, games, that kind of thing. There was always a bad element there though, older guys hanging around. When I heard what happened to Josh, I can't say I was surprised. Horrified, sure. But not surprised."

"Is that where his brother was abducted?"

"Yep. He saw the whole thing."

She remembered Josh that night on the bayou, his head tilted up to the sky, the way he'd turned suddenly to look at her. *I was there.* So Josh had his own dark place as well. A dark place he remembered.

"Did they ever find the brother?"

"The guy never told the cops where he put the body."

All the pieces were sliding into place. Josh's absences from the evidence room, the long silences between them.

"The bones, the ones they found by Baboon Jack's," Aurora said quietly.

Bobbie nodded. "They think those bones might be Jesse. They ain't sure, though."

"He never told me."

"Oh, sugar." Bobbie scooted her chair closer to Aurora's. "You know how men are. They never want to show you the weak parts. I know he cares about you, I could tell the way he talked when he came to see me. They're not complicated creatures."

"You're right, they're not." Aurora felt something loosening inside her, at ease in a way that she had not been in a long time.

"I know what I wanted to show you. Wait right here, sweetheart."

Bobbie disappeared into the house, leaving Aurora to watch the bayou. The water was thickening, the trees shuddering and retreating from its edges as though the water itself was gathering strength, the night building towards some grand crescendo.

Bobbie reappeared with a clay jar. Aurora recognized it from the top of the secretary desk in the living room. A delicate design, a sunburst of tiny iridescent lines was scored into the sides, a cherub that had shed much of its golden skin reclining on the stopper.

"What is it?"

Bobbie set it on the table between them. "Your grandpapa didn't like to talk about voodoo," she said, "but he went to see Charlsie, way back when."

"He thought the Crumplers had put a curse on him."

"Yes," Bobbie said. "Your grandpapa was a strong man. He didn't back down from nobody, not even the Crumplers. He told them to go to hell, and they put a curse on him, right before your mama died."

"Do you think they killed her?"

Bobbie shrugged. "They're behind most of the evil in this town. It wouldn't surprise me. Nobody in this town ever stood up to them, until your grandpapa did."

She twisted the vase around so that the cherub faced Aurora. "When we die," she said, "in *voudon,* we believe that it's just a change, from one condition to another. There's two parts to the soul, the *gros bon ange* and the *petit bon ange.*

When you die, the *gros bon ange* goes back up to the sky, to the cosmos."

"And the *petit bon ange*?"

"That's the part of the soul that makes you who you are: your personality, your hopes and dreams. After death, it hangs around the body for a few days, and you can capture it in a jar, like this one. Your mama's *ti bon ange*, it's in here, sweetheart. Your grandpapa and I captured it."

"Then what happens?"

"You're supposed to burn the jar, to release the soul into the land of the dead."

Aurora touched the top of the jar. "But you didn't."

"We couldn't, sweetheart. We just couldn't do it."

Aurora held the jar in her hands, the clay firm between her fingers. Her own mother, trapped in death in this vessel. Why would her grandfather leave this behind? Why was Bobbie telling her this? The questions rose and then died in her throat, the answer imprinted on Bobbie's tearful face.

She would be the one to solve her mother's murder, and she would be the one to let her go.

CHAPTER THIRTY-SIX

"Do you think he'll show?"

Samba and Josh sat in the Corvair in front of the Craw Lake detention facility, a concrete structure painted a soulless shade of brown that overlooked a marsh choked with kudzu so thick you could barely tell there was water somewhere underneath.

"If there's something in it for him, Doyle will show," Josh said, opening the door. "I told you, though, I think this is a waste of our time."

"How'd he end up back in jail so fast?"

Josh chuckled. "Doyle was always reliable that way. He didn't waste any time getting picked up again."

Josh's vote had been to go to Davis Gentry's office in Tampa straightaway, but Doc Mason had talked him out of it. They needed more information first, something solid to connect all the pieces. The Crumplers were the ones harassing Aurora at the house; they could have been involved in the murder too.

Back in the evidence room, this had seemed like a good idea. You wanted intel on local crime, Doyle Hudson was a good source. But now Josh wondered if it all had been some terrible mistake.

"When's the last time you saw your father?"

There had not been a trial. On the advice of his attorney, who was probably a bigger huckster than he was, Doyle had pled guilty to all of the charges against him. Assault with a deadly weapon; extortion; fraud. Liana had been long gone by then, and his mother was in treatment for the cancer that would eventually take her life, so only Josh, aged fifteen, had been present in the courtroom for the sentencing. They had given Doyle an opportunity to speak, to apologize to the people he had conned, to say a few words to his own family.

He had said nothing.

"Fifteen years," Josh said. "I'm only here for Aurora." It was a one-in-a-million chance, but those were the ones you had to take, weren't they? No matter what the cost.

"Well, that sounds like a good reason to me. I hear there's a place with the world's greatest banana pudding about a mile down the road," Samba said. "Call me when you're ready to go."

Josh nodded. One of Samba's best qualities was his ability to know when to leave things alone.

Inside, a woman with curly red hair pulled into a bun slouched next to the metal detector and gave Josh the once-over.

"I'm here to see Doyle Hudson," Josh told her, depositing his keys in the tiny plastic bin.

She raised an eyebrow. "Huh. Well, Doyle's just Mr. Popular this week, ain't he? Inmate of the month or some shit."

"Is that right? Who else has been to see him?"

"Some pretty little blond girl with legs up to here. Poor thang. I see it all the time, girls with a man in prison. These men in here act real sweet, but as soon as they cut them loose, they're out there screwing everything that moves."

Pea. It had to be.

"Not all guys are like that," he told her.

"I ain't never met one inside who wasn't."

"Well, you're working in the wrong place."

She beamed at him and held open the door to the visiting room, where Doyle Hudson waited behind a pane of filthy glass. Josh sat in the cracked plastic chair, and the two Hudsons regarded each other. His father had lost weight in prison, his skin tight against the curve of his cheekbones, but there was something else. He no longer held his chin and shoulders in an arrogant tilt, but slouched back against the chair. His hand curled around the telephone receiver, and Josh mirrored the movement.

"Good morning, son."

Josh steeled himself against the tide of anger, but it never came, just the same suffocating inertia that he'd been mired in since the day his father went away.

"Hello, Doyle."

His father bristled at the use of his first name. "You're looking well."

"I need some information from you."

His father nodded, expecting this reaction. "I have some things I'd like to say to you first."

"I'm not here to help you make amends."

"Jesus has forgiven me."

"Well, he's a better man than me."

Doyle leaned forward. "You're a good man, Josh. I know my opinion ain't worth shit to you. I know that. But here you are."

"You're right, your opinion ain't worth shit to me. I'm not

here to talk about the shit you did to our family, or how you had your little girlfriend Pea swindle me. I'm here about the Atchison homicide."

"Now, hold on a minute." Doyle pointed a finger at Josh. "I didn't ask Pernaria to take your money. She swindled me too, son. She told me she could find Liana—"

"Don't you fucking dare say her name."

Doyle held up both hands, a spiderweb of tattoos wrapped around the white insides of his forearms.

"I'm not the man I was, Josh."

"I'm not here to talk about you."

Was it pain on his father's face? Josh wasn't sure. There was something pathetic in his father's expression.

Doyle gripped the phone receiver with both hands. "What about you, son? You been taking care of yourself?"

Josh held the receiver away from his ear. It had been a mistake, coming here. In front of him, Doyle frantically tapped the glass. The guard raised his head from his newspaper, ready to end the visit. Josh turned back to his father, who was mouthing the same word over and over.

Wait.

"This is your last chance, Doyle," Josh said into the phone. "I'm here for information about the Atchison homicide. Nothing else."

"All right, all right." Doyle slumped back in his chair. "I want to do the right thing here. Help you bring the right person to justice."

"If you know where Wade Atchison is, Doyle, you best speak up."

"Wade ain't the one who done this."

Josh had been right. His father knew something.

"We're looking at other possibilities. We may have a witness."

"Who's that?"

Josh hesitated. "Pearline Suggs," he said. "She was working at the mini-mart, found the little girl after the murder. We think she may know more than she's telling."

"Well, just remember you can't trust nobody."

"Yeah, I learned that lesson pretty early, thanks to you."

Something like hurt flickered on Doyle's face. "I'm talking about Pearline."

"You know her?"

"You remember Trace Crumpler?"

Trace had been the town football star, someone the scouts rode out to the boonies to see before he'd blown out his knee in the last game of his senior year. Summers, he was the lifeguard at the town pool where Josh's mom took them for swimming lessons. Nowadays, Trace picked up odd jobs around town and spent the balance of his days grandstanding at the bar at Baboon Jack's, regaling the clientele with old game stories, Trace the hero of each and every one.

"Sure, I remember him."

"You remember all that talk about Trace back when he was in college?"

Something clicked in Josh's memory. "He got some girl pregnant, didn't he? Some underage girl?"

"Not just any girl. Pearline Suggs."

"So what?"

"So the Crumplers have been taking care of her ever since. They got her that job at their mini-mart, then paid for her to go to get her paralegal certificate. She used to run around with Burdette too; he's carried a torch for her for years. They're all close."

Josh sat back and let this information sink in. The Crumplers weren't on the short list for heaven. They were thieves; one of the brothers had been busted for writing bad checks and stealing credit cards from Baboon Jack's; another did a spell at Craw Lake for running meth in Kervick County. When Josh was a kid, there was a boy who had stood up to Padgett Crumpler, and they'd beaten him near death and left him in the swamp. There was a whole criminal mythology surrounding the family; they were like some kind of twisted redneck Mafia. It wasn't a big step up to murder.

"So they killed Raylene?"

"I don't know that. I'm just saying, you check into the Suggs girl's story, because she's a mouthpiece for them. She seen something different, she ain't gonna say so."

"All right. I do appreciate it."

"Are y'all investigating it over in the PD?" His father didn't know, that was plain to see on his face.

"No. They put me on leave because of your friend Pernaria."

"That goddamn bitch." He said the words with such venom, Josh was beginning to believe that she had swindled him too.

"It was my choice. I'll figure it out." Josh leaned forward, studying his father's expression. "So you're a changed man?"

"People can change, Josh. The world ain't as dark as you think it is."

"I hope you're right."

"Be careful, son. The Crumplers—they're dangerous sons of bitches. I mean, I should know, right?" His father grinned.

"Take it easy, Doyle."

Josh hung up the phone. He walked out without meeting his father's gaze and closed the door behind him, but it was

too late, something was splintering inside him. He'd been clutching the dead man's switch of his grief for so long, and now
Doyle Hudson, of all people, had loosened his grip.

The redhead sat behind the entry desk, mesmerized by
something on her computer screen. On the closed-circuit television, Josh watched his father being led back to his cell.

"How does it work," he asked her, "putting money in an
inmate's account?"

She tore her eyes from the screen. "I can help you with
that," she said.

Josh peeled a twenty free of his wallet and handed it over.
"Doyle Hudson," he said. "For cigarettes, or whatever."

"You bet," she said, returning his smile.

Outside, Samba sat on the hood of the car in the sunshine,
facing the remains of the lake. Josh climbed up and took a seat
behind him.

"How was that banana pudding?"

"Well, it's just like anything else in life," Samba said. "A
little better and a little worse than I thought it was going to
be." He rubbed his belly. "But all in all, it was worth it."

Josh laughed. "You're a philosopher, Samba."

"Naw, I'm just a crazy old man. Now, what about your pop?
Anything useful in there?"

Josh pulled down his sunglasses. "Tells me he's a changed
man," he said. "You believe in that garbage?"

"You mean second chances?"

"More like a hundred."

Samba chuckled. "I do."

"My dad says that Pearline Suggs is in the Crumplers'
pocket," Josh said. "But this is coming from a career criminal.
I have no reason to trust him."

"What does your gut say?"

"That it's worth looking into."

"Then we're trusting your gut, not your pop," Samba said. He tossed Josh the keys to the Corvair. "And that's good enough for me."

CHAPTER THIRTY-SEVEN

James and Aurora sat together on a bench outside the evidence room and waited for Malachi to arrive.

Fifty feet below, the bayou stared back up at them, a blank oval, a featureless face, its surface broken only by an airboat churning towards the opposite shore.

"He didn't say anything on the phone," James explained, "but he wanted to meet in person." He tried not to let the concern seep into his voice. "I figured whatever he had to say about your father, you would want to be here." The truth was, he had no idea why Malachi wanted to come in person. It was all very cloak and dagger, the kind of thing that made James nervous.

"So he ran the samples for you on the sly?"

James reddened. "Yes." He cleared his throat. "When he was a student, I helped him out. He was returning a favor."

"I can't believe you took that risk for me."

James shrugged, but could not help the smile on his face. "Sometimes you have to bend the rules a little bit," he said.

"I'm not sure what we're looking for," Aurora said. "You

think Gentry was botching autopsies on purpose? That he was covering up for someone?"

"I wouldn't put it past him." James scoffed. "Hanlon's Razor. Never ascribe to malice that which is adequately explained by incompetence."

Aurora nodded. "I like that expression. It definitely fits a few of the people I work with too. So what was this Gentry guy like?"

James summoned up an image of Davis Gentry in his mind, his off-color jokes, his cowboy hat, his condescending smile. *A snake-oil salesman,* that was the term he was looking for. Slippery. Dishonest. And somehow nobody seemed to catch on, or if they did, they didn't mind. Gentry could waltz into any public event and command the room's full attention, a clutch of women in his wake. James had dreaded these events and observed them from the edges of the crowd like a visitor from another planet.

"He was one of those guys who always has an agenda," James explained. "He was only interested in things that would further his career."

"So he leaves his job here, and then what?"

"He left because he got appointed to the Fish and Wildlife Commission. The last I heard, he was running for City Council or something like that." Politics seemed a natural fit for someone like Gentry.

"Fish and Wildlife," Aurora repeated. "What do they do?"

"They issue hunting and fishing permits, that kind of thing."

"What about for alligators? Alligator hunting?" The expression on Aurora's face went beyond inquisitiveness; it was excitement. She was making some connection, he was sure of it.

"Sure. Alligator hunting is big business."

"Doc!" Malachi rounded the corner and grasped his hand, pulling him into an embrace. Like James, Malachi was enthralled by his work and gave thought to little else; his dreadlocks tucked into a baseball cap, frayed shirt, and voluminous backpack gave him the windblown appearance of an exuberant student.

"Great to see you, Malachi. I'd like you to meet a friend of mine, Aurora Atchison."

"Nice to meet you, Aurora."

"You too."

"So you went out to Weir Island and dug up a grave, huh? Badass."

Aurora laughed. "I can't confirm or deny that."

Malachi sat next to Doc and hoisted the black backpack onto his lap. "Well, I know Doc wants me to get right to the point, so here it is." He pulled a manila folder free from the bag.

"The biological material in the grave is a match to Wade A. Atchison," he said. "The sweatshirt, and also some samples from the coffin itself. Based on the information Doc gave me, the stats on the unidentified body . . ."

"It was Wade Atchison in that grave." James said what Malachi could not. Beside him, James heard Aurora suck in a breath.

"Yes," said Malachi. "I'm so sorry, Miss Atchison. I know that's probably not what you wanted to hear."

Aurora nodded. "You know, I'm not sure if it is or not," she said.

"Anyway, as Doc here can tell you, I've always been a little aggressive when it comes to typing and sampling. You know, never leave any stone unturned. I learned that one from him."

James felt an unexpected surge of pride. "I can't take credit for your work ethic, Malachi," he said.

Malachi did not answer but pulled three plastic bags from the backpack. "So we have three pieces of evidence here from the burial site, besides the coffin itself. The sweatshirt, a rag, and a small set of keys. The samples from the sweatshirt are a match to Wade Atchison, and your other contributor is female, right here on the cuff. Not Raylene Atchison, not a relative, but otherwise I don't know who she is. But look at the sweatshirt. Nothing remarkable about it. Standard issue, polyester blend, boring." He put that bag aside. "Second, we have this rag. There's some kind of film on it, this black goopy stuff. I had it tested, and it appears to be motor oil, the kind commonly used for boats. And last but not least, we have these two keys."

"I don't remember cataloguing those," James said.

"Me either," Aurora echoed. "Where did you find them?"

"That's where this gets interesting." Malachi held the sweatshirt up again. "They were tucked inside a rip inside the left cuff of the sweatshirt. Concealed."

"Concealed by whom? The dead man?" James inspected the keys, a tiny set, the kind used to open a lock on a garage or shed.

Malachi shrugged. "That's up to you guys. I just run the evidence. Well, I guess I should say I *used* to run the evidence."

James looked at him in surprise. "You're not working at the lab anymore?"

Malachi nodded. "That's why I asked to meet you in person. Someone found out that I was working this case unauthorized. I thought they'd just give me a slap on the wrist, but they canned me."

"Oh, Malachi. I'm so sorry. I asked you to break the rules, and—"

Malachi waved him away. "That's the thing, Doc," he said. "You wouldn't believe how often people break the rules. They run paternity tests, that kind of stuff. It was something about this case."

"What makes you say that?" Aurora asked.

"My supervisor followed me out of the building," Malachi said. "Told me to stay away from this one, and to be careful. It freaked me out, I'll tell you that."

The words startled him, a perplexing terror beginning to take hold. Behind him, the sun was beginning to set over Weir Island, dislodging a memory in James's brain. When James was a child, the other kids had dared each other to take their boats out there, to touch a corner of the crumbling dock, to peel off a sliver from the moldy skin of the decaying trees that reached across the graveyard. James's own mother had told him that because no masses were said for the repose of the souls in that place, they would always be wandering the earth. The lack of a body in Wade Atchison's grave made this a possibility even more alarming. Wade was dead; but there was someone else, someone who wanted to make sure that this case was never reopened. Someone who might be a killer, who knew that Aurora and James and Josh were asking questions.

And that person was very much alive.

CHAPTER THIRTY-EIGHT

Too much evidence.

"It's a good problem to have," Josh assured her. The three of them—Aurora, Josh, and Samba—sat in a semicircle at the peeling Formica table in the evidence room, their loot set in front of them. The phone records from the night of the murder. The sweatshirt. The keys. Malachi's lab results. They were like talismans waiting to be deciphered. The fear that had smothered her at the house had been replaced by a kind of quiet exhilaration. For the first time, she was awake to the possibility that they would solve the case. There had been two murders that night on the bayou. Her father wasn't out there trying to scare her away from learning the truth about that night.

But someone was.

Above them, a bird sputtered around the ceiling, emitting a shrill, terrified cry. What was it that they said about a bird indoors? A harbinger of death? There was already too much death in this room. She wondered about the box with the contents of Josh's case. *They think those bones might be Jesse,* Bobbie had told her. He was in limbo, just like she was, seeking the answer but shunning it at the same time.

Josh tapped the phone records. There was a brightness in his eyes, an easy confidence in his voice. He was right. They were on the right track.

"Pearline Suggs knows something," he said. "She knows more than she said that night, and she knows how Wade Atchison ended up in that grave. I hate to admit it, but I think my dad was right." He held up a file. "Ongoing investigation into the Crumplers' financial activities from Boone, my partner. This shows that they were paying Pearline. Every month, like clockwork, for her son, Curtis. I think this is why she hasn't been returning our calls."

"So Curtis isn't Dale Holder's kid?" Samba shook his head. "That was the guy Pearline shacked up with after high school, the one who died in Iraq. I wonder if he knew he wasn't the father? And that kid's wrecked his four-wheeler out on Route 41 five times. He's got to be in his twenties now. Who the hell pays child support for that long? And where are the Crumplers getting that kind of money?"

"Maybe it's hush money," Aurora speculated. "Maybe it's less about the kid and more about keeping her quiet."

There was something like admiration on Josh's face. "I thought the same thing. The Crumplers have plenty of money from their criminal enterprises. And Burdette lied to me, said they were in contact with Wade Atchison, when he was six feet under. They definitely know more than they're saying."

"Where does Pearline fit in?" Samba asked.

"At the time of the murder," Aurora said, "she's working at the mini-mart. She sees something she's not supposed to see. She's terrified."

"Right," Josh agreed. "Sixteen and scared out of her wits. So she gets on the phone and calls the morgue. Several times."

"Do you think it was some kind of signal?" Samba asked.

"Maybe she thought someone would be there, someone that could help her. No offense, Josh, but the cops here are sometimes pretty out to lunch."

"None taken," Josh said with a smile.

"Wait a second," Aurora said. She paged through the file. "Doc thought she might have been trying to reach the other person who worked there. The other medical examiner."

"Davis Gentry," Josh said.

She laughed. "But why? Why would he be the first one she tried to call?"

The three of them sat in silence.

"We need Gentry," Samba said. "I say we march down there and just bust into his office. We could just tell him—hey, we know everything. Start talking."

"That only works in movies," Josh said. "A guy like Gentry? In real life, he's got some hard-assed attorney on speed dial. We wouldn't make it past the receptionist."

"What else do we know about him?" Aurora asked.

"What do you mean?"

"Gentry. There's got to be another way. There's always a way."

"Atta girl," Samba agreed. "She's right, Josh."

Josh flipped open the laptop. "Davis Gentry. They've got his bio up on his campaign site. '*Vote Davis Gentry for City Council. A Friend to All.*' All the standard political bullshit. He likes hunting, doing good work in the community, attending church six days a week, and spending time with his beautiful family."

"You can't trust the government any more than the cops," Samba said.

"Ah, Samba. You better watch yourself, old boy. You're

gonna end up wearing a tin foil hat and getting messages from the TV," Josh joked.

Aurora interrupted Samba's retort.

"What does it say about the wife?"

Josh's face grew serious, and he turned back to the computer screen. "Ex-wife. Ash Gentry. Married forty years."

"You don't last that long without knowing a few secrets," Samba said.

"And Davis has got a few," Josh agreed. He turned the laptop to face them. "Lots of rumors of infidelity, and one love child, up in South Carolina. Born during a difficult time in his marriage. Since then, the Lord Jesus has made his crooked paths straight."

"Not fucking likely," Samba chortled. "Maybe we could talk to the love child?"

Josh shook his head. "Are you kidding me? She's probably cashed up to the gills and signed an airtight confidentiality agreement. She's not going to give us shit."

"Tell me more about the wife," Aurora pressed.

"Looks like Ash is from Kervick County. Daughter of the Confederacy."

"That's a thing?" Aurora was incredulous. "Seriously?"

"Oh, yes," Samba told her. "People here remember the War of Northern Aggression pretty differently than your friends up in New York."

"Daughter of the Confederacy," Josh repeated, "Garden Club. Gun Club. Welcome Wagon. Event planning and charity. Her favorite thing to do is embroidering."

"She's probably got an embroidered set of her ex-husband's balls," Samba observed. "Gun Club! I would say we should try and talk to her, but she's probably a better shot than me."

"Don't sell yourself short, Samba," Aurora said. "I heard you almost put down Josh when he came in here after hours."

"Now, that's the truth," Samba agreed. "So where's Ash Gentry now?"

"Hang on, guys." Josh held up a hand. "It looks like she's still local. Got a family estate just north of Hambone, right on the water."

Samba whistled. "That's a nice area."

"Did you say Welcome Wagon, Josh?"

Josh checked the article. "Yep."

"Well I just happen to be new in town," she told them. "I can pay Ash a visit."

CHAPTER THIRTY-NINE

Josh sat in Rush's office. It felt like it was years ago since he had last been here, the day he was given his assignment in the evidence room. Now that place felt like home, and being here felt wrong somehow, as if he were going backwards. He wanted to go with Aurora to see Ash Gentry, to keep her safe, but at the same time, he knew that it was something she wanted to do herself. There was still danger out there, there was no doubt about it.

The train that's comin' for you, boy? You got no idea.

He tugged one of the vertical blinds aside and peeked into the main room. Boone was nowhere to be seen. If he'd known something, he would have given Josh a heads-up about the visit. There were any number of activities that Josh had undertaken in the last month that would merit taking away his badge forever. The things he had done in pursuit of Raylene Atchison's killer were at worst illegal and at best colossally stupid.

And he didn't regret a single one.

Photographs of Rush's family covered the desk, piled high with uneven mounds of paperwork. From inside a clay frame that looked like it was melting, Rush's seven-year-old, Drew, grinned from a perch high atop a bright yellow slide. Josh recognized Baboon Jack's. He had been at that birthday party. The other adults had lounged in the snack food area, drinking the cardboard-tasting beer, while Josh had spent the entire time on the lookout for predators, scribbling down the plates of every guy who looked like he didn't belong. Not exactly the life of the party.

"Hey, Josh!" Rush entered the room, as always, a little out of breath. He extended a hand, and Josh shook it. A plastic bracelet that read BREATHE clung to Rush's wrist.

Josh pointed to it. "Nice," he said.

"Oh, yeah. I'm supposed to snap it every time I'm thinking about Emily Jo, or the divorce, or blowing my brains out," he explained.

"And how's it going?"

"Surprised I still have a goddamn wrist left."

Josh smiled. "It's good to see you, man."

And then Rush took out the folder.

"How's everything going out there at the evidence room? Do you feel like it's clearing your mind out a little bit?" The words sounded far away, as though Rush were shouting them down an empty hallway. All Josh could focus on was the folder on his desk.

Hudson, J.

"It was Jesse," Josh said in a low voice.

Captain Rush stopped midsentence, his silence saying everything Josh needed to know.

"The bones," Josh managed. "They were Jesse. Is that what you wanted to tell me?

"I'm so sorry. The report came in this morning. I hoped— we hoped it might bring you some measure of peace."

"Peace," Josh repeated. It was a bullshit concept, just like closure, something people said. People like Rush, who didn't understand. His little brother, who mailed coupons to Santa and wanted to be a tollbooth operator because he liked quarters and thought they got to keep the money, was dead. Josh remembered the days after the funeral, the shock of starting a new year at school a few weeks later, with new socks and binders and sharpened pencils. It seemed unbelievable to him then that his brother was really gone, that there was a Jesse-shaped void in the universe. *It's like going blind*, he remembered their pastor telling his mother at their kitchen table. *You find a new way of living, but nothing is ever the same again.* He had been right about that.

They'd had a memorial service for Jesse. There was a tree for him, back at the elementary school, with a plaque that was now faded. Jesse was dead; the Shadow Man had told them that much. But hope was a resilient thing, treacherous and comforting, and it had burned in the back of Josh's mind without him even knowing it.

And now here was the truth. The Shadow Man had carried his unconscious brother out of Fun World to his trailer two counties away; when he was finished with him, he had killed him, shoved him into a duffel bag, and thrown it in a river. The Shadow Man had smirked and laughed when the cops had asked him to lead them to Jesse's body, as though there might be some undiscovered spark of compassion inside a person who was pure evil. *Give the family peace,* they'd pleaded, and he'd laughed. And now the case was finally closed. Another box in the evidence room. Peace.

"I'm so incredibly sorry for your loss, Josh," Rush said. "And there's actually another reason why I called you here today. A good one."

He palmed his sweat-stained breast pocket and then extracted a key, which he used to open his top desk drawer. He removed an object and slid it across the desk to Josh.

Josh's gun.

Josh could not believe what he was seeing.

"Sir?"

Rush grinned. "Your old friend Pernaria Vincent came back in here for a chat yesterday. It seems that she had a visitation from an angel, who advised her to start talking. She told us that you weren't involved with any of her and Doyle's criminal activities, and that confirmed what our internal investigation already found. You're clear, Josh. Welcome back to work."

A few weeks ago, he would have been leaping out of the chair with joy, but today Josh was rooted to his seat. Jesse was dead, and Liana was missing, and Aurora's case was still unsolved.

"Did Pea—did Miss Vincent say anything about Liana?"

Rush shook his head. "I'm sorry, Josh. You have to understand, Pernaria Vincent is a con artist. She'll say whatever a man wants to hear as long as he's got money in his pocket."

"But the picture. She had a picture of my sister."

"I'm sorry, Josh."

"I saw it, Cap. It was authentic. My sister's alive."

In his mind, Liana loomed larger than anything alive, seventeen and shoving clothes into a roller suitcase in her bedroom in Tennessee. *Come and find me,* she'd said to him that day, and he'd looked away, down at the whites of her forearms that framed him, the right one embroidered with a smudged Magic Marker tattoo, a single word over and over in her old-fashioned curly handwriting.

Courage.

She was still out there—he knew it. He had tried to put the thoughts aside, focus on Aurora's case.

"I know you'll still work on your sister's case, Josh. I respect that. I do. But can we agree that Pernaria Vincent and people like her are not the way? You know better, Josh. I know you do."

Josh slid the gun across the desk.

"I appreciate the gesture, Cap," he said, "but there's a case I need to close out in the evidence room. I'm not ready to come back. Not just yet."

CHAPTER FORTY

James ignored the flashing light that indicated the presence of a voice mail. It was the State Board again, he was sure of it, but he didn't care. Ruby could stave them off for a while longer.

There was something he could have done.

The words thrashed at his consciousness, unforgiving in their truth. He had worked here alongside Davis Gentry, in this very autopsy suite, written reports with the man, attended conferences, even a few mandatory social events, and he had seen nothing. Perhaps there had been some sign, some clue that he could have seized on. Perhaps some action could have unraveled the series of events that led to Raylene Atchison ending up on this table. He had failed her somehow, and this knowledge bore into his chest and caught his breath. He had always imagined that this job had made him a better judge of people, that in all their infinite wisdom, the dead had taught him something about the living. They had not.

James turned the pages of his work diary back in time until he reached the night of the Atchison murder. He'd told Ruby it was for ethical and legal reasons that he recorded the things he did each day in minute detail, but the real reason was some visceral need to commemorate each of his patients. All of the details he had shared with Josh Hudson were there; the teenagers in the accident on the causeway in the pickup truck, the waiting as the jaws of life separated the cars, the appearance of Detective Rossi at his doorstep, hand in hand with Aurora Atchison. He had seen so much death since then, but somehow that night had always stayed with him, because of Raylene and because of Aurora.

He'd made notations about Gentry too; there they were, at the bottom of the second page. *Gentry receiving Community Award for Excellence in Service Tonight. Bullshit,* he'd added unceremoniously beneath the words, underlining them three times to drive the point home. James scoffed at the title—it wasn't as though Gentry was feeding the hungry or clothing the poor, he was doing a job, same as James, only with the least effort and the most complaining possible. Gentry's reports were indecipherable, his medical knowledge shoddy, and he had the horrifying habit of making jokes over the dead and then writing them off as *the only way to cope,* as though the patients had ever stirred any type of emotion in him. So he had skipped out on work that night to attend a fund-raiser—did that mean he could not have been out on the bayou with Wade and Raylene?

A few pages later, James had his answer—there was the *Bayou Bumblebee* story about the event, a Casino Night at the Shrimp Shack. James frowned at the photograph. The Shrimp Shack had been a terrible restaurant, with a floor that was sticky underfoot and drinks served in plastic buckets with shovels sticking out of them. The place had burned down in a suspicious fire with nobody inside, its charred entrails remaining until some featureless chain restaurant had taken its place.

James peered at the photograph that accompanied the article. There were all the local politicos, Royce Beaumont, and there was Gentry, front and center in a cowboy hat and a silk shirt unbuttoned almost to the navel. James skimmed the article. The Casino Night had been a rousing success, and at the end of the evening, the award had been presented. It was as airtight an alibi as you could get. Gentry could not have done this.

But he must have known who did.

The personnel file on Davis Gentry was relatively slender; pay stubs, copies of the autopsy reports he'd done. James paged through them. Davis was the one who had insisted on a seal for the medical examiner's office. The office didn't have enough prestige for him, that was for sure. James read each report. They were woefully brief and incomplete, just like Raylene Atchison's had been. There was no indication that her case had been special. It hadn't set off alarm bells when he'd insisted on doing her autopsy; James had been relieved, scared of what the sight of Raylene on the autopsy table would have done to him. Now he wished he could have been with her on her last day on earth. He would have put aside his feelings and made sure to annotate every detail, anything and everything that would catch her killer.

James opened the locked drawer, where he'd tucked Malachi's printouts and Wade's samples into a Java Jive reusable lunch bag. That was the puzzle of it all; how had Wade's path crossed with Gentry's? Gentry had lived up the bayou in some decaying wreck of a plantation house that he was rebuilding into a modern monstrosity, digging up a grove of magnolia trees to put in a swimming pool. Those from down the bayou—including James—were of no use to him, and he made no secret of it. So what did he want with Wade Atchison, a small-time criminal?

Unless it wasn't Wade he was after.

Raylene. He recalled the image of her approaching him on the skiff out on the bayou that day; something startling and unearthly in her beauty, something childlike in her manner that told him she was not aware of this beauty, a quality that only deepened her loveliness. James had seen it. Wade Atchison had seen it. It was not a stretch to think that Gentry had seen it too.

Town gossip. It wasn't something he had ever been plugged into, but lucky for James, he knew someone who was.

"Ruby, can you come in here for a moment please?"

"Sure, Doc."

He glanced up at the clock. Four forty—she would have already begun her preparations to end the day, an elaborate process that started with shutting down her computer and ended with the application of makeup.

She opened the door and leaned in, the scent of her perfume overwhelming the antiseptic smell of his suite. She smelled of vanilla, of warm baking smells and safe, sweet things.

"I have a question that you might be able to help me with. It involves some—well, some unsavory matters."

She raised an eyebrow. "Go on."

"I want to know about a rumor that may have been around town a number of years ago—1989, to be specific."

Ruby frowned.

"Of course," James continued, "you would have been young then."

"Very young."

"Very young," he echoed. "But you know, I know how social you are, and I thought you might—oh, forget it."

"No," she said. "Who is it about?"

"Davis Gentry," James said. "I want to know if you ever heard any rumors about him being a philanderer."

"A what?"

"A cheater. A louse." He did not understand why she was smiling.

"Well, I did hear a few things. My friend Adrian did some construction work for his wife on their house. Ashley, Ashford, some rich white-girl name. He said she was like Hitler in a bra."

"So he might have been—um, stepping out on her?"

"I can't say I've heard that. But I did hear it about her."

"The wife?"

"Don't sound so surprised," she said. "Out there in her lonely house on the bayou. She keeps to herself. Nobody in town's seen her in years. I heard she had workers out there all the time, doing construction jobs and all other kinds of nonsense. You ask me, she was scouting the local talent."

"I see. Well, um, thanks, Ruby." He averted his eyes, sure that this conversation violated some sort of employer-employee code of ethics. "I appreciate the information."

"Anytime, Doc," she said.

She palmed the light switch on her way out and called to him over her shoulder. "Don't be sitting here in the dark for too long," she scolded. "You're gonna hurt your eyes, you know."

It was the little things like this that made James grateful for Ruby.

"Be safe out there. See you tomorrow."

Alone in the office, he watched the sun slip beneath the surface of the bayou, Ruby's words echoing in his ears.

He pinned Raylene's X-rays to the light board. Someone had strangled her, an act that was both horrifyingly violent and extremely personal. They had watched the life leave her body. He had never considered the possibility that it could have been a woman.

Your other contributor is female.

Malachi had found another sample; what if it was Ash Gentry's? Wade Atchison had nothing to offer Gentry, but he had something to offer Ash.

James removed one of the photographs of Wade from the file. He was grinning from the passenger seat of a pickup truck, one muscled arm draped out of the window. Even James knew he was the type of man that women found attractive. And Ash had an eye for the local talent, as Ruby had described it. Was it too much of a stretch to think that Ash had noticed Wade or stepped out with him? Maybe Raylene had found out about the two of them, had followed Wade and Ash out to the bayou that night, where they'd snuck out while her husband was away. Gentry would have helped her cover the murder after the fact; he would have had plenty of time after the casino night was over.

James reached for the phone and called the evidence room.

"We're one step ahead of you," Josh said, after James had explained his theory. "Aurora's visiting Ash Gentry, see what she can find out."

"Alone?"

"She can handle herself, Doc."

Josh was right. Aurora was a grown woman, not the child that he had cared for all those years ago. He had known nothing about children then and knew even less about women now. But that didn't mean that you packed someone off into a car and sent them driving straight into danger either, did it?

"I know you're right," he said finally.

James turned back to the window. The Gentry place was

miles from here, where the bayou stretched into two arms of a coffee-colored river, its bleak beauty stripped bare at the foot of green hillsides dotted with collapsing sugar plantations, where people peered at the water around heavy curtains. This was where Ash Gentry had shut herself away from Cooper's Bayou and the past. What would she say when Aurora Atchison appeared on her doorstep? Captain Rush's words echoed in James's memory. *Leave this one alone.* It was a warning, and they had all ignored it. Someone was going to pay the price for stirring up the past.

He prayed it would not be Aurora.

CHAPTER FORTY-ONE

Soon.

Someone had used a finger to carve the words in the dew that spread across the back windshield of Aurora's rental car. She'd stood there in the driveway, momentarily rendered immobile by the precise, clean letters and their ominous meaning. A week ago she probably would have wilted right there in front of the house, sat underneath the peeling limbs of the crape myrtle in the front yard and wished for home.

But not today.

She remembered Josh's face, the curve of his split lip as he smiled up at her, pointing at the picture of Niney Crumpler. He was right; they were on the right track. They were getting closer to the truth. Aurora felt her senses sharpening, the way they did when the trauma calls came in at work and she had to shed every anxiety, any distraction that might interfere with the work at hand. She had a job to do. She was going to see Ash Gentry. They'd talked about the different ruses she could use; she could give a fake name, pretend to have just moved to town. In the end, Aurora had told Josh and Samba she was going to be honest, lay her cards on the table for Ash Gentry, pray that the woman would tell her what she knew. It was the only way to find the truth. And she wanted the truth.

She twisted the key in the ignition, and her cell phone lit up. Ruby.

"Aurora. I'm glad I caught you. You all set?"

"Yeah, thanks."

"And Doc wanted me to remind you again to be careful."

"Yeah, thanks, Ruby." Aurora pulled onto the tangle of back roads that would eventually lead her to the interstate. "Tell him I'm fine."

"You know what you're gonna take from her?"

Aurora hadn't thought this far ahead. "Tissues? Something from the trash in the restroom?"

Ruby humphed, a disapproving noise. "Toothbrush or hairbrush would be the best." How did she know this stuff? Had she done this before?

"Got it." Have you heard anything from Josh, Ruby?" She tried to sound casual. He hadn't been picking up his cell. She imagined him melting into the shadows in some dark alley somewhere, asking questions about Liana, heedless with grief about Jesse.

"Nada," Ruby answered. "I'm sure he's fine. You just be careful and you let us know when you're on your way back."

"I will," Aurora said, and ended the call.

All around her the landscape was changing, the bayou receding, dun-colored housing developments appearing in its place. *Soon.* It was amazing how one word could be so ominous. The shuttered gas stations, the rusting water towers, the cars on cinder blocks in front yards—all of these ordinary things suddenly seemed threatening.

She almost missed the turnoff. AMARANTH. The name was written in fading script across two scalloped metal gates pressed together like palms. A green pickup truck with a Confederate flag front license plate, the truck bed laden with paint cans and machinery, was parked where the road met the gravel.

Aurora put the rental car in park and was still searching for an intercom button when the gates began to fold open. The ancient limbs of the oak trees that lined the driveway reached across her path and drew their leaves across the roof of the car. At the end of the long driveway, the house came into view, a stark brick structure half hidden by the Spanish moss that hung from surrounding trees, its windows unencumbered by shutters so that they appeared to Aurora like unblinking eyes. A lone figure stood in the half-open doorway, watching Aurora's approach.

She pulled the car half onto the grass and stepped outside. There was no trace of the swampy air from Cooper's Bayou, just a delicate breeze.

"Good afternoon," said the woman on the steps. She descended slowly. "Welcome to Amaranth."

This had to be Esma, the housekeeper Aurora had spoken with on the phone. *I'm new in town, and I think she might remember my family. Aurora Atchison.* Her name had meant something to Ash; Esma had come back to the phone quickly, something urgent in her voice. *Miss Ash would like you to come to the house this afternoon, if possible.*

"Thank you so much for having me." Aurora held out the bottle of white wine she'd purchased the previous evening at the supermarket, even though they didn't have much to choose from. Nana had taught her never to show up anywhere empty-handed.

"How nice. I'll just put it in the refrigerator to chill. Please follow me."

Esma led her into a large living room. The interior of the house was dark, and all of the heavy brocade curtains had been pulled across the windows. Garlands of flowers that spilled from disembodied hands were scored into the walls surrounding the fireplace. Aurora bent down to read what looked like handwriting scribbled on the door frame.

"Isn't it marvelous?"

Ash Gentry's voice startled her. Like the house, she seemed to be sheathed in half darkness. She crossed the room in a few strides and stood at Aurora's side, pointing to the markings on the wall. Even in velvet flats, she towered over Aurora.

"Heights of the children who lived in the house," she explained, drawing a pink varnished nail down the edge of the door frame. "How could I paint over it? All that family history. There's a difference between renovating and restoring, you know. I never let my workmen forget it. It's important to me that things stay the same." In the light from the nearby antique lamp, Aurora could make out the years. *Kitty, age 5, 1906. James Edward, age 8, 1910.*

"Your family?"

"Yes," Ash said. "I used to spend summer vacations here. My great-great-great-granddaddy built this place for his bride. Restoring it to its original glory has become my life's work. I mean, it's not like I do anything useful otherwise." She laughed. "Aurora Atchison." There was something clenched in her face when she spoke Aurora's name. "I must admit, when Esma told me you were calling, I was caught very much by surprise. Please, come sit down."

Aurora perched on the edge of a raspberry-colored chaise. All of the furniture looked antique, as though it might crumble under your fingertips. Across from her, Ash sat on a high-backed mahogany chair.

"You remembered me."

"Oh, yes. Nobody could ever forget what happened to you. It's all anyone talked about for years! A body in the bayou, a murderer running free, an abandoned child. It shook everyone up." She leaned forward and pressed her hand into Aurora's. "I think it's wonderful that you came back. But tell me, why did you?"

Aurora stared at the woman's pale hand in her own. "My grandfather passed away. I came to settle his estate."

Ash appeared pleased by this answer. "I'm so sorry for your loss. I'm sure being back here must be difficult."

Aurora hesitated. There was no easy way to ask the questions she needed answers to, but she had to try.

"Miss Ash," she began, "since I arrived here, I discovered some things about my mother's murder. I think the story that I've heard all my life has been untrue."

To Aurora's surprise, Ash nodded. "I think you're right," she said. "It never made sense to me either."

"What makes you say that?"

"Wade."

Something softened in Ash's tone when she spoke Aurora's father's name.

"You knew him?"

Ash smiled. "It was so long ago," she said. "I was a young politician's wife, still naive enough to think that I could be happy with Davis. This was before he put me out to pasture and took up with some waitress from Kervick County. Back then, I made it my mission to be the picture of a Southern lady."

"It seems to me that you are," Aurora said before she could stop herself.

Ash chuckled. "It does seem that way, doesn't it. But there was only one thing that fulfilled me, one thing that could take me away from planting flowers and organizing luncheons. I found it at St. Simeon's."

"Christ?"

"Oh, Lord mercy, no." Ash's eyes gleamed. "It was men. The pastor at St. Simeon's was always trying to better the men of the community. He gave them jobs, put together men's groups where they could talk about their problems. Rooms full of men, shrimpers with their tan muscles, sitting around talking about their problems." She laughed again.

Aurora wasn't sure she wanted to hear the end of the story. "And that's where you met my dad?"

"Yes. But he wasn't there to flirt with me, Aurora. Your dad was trying to turn his life around. He had made mistakes, but he was fixing them. He had big plans to get you and your family a better life."

"What do you think happened?"

Her face darkened. "I don't know. I think he was involved in something bad, something he couldn't get away from."

"Do you think your husband was involved in any way?"

To Aurora's surprise, Ash did not flinch at the question. "I thought about it," she said quietly. "Davis is the kind of man who won't let anything stand in his way. I just can't imagine what your daddy would be standing in the way of."

"I know." A politician and a shrimper. How had their paths crossed? It was the part of the story she could not seem to uncover.

"Miss Ash?" Esma appeared in the doorway. "I'm so sorry to interrupt. The *Bayou Living* photographer is here."

"I forgot that was today! Thank you, Esma."

Ash sprang up and grasped Aurora's hands. "I don't know what I'd do without Esma keeping all my appointments. When

Davis and I got divorced, I told Royce Beaumont, who handled the whole mess, Esma has to come with me. Anyway, Aurora, I hope you'll come by again. I'm sorry I couldn't be more help."

"No, no. Thank you for seeing me. You have a beautiful home."

"Thank you." Ash appeared genuinely touched by the compliment. Together they stood at the top of the steps. For the first time, Aurora saw a smaller structure, tucked far behind the house on the lip of the river.

Ash followed her gaze. "Yellow fever," she said. "My great-great-great-grandfather built a house for the family doctor after his daughter died of yellow fever. For protection, you know. To keep his other daughter safe from disease. But then she ended up drowning farther down the bayou."

"That's so tragic."

"I guess the world finds all of us," Ash said. "I hope you'll enjoy the rest of your visit in Cooper's Bayou, Aurora. I'm so glad you came to Amaranth."

"I am too." And she was.

To hear someone speak kindly about Wade had rejuvenated her. They were on the right track. He had been trying to improve his life. He was innocent.

Aurora pulled the car back onto the oak-lined drive. The drive to see Ash had been longer than she thought; the afternoon was fading into twilight and had begun to wrap the road in darkness.

She reached for her cell phone. No service. Of course, she was in the middle of nowhere. Telling Josh and Samba about Ash Gentry would have to wait. She fiddled with the radio until the lumbering drawl of a country song filled the car. *The*

world finds all of us, Ash Gentry had said, something despon-
dent in her tone, as though she had tried to hide from something
in the ruined hulk of her family plantation.

High-beam headlights illuminated the interior of the car.
Someone was behind her. A truck, one of those ones with the
custom wheels that lifted them far off the ground. Aurora smiled.
She and Josh would laugh about it. She slowed down to let the
truck pass, but it moved closer behind her so that it was right on
her bumper. All she could see was that it was a dark color; and
then she saw the front plate.

A Confederate flag.

The truck from Amaranth.

Had he been watching her the whole time he was at Ash
Gentry's? Aurora pressed the gas pedal, and the rental car stuttered, then shot forward, the truck close behind. Aurora felt
the adrenaline rising in her throat. From his vantage point, he
could see into the car. He could see she was alone. The turnoff
for Cooper's Bayou wasn't for miles. She peered into the growing darkness. The only houses around here were miles from the
road, behind gates. There was no time. She was going to have
to outrun him.

The first hit to her bumper jolted her. She kept her hands
firmly on the wheel, praying that the rental would hold the
road. In the rearview mirror, half-blinded by the lights, he was
just a featureless shadow behind the wheel. He was just trying
to scare her, but after what she'd seen in Cooper's Bayou, she
didn't scare that easy.

Aurora floored it at the same time he hit the bumper again.
The rental car skidded and then she felt the wheels leaving the
road for the soft earth of the marsh, the headlights illuminating
the trees all around her, until the car finally came to a stop in
a thicket of reeds.

She pushed open the door and stepped into ankle-deep brown water. Above her, the pickup idled at the edge of the road. She could not see the driver.

"Hey," she shouted, the adrenaline coursing through her, an uncharacteristic boldness in her voice. Let this man, whoever he was, come at her face-to-face, not hiding in his truck. She was not going to run.

Behind her, another truck appeared around the bend and began to slow. The driver had probably seen the lights, seen Aurora's car in the ditch. The driver of the green pickup revved the engine one last time and sped away into the darkness.

"Is anyone down there? Hello? Do you need some help?"

An imposing man in a checkered shirt began to shuffle down the hillside towards her, his flashlight finding her where she leaned against the half-sunk car, the bayou glowing incandescent all around her in the headlights.

"Ma'am? Are you okay?"

Aurora held up her hands. Someone was trying to hurt her, or worse, but she felt strangely alive, how she imagined Josh might feel when he was on the verge of solving a case, as though everything was right at her fingertips.

"I'm fine," she said. "I just need a ride home."

CHAPTER FORTY-TWO

Aurora was in danger. Maybe Wade Atchison wasn't pulling the strings.

But somebody was.

Josh sat at the center table of the evidence room, elbow deep in Aurora's case file. The dust-furred lights above had sizzled and burned out one by one, so that only two remained, casting a patchwork luminescence on the space where he and Samba worked across from each other. He struggled to focus on the file; instead, Aurora's description of the previous evening's events played over and over in his mind. He imagined the person following her, her car leaving the road, the bayou below waiting to swallow them. She had stopped the car, he reminded himself. She wasn't hurt. Someone had happened upon the scene. She had gotten lucky. But whoever was in the truck wasn't giving up.

Samba had not questioned Josh's absence the past two days or his sudden reappearance, and had swooped down on *The Bayou Bumblebee* the second it was delivered to their doorstep, almost quickly enough for Josh to avoid seeing the headline, *Bayou John Doe ID'd as Jesse Hudson: Tragedy of*

Henry Lee Cates's Third Victim. He never thought about the Shadow Man by name, because a name implied that he was a person, had once been a baby that somebody loved, had feelings and friends and internal organs. These things could not possibly be true of the man who had killed his brother. He wondered if somewhere Liana was reading the headline, if the identification of Jesse's body would draw her out somehow.

"Well, Josh? You wanna know the good thing about criminals?"

Samba's hovering catapulted Josh back into the present. "Absolutely," he said. "Please tell me the good thing about criminals."

"They're human."

"Okay." Josh wasn't sure where this was going, but he was willing to give Samba as much leeway as he needed.

"See, the thing about us humans is, we think we control everything. We plan things to go a certain way, and they never do, because we can never account for everything." His eyes glittered with the excitement of a charismatic preacher midsermon. "So, we just have to find out what Raylene's—or Wade's—killer didn't account for. It's got to be in here. The truth isn't out there, in what people are saying. It's in here, it's in something that was left behind."

Josh agreed. Detectives were supposed to talk to people, solve fresh cases by hoofing it out on the street, tracking down leads. But cold cases were a different animal altogether. Wade Atchison had no remaining relatives, other than Aurora; Pearline Suggs was in the wind. Everyone else was dead or had left town. This case was cold for a reason. There was a moment on the cases he'd worked before when everything slid into place, but in Josh's head, the images from this case swam together with those of his own; Jesse's bones beside Raylene on the shores of the bayou; the Shadow Man accelerating towards Aurora in a green pickup.

Aurora appeared in the doorway. She smiled, but there was something drawn in her expression. Josh felt a dull pang in his chest. He hadn't kept her safe. Doc was right; she shouldn't have gone to Ash Gentry's alone.

"Hey! Josh told me what happened." Samba ushered her to a chair. "You okay?"

She pulled out a chair between them. "I'm fine. I just wish I'd gotten his license plate. I asked Roger, but—"

"Roger?" Josh asked.

"He's a plumber from Hambone," Aurora explained. "He's the guy who pulled over when he saw my car go off the road."

"And what do we know about him?" Josh pulled out his laptop. "What's his last name?"

Aurora put a hand on his shoulder. "He just stopped to help," she said. "There's still good people in the world, Josh."

"Sure." He wished it were true. He would look up Roger's name later.

"What do you remember about the truck?" Samba leaned towards Aurora. "I know it was dark, but did you notice anything about him?"

Aurora shook her head. "He was just a shadow." The word reverberated in Josh's memory. "The truck was green, had a Confederate flag on the front plates. Older model."

Samba raised an eyebrow. "Crumplers have a vehicle like that, Josh? I can't recall."

"Probably. Them and every other redneck in this county." He wasn't sure which possibility was more frightening, the

Crumplers or someone else. They had contacts in other counties; who knew how far this case went?

"You think Ash Gentry sent someone after you?" Samba frowned.

"I don't know, but I don't think so," Aurora said. "Why would she agree to see me at all, then? And she didn't give me much, but she told me flat out she doesn't think my father is responsible. And she definitely doesn't trust her ex-husband."

"She knows something," Josh said. "There's got to be a connection here; we're just not seeing it." There was some dark link between all of them: the Crumplers, the Gentrys, Wade and Raylene. The case was more complex than they had imagined, more dangerous than they had feared. It wasn't just a feud with the Crumplers; it went deeper than that.

The train that's comin' for you, boy? You got no idea.

Samba broke the silence. "I think you're right, Josh. Check out what I was looking at this morning. He set a box on the table with a resounding crash. "Fish and Wildlife records. Didn't even know we had them, but there was a flood in the county records department a few years back, and they moved their files here and never got 'em back. I was thinking there's probably some information on Gentry in here."

"That's a good find, Samba," Josh said. He peeled open the first box, embossed with the state Fish and Wildlife emblem, a rendering of a bird, a deer, and a fish, swirled in a circle. Something was missing from the picture. And then it clicked.

"Alligators," she said. "It's the connection between Gentry, my dad, and the Crumplers. This has to be the answer. Something about these files."

"It's too bad your grandpa isn't here," Samba said. "This hunting stuff, I don't know too much about this area of the law. The alligator man, now, he's the one to ask about this stuff."

"What if there was a way we still could?" There was something triumphant in Aurora's face. "I've got all his notes, his journals, in my car. I went through them, but maybe I was looking for the wrong thing. The caretaker told me—the answers are in the house. Maybe he was right."

For the next couple of hours, the three of them pored over Hunter Broussard's logbooks and notes. He had taken his appointment as the alligator nuisance man seriously; the ledger listed every call he'd gone on. As per state law, he'd relocated any gators less than four feet long and only killed the larger ones for meat. The animals had been protected under the law until 1988, when alligator hunting was made legal after the gators began showing up in backyards and playgrounds, a sign that their numbers were flourishing.

"What year was Davis Gentry appointed to the Fish and Wildlife Commission?" Josh looked up from the book.

"The year of the murder. Eighty-nine."

"Listen to this." Josh read from the journal. " '*State is instituting a lottery for hunting tags. No idea how the Crumplers are getting away with this, but Wade says he's gathering enough information to turn them in, it's just a matter of time. I'm afraid they know someone with the state. Secured the property, warned Raylene about going out after dark with the baby. Wade says the law will protect us.*' "

"So my dad was turning the Crumplers in, and Gentry knew about it." Something in Aurora's face flickered open.

They were still missing a piece, something that couldn't be found in one of the boxes.

Josh's cell buzzed on the table, turning itself in a circle. A text from Boone. Ever since the news about Jesse, Boone had been trying to track Josh down. Laura Jane had left a basket on his doorstep with a sympathy card attached the day before. Acknowledging these kindnesses would mean he'd have to begin shouldering the grief, and he wasn't ready. Not yet. He reached out and hit the button to display the message.

Pearline Suggs is a missing person. Hasn't shown up for work in three days. No answer at the house, no contact with family. Thought you'd want to know.

Josh held up the phone to Aurora and Samba. "Check this out."

"There's got to be a connection," Aurora said. "But what?"

Something clicked in Josh's memory. "I think I'll take a drive over to the Crumpler compound," Josh said. "I have a feeling one of the Crumplers may be up for talking."

CHAPTER FORTY-THREE

Four miles south of the evidence room, beyond the knots of roads behind the bayou, at the heart of a tumble of four-wheeler paths, the gates to the Crumpler compound rose out of the marshy earth. A sun-bloated truck tire hung from a frayed rope in the center of the gate, painted with the words NO TRESPASSING in trembling yellow letters. The main house and outbuildings were partially obscured behind a small rise.

Josh had been here twice: once as a kid, when his dad had told him to wait in the truck while he went and did business with Niney Crumpler. The second time had been with Boone to deliver a warrant for Dean Crumpler's arrest. Both times had involved gunfire, and neither was a pleasant memory.

If you were going to battle on the Crumplers' home turf, you needed ammunition, and Josh had some of a different kind from an unlikely source. The visit to Doyle had been helpful after all. Samba was right; every criminal made mistakes, everyone had a weak spot. Burdette Crumpler's hadn't been hard to find, and it was no surprise to Josh that it was a woman.

Pearline Suggs.

Josh hit the buzzer on the gate and glanced up at the camera that swiveled to face him; he gave whoever was on the receiving end of the video a little salute.

"Hold up the warrant," a voice growled through the speaker.

Josh held up his hands in surrender. "No warrant, boys. Just want to talk to Burdette."

The voice on the other end of the line snorted. "And why the hell might that be?"

"Just a friendly chat. I ain't here on police business."

"A friendly chat, huh. Well, you just hang on a minute there, Detective Hudson. Let me go see if Burdette has any openings in his calendar."

The speaker clicked off, and Josh retreated to the Jeep, leaning against the dirt-speckled hood. He was banking on a tiny glint of humanity that he'd recognized in Burdette Crumpler, but he'd been mistaken before—Pernaria Vincent could attest to that. Above him, an osprey dove in a perfect, unbroken arc to pluck its prey from the tall grass around the bayou.

A figure came into view on a four-wheeler, cresting the hill behind the gate. Josh recognized the red hair and waved, and Burdette Crumpler waved back. He coasted up to the gate but made no move to unlock it. This time the eyes he turned to Josh were clear; he wasn't high on anything. But the smirk he'd worn at their last meeting had been replaced by a new, troubling wariness.

"You shouldn't be here, Josh."

"Well, it's mighty fine to see you too, Burdette," Josh said lightly.

"I ain't messing around. You got no business here. I'm telling you, because I like Doyle. Get out of here." Burdette glanced behind him. "I mean it, Josh."

"I can't do that, Burdette. Not while someone is bothering a lady. Miss Aurora, someone ran her off the road last night. Now, you tell Lionel, he has a problem, he can come settle it with me. He needs to leave Miss Aurora alone."

"I *told* you. You need to talk to Wade Atchison about that."

Josh laughed at Burdette's grave expression.

"You see, Burdette, I tried doing that, and Wade Atchison didn't help me too much, on account of the fact that he's been dead some twenty years."

"What?" Burdette chewed his lower lip. Josh was willing to bet he hadn't known Wade was dead. But he knew something.

"That's right. Now do you want to tell me what you know about what's going on here?"

"I can't, Josh." He closed his eyes. "I can't. And if you're gonna hassle me, I'm gonna have to call my lawyer." He revved the engine on the four-wheeler.

"All right, Burdette. I just thought since Pearline Suggs was involved, that—"

It was barely perceptible, but Josh saw Burdette flinch at the sound of her name.

"What's she got to do with this?"

"Pearline Suggs is missing, Burdette. Now, I know that you care about her."

"You don't know shit," Burdette spat.

"I know that she was the one who took care of you. After the truck accident."

"Accident?" Burdette snorted. "Is that what somebody told you?" He leaned forward, and Josh saw it plain on his face, the old pain dressed up as anger. "It wasn't no accident." It had defined Burdette's life, just as the Shadow Man had defined Josh's, a nightmare that had cleaved a life in two. Before and After.

"Wade pushed you out of a moving truck."

"He did. And you know what? If he's dead, like you say he is—I'm glad. He was a motherfucker."

"And Pearline helped you get better."

"Everyone was so nice to me after I came home from the accident. I just stayed in bed, and people brought me shit because they felt bad. But Pearline didn't." Burdette chuckled. "She busted my balls, you know? Started bugging me about work and asking me when was I going to get fitted for the chair. She's the reason I got better. She made me deal with things."

That was what the love of a woman could do, Josh thought. He thought about Aurora, her offer to help him with the search for Liana, their easy banter in the evidence room when they went through the files.

"Jesus." Burdette slammed his fists on the steering wheel of the four-wheeler, startling Josh. "She's really missing?"

Josh nodded. "Hasn't shown up for work at Royce Beaumont's in three days. He called the police station. They got no leads, Burdette."

"Shit." He saw Burdette consider his options, but he knew the girl would win out. They always did.

"What do you want to know?"

"Everything you know about Wade Atchison."

"Fine. And this is gonna help Pearline? How?"

"I promise you, Burdette. You tell me what you know, I'll do absolutely everything I can to make sure she gets home safe. You have my word on that." He offered his hand, and Burdette took it.

"All right, man." Burdette cut the engine on the four-wheeler and reached back to unlatch his chair. "Not here, though. Let's go down by the water."

Burdette unlatched the gate, and Josh held it open so he could roll through. Together they made their way back down the path Josh had taken, towards the bayou.

"Like I told you, Wade started out helping with the gator poaching. His father-in-law bein' the alligator nuisance man, he had information that we could use."

"So y'all had an arrangement."

"Yeah. And it worked out for a while, but then something changed. Wade decided he wanted more cash, and my family didn't want to give it to him. So he threatened to go to the cops, you know. The animal cops and shit."

"The animal cops?"

"Fish and Wildlife," Burdette explained. "That pissed Niney off so bad, he started chirping about how we owned those guys already."

Something clicked in Josh's mind. "Because of Davis Gentry."

"Yeah. The Grim Reaper guy from the morgue. He was taking our business to the next level, and he was getting appointed to Fish and Wildlife."

"And Niney told Wade about him." Wade Atchison wasn't an idiot. And Gentry had flashed his wealth all over town, Doc had told them that. Wade had seen deeper pockets. He was an injured shrimper with a wife and a little child. There was no way he could have resisted squeezing a man like Davis Gentry for all he had.

"Yep. And then Wade started threatening Gentry."

"So y'all started bothering Hunter Broussard and his family. All that voodoo shit."

Burdette held up his hands. "It wasn't me," he said. "They thought Wade might back off if people threatened the nuisance man."

Josh thought about the journal, about Hunter Broussard lighting candles in the house on the bayou, trying to protect his family. "He didn't know, Burdette. Hunter wasn't in on it. He was just a man trying to do his job."

"I told you, Josh, I ain't had nothing to do with it." Something caught in his voice. Josh had no reason to, but he believed him.

"So tell me what happened next."

"Gentry didn't want to pay Wade, but Wade wouldn't shut up."

"So Gentry killed him that night on the bayou." It made sense. Wade could have played it smart, maybe even gotten a payday out of it, but that wasn't who he was. A man like him— a cocky, brash loudmouth—he was way too much of a loose end to someone like Gentry. But Raylene? Bobbie Sharpless's sugared drawl played in his head. *Raylene and the baby, they weren't even supposed to be there that night.* Wade had brought his wife and daughter to the meeting with Gentry. The sick son of a bitch had tried to use his own family as a shield.

Burdette frowned. "That ain't what happened. The way I understood it, they came to some kind of agreement. Wade was always beating on Raylene, and he's the one that killed her. You're sayin' Wade died that night?"

"He's been dead this whole time."

The expression on his face told Josh that he had reached the end of Burdette's goodwill.

"And now I'm done talking until you tell me what the hell this has got to do with Pearline."

"I'm not sure," Josh admitted. "But what you've told me, Burdette, it's gonna help us find her."

Pearline had been there that night. And Josh and Samba had started asking questions around town, looking for her. If word had gotten back to Gentry, then Josh and Samba had turned Pearline into another loose end.

"She's going to be okay, right?" Burdette was shouting at him now. "Do something. You have to do something."

"I have to go, Burdette. I will be in touch." He took off for the car at a full run, opening his cell phone. They were running out of time.

CHAPTER FORTY-FOUR

Pearline Suggs's house was down the bayou, about a mile past Baboon Jack's, a converted trailer on the edge of town. Aurora followed Josh up the steps to the front door. Samba was still plowing through the files in the evidence room, hoping to find some clue that would lead them to Gentry. Josh had filled Aurora in on the way over about his visit to the Crumplers and the confirmation that her father had been threatening Gentry and probably walked right into a trap that night on the bayou, with Aurora and her mother in tow. She tried to muster up a surge of anger at this revelation, but all that she felt was compassion for Wade Atchison, a man who'd been labeled a criminal in life and a murderer in death although he'd only earned one of those titles.

"Locked," Josh said, turning away from Pearline's front door. Yellow blooms sprang from clay flowerpots on each step, and a wreath of wildflowers adorned the door. To the right of the steps, a statue of an eyeless angel held a harp towards the heavens. "Looks like nothing's out of place here."

"Maybe they followed her to work?"

Josh frowned. "I don't know. Baboon Jack's is pretty busy. It seems like it would be too risky."

"So what now?"

Josh vaulted over the railing and cupped his hands against the window. "Nothing to see, really. Laptop's open on the couch. Now we just need a way in."

Aurora tipped the angel statue to one side and slipped a hand underneath, peeling back a slice of tape so that a key dropped into her hand. "Got it." Josh looked at her with admiration as she fitted the key into the lock.

Inside, the floor was spotless, the afghan draped in a straight line across the couch, the mail and bills stacked in a neat column next to the phone. Iola Suggs, hand on hip, raised a champagne flute at Josh from a framed picture. Miss Iola had to be Pearline's mama. Josh smiled at the memory of the day of the carnival.

"Nu Life Center for Addiction," Aurora read from the top envelope. "Must be for her son?"

Josh whistled. "Damn. Have you seen that place?"

"What is it?"

"It's in Kervick County. It's a five-star rehab resort. Come in addicted to pills, leave addicted to other pills."

"Wow. That's quite a business model."

"They rake in the cash. I think it's thirty grand just to get in the door."

"So how does Pearline Suggs afford a place for her son to dry out that's thirty grand a year on a legal assistant's salary? Royce Beaumont's a nice guy, but I doubt he pays her that well."

"Well, she lives pretty simply." Aurora opened a cabinet. "You said Lionel's dad is Trace Crumpler, right? Maybe he helps out."

"I doubt it. He's drinking every dollar he earns." Josh hesitated. "Burdette, though. He could be helping out with some funds from the family business."

Josh riffled through the rest of the envelopes. "Burdette could definitely be helping her. Between the steamboat and his little meth business, I'm sure he has some cash."

"And he loves her."

"Sure."

"Enough to help her out with another man's kid?"

Josh tilted his head to one side. "His nephew."

"Could be."

Aurora circled around the couch and connected the laptop's power cord. "It seems weird that she wouldn't put this away." She pointed to a zippered case that lay open on the love seat.

"Yeah." Josh sat beside her on the couch. "Let's see what she was looking at on here."

The screen came to life, revealing several open windows. "*'Your Toughest Decorating Dilemmas—Solved,'*" she read.

"Fascinating," Josh agreed.

She clicked the window closed. Behind it was a message board. "Looks like some kind of a group for mothers posting about their troubled sons," she said.

Josh leaned over her shoulder. "This one must be her. PearloftheSouth458. 'My son came home last Wednesday with bloody knuckles, like he'd been in a fight. He freezes me out at every opportunity and refuses to stay in rehab,'" Josh read. "'Should I be worried that he shows signs of increasing violence? I am a single mom. Please help.'"

"That was the night of your attack," Aurora said. "Do you think Lionel could have done this, too? To his own mother?"

"He was acting under orders—probably Gentry's—when

he came after me." Josh said. "It's one thing to do that, but coming after a family member? I don't know. He *is* a Crumpler, though, so anything's possible."

"Did the police question him?"

Josh nodded. "Boone said his alibi was pretty solid. He hasn't taken off or anything. I don't think this is him."

Aurora clicked on the next window. Cooper County Bank. The session had been timed out due to inactivity. She clicked on the login button.

"What was that name from the message board?"

"PearloftheSouth458."

Aurora typed it in.

"We don't know the password, though."

"Come on, Detective." She typed 'Lionel' in the password box.

" 'Retrieving account . . . one moment please,' " Josh read. "Damn. Nice work."

"Whoa." They both exclaimed at the account summary page. Pearline had almost two hundred thousand dollars in savings, along with fifty thousand in her checking account.

"Maybe we've been looking at this all wrong," Josh said. "Maybe Pearline Suggs is the criminal mastermind here."

"Legal secretary by day, drug kingpin by night?"

"Like I said, anything's possible. Let's look at her last statement."

There were regular deposits into her account from Royce Beaumont's law firm, an amount that looked like her paycheck, and then there were regular deposits of a much larger amount.

"Esma Lee Bedgerton," Josh read. "Who do you think that is? A wealthy relative?"

"Oh, my goodness. Esma is Ash Gentry's housekeeper," she

told Josh, her voice crackling with excitement. "She said that Esma had been with the family for years."

"So Gentry's paying her too. Damn."

"Hush money," Aurora said. "She must have seen what happened to my father that night at the minimart."

"But if she saw Gentry kill your father, why didn't she tell the police then? Why did she call the morgue from the minimart that night? Because they paid her off right away?"

"I don't know. All I know is, we've got to find her, Josh. She knows what happened that night."

"Let's go back to the evidence room. Maybe Samba's got something on Gentry. He's a hunter. Those guys always have a cabin or something out on the bayou. There are places we could check." Aurora folded the laptop back up and they both stood. "We're close, Aurora. We're getting close." The shuttered expression that he had worn the day they'd walked past her childhood home was gone.

"I know," she said, resisting the impulse to grab his hand.

She slipped her phone out of her pocket. Jefferson Gibbs. Sixteen missed calls. Something cold began to spread its tentacles throughout her chest.

"Josh," she said. He turned in the doorway in front of her. "The house." Something was wrapping itself around her voice, so that she could only force out her words in staccato bursts. "We have to go. Now."

CHAPTER FORTY-FIVE

"I have to tell you something," Aurora said when they were in the car.

Josh's mind was ticking furiously, trying to stitch together all of the free-floating pieces that made up this case. In his mind he saw Raylene Atchison's bloodless face in the autopsy photo, Burdette Crumpler flicking ashes over the side of the steamboat, Doc Mason standing over Wade Atchison's empty casket. Every day had brought more questions.

"What?"

"The house." In the passenger seat, Aurora watched him, some unreadable anxiety on her face.

"What is it?"

"The other day. When I went to see Ash Gentry. Someone—I think someone had been at the house."

"*What?*" It was all Josh could do to keep the car on the road. "What happened? Why didn't you say anything?"

"I'm sorry. I just—I didn't want to upset you. It was the day they found Jesse, and I didn't want to bother you with it. Someone wrote the word *soon* in the dew on my car."

"It's okay." She had been trying to protect him. "I know I

kind of fell off the map there for a minute. I didn't know what else to do."

"What else could you do?" She reached out and gripped his shoulder. "They pulled your brother out of the bayou, for God's sake. It's like you said to me, Josh. You did what you had to do. You survived."

"I didn't, though, Aurora. That's the difference between you and me. I stood there. I could have called for help, I could have tried to fight him. And I did exactly what he said to do." He was shouting now. They were the words that he had feared she would hear from someone else, and now he was telling her himself. It should have felt like a betrayal. Yet in a strange way, it was a relief.

"I wasn't a survivor, Aurora. I was an *accomplice*."

She was quiet for a moment. They were near the turnoff for Spotted Beebalm Drive now; whatever awaited them at the house, they'd see it for themselves in a few minutes.

"Josh. Oh, my God."

A Cooper's Bayou police cruiser was parked in the front yard, lights flashing.

"Stay here," he told Aurora.

"Like hell I will."

Boone met them at the door, his expression grim.

"Aurora, this is Boone. My partner."

Boone took Aurora's hand. "I wish we were meeting under more pleasant circumstances, Miss Atchison." He paused. "Jefferson Gibbs, the caretaker, called us. He came by the house to fix the burned-out porch light, and that's when he noticed it."

"Noticed what?"

Boone gestured for them to follow. "Two of the windows that face the bayou were busted in. Looks like they might have used a rock or something, smashed it in."

"Was anything taken?"

"I'm afraid you'll have to verify that for us, ma'am," Boone told Aurora. "We noticed some papers on the floor in the bedroom. Maybe some of your grandfather's personal papers."

Aurora and Josh exchanged a glance, not unnoticed by Boone.

"What?"

"They may have been looking for some of her grandfather's logbooks. Aurora brought them to the evidence room."

"For safekeeping," Aurora added.

"Safekeeping," Boone repeated. "Well, Miss Atchison, Y'all need to step aside while we secure the scene here and finish writing up our report."

Aurora stepped in front of Josh. "I appreciate what you're saying. But the police haven't done anything about my mother's—and my father's—murder for twenty years. Your partner is the first person who got anywhere on the case. So with *all due respect*, Boone, please step aside. In fact, please leave."

Josh tried to hide his grin. Boone held up his hands in surrender, chastened. "If that's the way you want it," he said. "If you could make a list of what's missing, that kind of thing, that would be helpful. I've got two guys out in the yard, just snapping pictures for evidence. I'll tell them it's time to go."

"Thank you. It was nice meeting you."

Boone nodded at Aurora. "Josh." He jerked his head towards the door, beckoning Josh to follow, but Josh ignored the gesture.

"See ya, Boone."

After Boone left, they sat together on the peach-colored velvet love seat in front of the broken window. Without the barrier of the window, the bayou seemed to be even closer, the enchanted landscape like a living, breathing thing reaching for them. Aurora rested her head on Josh's shoulder and finally, the tears came.

When she was finished, she lifted her head and they stared out at the shadows that were beginning to stretch towards them across the bayou's surface.

"What are we going to do now?"

"I think Samba's right. The answers are here, in something that was left behind. We're just missing something." The box from the evidence room was seared into his memory, the key tucked into the sleeve of Wade Atchison's sweatshirt beckoning to him like some kind of charm. He would let her rest, he would go to the evidence room and hold out every fragment, every clue, until something fit.

He opened his mouth to tell her this, but to his surprise, she was already standing in the doorway. Aurora Atchison didn't need a savior; she was going to save herself. He was just going to help her do it.

CHAPTER FORTY-SIX

"So Wade Atchison was traveling light," Samba remarked. The three of them were gathered around the center table in the evidence room, the contents of Aurora's father's tomb laid out before them like an altar.

There was an urgent message from Nicky on Aurora's voice mail. Nicky had questions: when was Aurora coming back, had she abandoned the city for the bayou, was she safe? Aurora didn't know the answers to any of them. She was coming to the end of her allotted leave time; even a dead mother only bought you so much goodwill with her boss at the hospital. But there was no way she was leaving. Not now.

Aurora reached for the key and slid it towards herself. Her father had fitted it into the cuff of his sweatshirt. *Concealed,* Malachi had said. Meant for somebody to find.

She held it up to the light and the star-shaped hole in the top winked at her like a tiny eye. It was engraved with a skull and crossbones, the edges of the emblem faded with time, encrusted in a furred black sludge.

"Samba, do you have any acetone?"

Anyone else would have questioned this request, but Samba bounded out of his chair. "Back in a jiffy, Aurora."

Josh grinned at her. She should have been embarrassed, the way she'd cried on the couch, scared about returning to the house with no front windows, but having Josh here with her gave her a kind of invincibility.

"Bingo!" Samba held aloft a clear plastic bottle of lavender liquid.

"Nail polish remover?" Josh asked him.

"You gotta open your mind, Josh," Samba said. "This stuff is magical. It can dissolve paint and varnish. You can even use it to make meth or cut coke. Or so I've heard."

Aurora reached for the bottle. She pulled a tissue from her purse and dabbed some of the liquid onto it. With Samba and Josh looking on, she began to scrub vigorously, first one side of the key, and then the other, gradually bringing the image into focus; the border surrounding the skull and crossbones and some letters beneath it. She held it up under the light.

Josh squinted at the design. "Looks like there's some initials underneath the skull and crossbones. 'J' and 'A'?"

Samba's eyes widened. "I don't think that's an 'A,'" he said. There was a little twist of excitement in his voice. "I think it might be an 'R.' 'JR.'"

"You know what it's for?"

"Sure. It's that boat storage place at the marina."

Josh gave him a quizzical look. "What?"

"It closed a few years back. Before your time. Jolly Roger Boat Storage. You must have heard stories about Roger Beaulieu. Everyone made fun of him because he wore an eye patch, had some eye condition. Finally he just ran with it and went full

pirate. Parrot, gold tooth, the whole bit. Roger was a charac-
ter." Samba patted one of the steel evidence lockers. "Before
we had these babies, he used to give me extra boxes they had
lying around. He was a good guy."

Aurora stared at him, openmouthed.

"Where was the boat storage place?"

"Right across from Weir Island," Samba said. "The other
side, right near the mini-mart."

Near the scene of the murder.

Josh and Aurora looked at each other. Samba had just
cracked the case wide open.

CHAPTER FORTY-SEVEN

In any other place, the remains of Jolly Roger Boat Storage would have been razed, a soulless strip mall or discount buffet restaurant rising from its ashes.

Not in Cooper's Bayou.

The skeleton of the building remained, cypress trees poking through its empty windows, kudzu strangling what was left of the painted exterior, its wooden boat ramps leading to the bayou sun-bleached and soft with rot. When the place had first closed down, Roger Beaulieu had shoved whatever he couldn't sell into the water. Now a fleet of abandoned boats, tilted at dangerous angles, surrounded the entry in a ghostly ring, the bayou slowly pulling their rusted remains beneath its syrup surface.

The key smoldered in Josh's pocket. There were answers behind the door it opened, he was sure of it. The thought of it propelled him forward, sending a fresh tide of adrenaline roaring through his veins. More than anything else, he wanted to bring Aurora answers, bring her peace, but he knew it would be a hollow kind of peace, the same kind given to him when he had held the threadbare remains of the duffel bag, aware that the browned bones inside were Jesse.

"Wait up," Samba called, charging up the bayou banks, poking the trash aside with a carved walking stick painted in psychedelic colors.

Josh tore off a NO TRESPASSING sign flapping uselessly in the breeze and paused in the entryway to the old building.

Any evidence exposed to the elements out here would be long gone; lucky for them, the red painted roll-up doors on the old units were virtually indestructible, although some enterprising people had managed to open a few. Josh saw the edge of what looked like a striped beach towel poking out from one of the units. It could be a lovers' retreat, or it could be a meth lab that would blow them sky-high at any moment.

"Too bad they let this place fall down," Samba called, his eyebrows tilted at an optimistic angle.

Aurora turned and Josh glanced out at the decaying armada of boats and wondered if they were seeing the same thing. He wiped the sheen of sweat from his face. "Beautiful."

"Well, the good news is, most of these don't have locks." Aurora grasped the handle of the nearest unit and jerked it upward, revealing a slumbering family of possums. Josh, Aurora, and Samba stood at a crossroads, a crumbling corridor branching off in three separate directions.

"All right, then. Let's each take a direction. Anybody sees one with the lock still on it, give a shout," Josh said.

"I'll take this way." Aurora headed north, Samba east, and Josh to the west. A coil of unease unwound in Josh's gut. They'd come here straight from the evidence room without a map or a plan. He patted the gun, its reassuring weight heavy in his waistband, filmy with sweat. It was the middle of the afternoon; they weren't likely to run into anyone out here. But if someone was already watching Aurora's house, how easy would it have been for them to follow her?

"Holler if you need anything, guys," he shouted in their general direction.

For the next half hour, the only sound was the scattering of bugs and the shriek of the metal doors sliding open. Josh opened the last door and stepped into the pot-scented interior, empty save for a broken stick of incense and a torn couch cushion, its fluffy innards strewn across the ground. None of the units in his section were locked, and all were empty. Josh sagged against the wall and removed the key from his pocket. Had they once opened one of these empty lockers? Had someone beaten them to it, the same way they'd beaten them to the body of Wade Atchison?

"Over here, I got something!" Aurora shouted. Josh sprinted in the direction of her voice. At the end of the hallway, she stood in front of a red door, a lock still attached to its hinges, bearing the skull and crossbones insignia. Samba trotted towards them, breathless, a few moments later.

"I think we might have hit the jackpot," Samba said.

As if in reply, a muffled squeak came from the interior of the locker.

"Please tell me that was a possum," Aurora breathed.

"Stand back everybody." Josh removed the gun from his waistband and rapped on the door. "Whoever's in there, this is the police. Open this damn door right now."

Silence.

Josh slipped the key out of his pocket and held it out on his palm to Aurora. Soundlessly she slid it into the lock and the three of them inched the door upward, revealing the cavernous, musty interior, boxes stacked against the back wall. He swung the gun around to each corner. Empty. It had to have been an animal.

"Hello?"

In response, a flurry of sound came from the back right corner, and a cold realization washed over Josh. It wasn't someone lying in wait to kill them. It was someone who needed help.

Aurora must have had the same insight. "Hang on," she called out. "Hang on. Help is coming."

All three of them rushed to the back corner of the room, desperately trying to locate the source of the sound. Aurora tossed aside the cardboard carcasses of boat supply boxes and threw back a tarp to reveal the hulk of an old steamer trunk looming in the corner. The sounds were getting louder.

Someone was in the trunk.

"I'm just going to smash the lock," Josh shouted. "If you can, just keep your hands away from this side, okay?"

Aurora held it steady and with one well-placed hit of the gun, Josh shattered the lock and threw it open to reveal a shuddering and terrified Pearline Suggs.

He froze, and Aurora leapt into action.

"You're all right now. You're safe now. You're safe." She repeated these words like a mantra, all the while removing the duct tape that was plastered around Pearline's wrists and the neon yellow slash of tape that covered her mouth. "Samba," she said. "Help me get her over to the grass."

"She's in shock," Aurora called over her shoulder to Josh. "We need to get her to the hospital. Fast."

Josh stared down into the depths of the steamer trunk, the layers of material that had bound Pearline Suggs. There was a plastic paisley tablecloth, the tattered remains of a baby blanket, and then something below it, something wrapped in a familiar-looking blanket, the kind they had in the back of their police cars for trauma victims. Something tightened in Josh's chest. He unfolded the blanket.

Cooper County Medical Services.

He peeled it away to reveal a cluster of brown bones. It was not a blanket. It was a shroud.

"I found Wade Atchison," he said.

CHAPTER FORTY-EIGHT

In the backseat of the Jeep, Aurora sat with Pearline's head in her lap. At the Jolly Roger, Aurora had done a quick assessment. Pearline had a few minor abrasions, but was otherwise unharmed.

Josh was speeding down a dirt road shortcut to the interstate, and each time the Jeep shuddered, Pearline groaned and closed her eyes. Aurora thought about her first-aid kit. There was a sedative in there, but then Pearline would be knocked out before they reached the hospital. What if she could tell them something?

"You guys still okay back there?"

Samba poked his head between the seats, and Aurora gave him a thumbs-up.

"Pearline, just relax. Keep breathing. In and out. In and out. We're almost at the hospital," Aurora soothed. She stroked the side of Pearline's head, tucked a stray strand of hair behind her ear. "You're safe now."

Pearline nodded, her eyes still closed.

"Can you tell us who did this to you, Pearline?" Josh called from the front seat. "Anything? We could really use your help."

His voice was thick with the desperation that she felt; she guessed they were all feeling it. So close, and yet the answers seemed to keep slipping through their fingers.

"Easy, Josh," Samba said. "She's been through a lot."

Pearline's eyes snapped open.

"He was going to kill me," she whispered, her eyes focused on Aurora, wild with terror. "Davis. He thought I was going to tell, but I wasn't. I *wasn't*."

Pearline began to convulse with sobs, wheezing and sputtering words that Aurora could not make out. She looked at Samba and shook her head no. Pearline was not in a condition to answer any questions. Not now. As much as they needed the information, they couldn't press her.

"It's okay. You're safe now. He can't hurt you now." Aurora looked out the window, where the bayou was drifting by, reduced to a caramel blur behind the mist and clouds. The truth was, they had no idea where Gentry was. He had the Crumplers in his back pocket; who knew what other connections he had around Cooper County? Aurora thought about the shattered front windows, the writing on her car. If he could kill her parents in cold blood with no repercussions, what was there to prevent him from coming after her?

"Gentry must have gotten wind of us being on the case through Malachi," Josh reasoned from the front seat. "He moved Wade Atchison's bones from Weir Island to the storage unit, to throw us off, make us think there was a chance Wade was still alive. He had the Crumplers believing it too." He whistled under his breath. "All this time, they were afraid of a ghost."

In the end, Wade Atchison had helped them.

Aurora thought about her father meeting Gentry that night on the bayou. They'd found the storage locker key in the lining of his sweatshirt. Had he stolen it from Gentry unnoticed, left it as a clue to his killer? They would never know. She wondered at what point he had known the game was up, that he had been lured out to the bayou not for a payoff, but to be slaughtered. Had he tried to save his wife and child and saved only one of them?

She looked down at Pearline, but there was nothing inscrutable in her expression, just horror. She had kept everything she had seen that night a secret, stayed quiet while everyone blamed Aurora's father. She had even taken a payout for her troubles, straight from Gentry himself. Still, she had been a sixteen-year-old kid in a small town, the mother of the child of a Crumpler. She probably didn't see another way out. *The lady led me to the steps,* Aurora herself had told the police on the night of the murder. Pearline had helped her, maybe even saved her life, and now she was returning the favor.

"Almost there," she murmured, and when Pearline opened her eyes, Aurora gave her the most encouraging smile she could muster.

"Pearline Suggs might not be an innocent victim here."

James had never been one to dance around the delivery of bad news.

On the other end of the phone, Josh unleashed a stream of expletives and then a series of rapid-fire questions. Cops were so predictable, it was tiresome.

"One thing at a time," James told him. "I told you there was female DNA in the sample we collected from the grave. Malachi let me know this morning that there was a match in CODIS. Apparently before Pearline was an upstanding legal secretary, she had a brief but prolific career in forgery and credit card fraud. The DNA was Pearline's."

"What about Ash Gentry?"

James removed his glasses and pinched the bridge of his nose. "Aurora was right about her. She's clean. Other than poor taste in husbands, there's no evidence to support her being there that night, and nothing to link her to Wade Atchison except town gossip."

"So you think she—you think our suspect helped kill Wade Atchison?"

"I can't say. But she was definitely present when that body was put in the grave." James consulted Pearline's rap sheet, which Malachi had attached to the report. "She's pretty petite. I can't imagine she overpowered anyone. She definitely didn't strangle anyone."

"So someone else was definitely there that night. One of the Crumplers?"

"Maybe." They were Gentry's henchmen, his personal redneck Mafia. But something about it still bothered James. The autopsy photos. Strangulation.

This was personal.

"What if we're looking at this the wrong way round? What if this wasn't just about Wade? What if this was about Raylene?"

"What do you mean?"

"I mean, maybe there was someone besides Wade who had it in for her. She was a beautiful woman who liked bad men."

On the other end of the line, Josh sucked in a breath. "Thank you, Doc," he said. "I think I know exactly who we're looking for."

CHAPTER FORTY-NINE

Josh and Aurora were headed back to the evidence room. They had delivered Pearline safely into the hands of the doctors and nurses at Kervick Hospital, who told them she would be all right. Samba had stayed behind so there was someone to meet Lionel when he arrived from rehab to see his mother.

Davis Gentry's assistant had told Boone that he hadn't been in the office; the guy could be on a plane to Brazil by now, but Josh doubted it. Sick bastards like Gentry couldn't resist sticking around to see the results of their mayhem. Josh would bet he was still in the state, maybe even still in the county. *Suspect is to be considered armed and dangerous,* Josh had added to the report. *Do not approach without backup.*

"I think Samba's right," he told Aurora. "The answers are all there, in the evidence."

"This was about my mom. Not my dad." It was amazing, the way she could distance herself from what was happening.

"It was about Raylene," he agreed. "Whoever met them out on the bayou that night had a connection to her too. I'll show you what I was thinking about."

Back in the evidence room, he pulled out the accordion file containing the records of interviews.

"Margie Belle," he proclaimed, lifting out a red file. "The older lady at the mini-mart. Remember, I went and talked to her. She mentioned that Raylene had a boyfriend before Wade."

"That's right. Bobbie said something about some guy bothering her too, right around the time of the murder," Aurora chimed in. "Maybe that guy is the key to this whole thing." She upended the file, spreading out the witness statements so they blanketed the table. "You're right. He's got to be in here somewhere. I'll pull the rest of the file. Samba had it over in the other workspace."

"Good idea." He spun through the statements in front of him. Would Raylene have taken up with one of the Crumplers? It seemed unlikely, given their feud with her grandfather, but then again, she had gone for the dangerous types. It wasn't out of the question.

A shuffling sound interrupted his thought. Aurora, with the boxes.

"What do you think about the Crumplers?" he said to the space between shelves where the noise was coming from.

"Never liked 'em."

A man in a cowboy hat stepped out of the shadows. A man with a very large gun pointed directly at Josh.

Josh reached a hand into his waistband, and the man fired a warning shot above his head. Josh heard the bullet strike one of the old metal fans, then clatter to the ground. In the interior space, the noise was deafening.

"Hands in the air, Detective Hudson. I ain't gonna tell you again."

The man took a step forward, and his features came into

focus. Cowboy hat, oversize belt buckle, every country song cliché come to life.

Royce Beaumont.

Josh raised his hands. "Well, hey there, Royce," he said. "What brings you over here to the evidence room? Any files I can pull for you?"

Run, Aurora. He tried to will her with his mind. There was an emergency exit between two of the rows of boxes at the back of the building. She would have heard the gunshot; she would have time to escape. A white-hot dread scorched his throat dry. She had to be all right. Had to be.

Royce chuckled. "You're a funny guy, Josh. You know, I liked you. Before you started digging into all this shit. You should have stuck to lost dogs and patrolling the state fair, and we would've never had any problem, you and I."

"Oh, well, now, I don't know about all that, Royce," Josh said. "I have a problem with a man who lays his hands on a woman."

"You got no idea what you're talking about."

"If that were true, I don't think we'd be in this little situation right now, do you? So tell me, Royce. I understand why you killed Wade. You were just following orders from Gentry, right? But why Raylene? That wasn't about the gators, now, was it?"

"Shut the hell up, Hudson."

"She wasn't supposed to be there that night, was she?" Josh pressed on. He hoped he was buying Aurora time. "So you must have been real surprised when she showed up with Wade and her kid. That must have really pissed you off."

"It wasn't about that. She would have turned me in. I couldn't risk it." Something wavered in his voice, and Josh knew he had hit the jackpot.

"Well, if that were true, then you would've taken her out with a gun like that," Josh said. "But you didn't, did you? You put your hands on her, squeezed her neck until she stopped breathing."

"I told her Wade and I had business to discuss. She wouldn't leave."

"And then you threatened Pearline Suggs, a poor teenage girl."

Royce laughed. "Is that what Pearline told you? She was in on the whole thing. Lionel ain't a Crumpler. He's Gentry's kid. She had her hand out just like everyone else, wanting a big payday. Only she got greedy, just like Wade."

"So you got rid of her."

Royce grinned. "Easy with those accusations, Detective."

"Huh. Well, you should probably know that we found her. She's at Kervick Hospital right now telling some nice police officer her whole sad story. It's over, Royce."

If the news surprised Royce, he didn't let it show. "See, that's where you're wrong. Detective Hudson. I'm just getting started."

Something moved in the shadows behind Royce, but Josh maintained eye contact until Aurora crept into his peripheral vision, one finger on her lips. She was holding aloft the syringe from her first-aid kit, the one filled with a powerful sedative.

"This is it, Royce. Don't make it harder than it needs to be."

Aurora plunged the needle into Royce's arm, knocking him off balance and sending the gun skittering across the floor towards Josh. He kicked it out of reach, and he and Aurora pinned Royce to the ground.

"I hate to see it end this way, Josh," Royce said, his eyes

flickering between Josh and Aurora. "We had so much left to talk about. Raylene. Wade. *Liana*."

He spoke her name in a sacred tone, like a promise, and then his body went slack between them, his cowboy hat tipping forward as he slumped to the floor.

CHAPTER FIFTY

They gathered to bury Wade Atchison for the second time on a September afternoon in Ti Bon Ange cemetery. He would be laid to rest next to Raylene.

James stood on the bayou side of the cemetery. He had never been much for funerals, but if Wade were able to observe his own festivities from some celestial perch, he probably would have been very pleased. Wade was one of those people who was greatly enhanced by death. They didn't call it the great equalizer for nothing. There was no mention of the crimes he had visited on Raylene and others, only a celebration of his innocence for the one that had taken her life.

James shielded his eyes against the sun and turned towards the bayou behind him, its blackberry water creeping slow as sludge through the flooded forest. Aurora steered a skiff towards the graveyard and lifted her hand in a wave. She had decided to stay in Cooper's Bayou and had already started working at the emergency room at the hospital in Kervick.

James waved back, remembering the little girl in the puffy pink jacket from all those years ago. He'd thought he had lost her; but by some miracle, she had returned to him after all these years. If he looked closer, if the light was just right, he could still see Raylene in the curve of her shoulders, the tilt of her chin.

"There we go." Ruby climbed down the hillside to his right, holding a wreath of Cajun hibiscus blossoms, a perfect unbroken circle. Together, she and Aurora gave it a push and watched it glide down the bayou, past the Broussard house, until it was carried around the corner and out of view.

Josh stood in the stern and watched Aurora turn the boat in a wide arc towards the cemetery, on their way to Wade Atchison's final send-off. In the end, Wade's crimes had been what had led them to the truth. Aurora had accepted his role and forgiven him the rest. *People aren't just one thing,* she'd said, and it was true. He was even allowing himself to believe it of Doyle, who was once again a free man for the time being, running alligator voodoo tours part-time off Burdette Crumpler's steamboat. Some disgruntled tourists might still label it a scam of sorts, but hey, at least it wasn't the kind of scam that would put him back in Craw Lake.

All around him, the bayou waters were retreating, exposing the silver-skinned land underneath, littered with soda cans and castoffs from the shrimping boats. The tide had brought Jesse's bones back to him, and he wondered about all of the other mysteries it still held beneath its shimmering surface.

In the bow of the boat, Aurora glanced over her shoulder and smiled at him. He believed in voodoo now, he told her, since it was what had brought her to him. When he drove to Kervick late at night to pick her up after her shift, he still circled the blocks east of Pernaria Vincent's beauty shop, peering out the dark windows of the Jeep at the women melting into doorways, scanning the sea of strange faces for a familiar one.

They came around the side of the cemetery, and Josh reached forward to slip his arms around her, their image stretched out in shadow across the shimmering surface of the bayou.

The jars containing the souls of her father and mother rattled at Aurora's feet, and at her side, the canister of Papa's ashes that had traveled with her from New York. In *voudon,* death was not a cessation of life but, like everything else, a change from one condition to another, Ruby and Bobbie had explained. Before she'd come to Cooper's Bayou, she would have dismissed such a statement as backwoods black magic, but now she was beginning to appreciate it the way Papa had.

The transition to life in Cooper's Bayou had been an easy one. Ernest Authement had been right; once the bayou got a hold of you, it didn't let go. Aurora had surrendered herself, and where had it left her? In the house on the bayou. Happy. Josh Hudson had come over the week after Gentry's arrest to help with repairs, and they were spending most evenings together.

She hadn't decided when she'd return to New York yet. She was still paying rent, and had taken a leave of absence from work. Of course she would have to go back sometime; but for now, she was content in the house on Spotted Beebalm Drive. She was making it her own and had even hung the pictures of Raylene and Wade they'd found in Papa's things. They had spent enough time in boxes.

Aurora maneuvered the boat between the coiled cypress tree stumps at the entrance to the cemetery. She cut the engine and placed the jars on the railing of the boat. When she opened the jars, she would release their souls together, into the land of the dead.

She felt Josh beside her, felt his fingers slide into the empty places between her own, the warm flat of his palm against hers. She had only been carrying the jars around for the past week, but the pain of not knowing what had happened to her parents had been with her for two decades.

She opened the lids and let them go.